CW00524719

**Just for
Krsna,
My only friend…**

NITIN MISHRA

THE LAST WIND

A Novel

AUSTIN MACAULEY
PUBLISHERS LTD.

A CIP catalogue record for this title is available from the British Library.

ISBN 9781785549403 (Paperback)
ISBN 9871785549410 (Hardback)
ISBN 9781785549427 (E-Book)

www.austinmacauley.com

First Published (2016)
Austin Macauley Publishers Ltd.
25 Canada Square
Canary Wharf
London
E14 5LQ

Contents

Chapter One

Born to be Alone

It was a regular Tuesday evening.

The unhappy clock hung at the corner of that inn's room indicating ten of the clock.

For some it was a time to get drunk, but for some the time was bringing more terrible times ahead. As usual the locals had gathered to quench their alcoholic appetite in their favourite inn that evening too. In no time, the small house got overcrowded as the darkness from the west moved in gracefully and majestically overpowered the day that was tiresome. As the visitors walked in one by one, the small insects started to play a live music that was terribly discordant; needless to say it was very unpleasant music but no one inside the inn bothered to care. And why would they?

That inn was really a hard thing to describe: both in words and thoughts. Describing it was a futile act because the house was a den loved by stubborn souls, and that is probably why it denied to be arrested in words. However, the visitors reported that it had two floors: the ground and the upper. The ground floor looked very common. It was here the commoners were served. But the upper floor looked better and it was further made to look much better for the affordable ones. No doubt, only the landowners, sheriffs, and some snobs from neighbouring villages would occupy the upper floor.

Huge tables and benches made the room look smaller. The scene in the room looked very dramatic; it was a complete picture of the world outside. Inside many would be heard shouting at each other, some were already in a deep slumber and some were about to come in, while some others were about to leave the place. A few people could be seen standing at the corner just waiting with exemplary patience for an empty seat. The place smelled of meats of all varieties: chicken, buff and pork. Customers had their own versions regarding the quality and taste of the food served. Needless to say, many would be heard complaining about the food being nasty, uncooked, repulsive and disagreeable to their taste. Others even said the food was bland, unfriendly and unsavory while it was always unappealing, unpalatable and repugnant. It was a mere habit.

Visitors smoked everywhere inside the inn. The smoke made them invisible, the smoke was thick as giant clouds lurking in the sky. A non-smoker would readily get suffocated to death under it. The day outside was sunny but the inside temperature was boiling. All the visitors were male except the owner, a stout and ever-grumbling old lady with two sons. Her long hair was as black as coal and plunged over her shoulders. One of her sons helped her in serving the customers, whereas the other had left the village years ago in search of a respectable profession and to lead a better life.

This was an every evening chore in this place. Most of the villagers were peasants; their wives would constantly try to stop them from attending the inn but no attempt was a success. Wives are always a nuisance for those who want to get boozed up, the males would complain.

That night was no different until a gentle looking man in his late-twenties rushed into the inn making straight for the counter. He seemed a bit worried and confused. He hurriedly threw some question to the owner; she in an unwelcoming tone pointed towards a group of peasants, almost intoxicated. He hurried towards the table and summoned one of the villager. He said something to the villager but it seemed as if he was unable to respond to such unexpected news. He hardly managed to pull the drunken villager out of the chaos. The lights of the inn were dim compelling him to stumble about a number of times.

The gentle man informed the drunken neighbour that his wife had died an hour ago and his only son was alone crying beside his dead mother. At first, it was difficult for him to understand. Intoxicated, he did not feel the news. For him, it was not news. But somehow this gentleman made him understand the whole situation. Cunningly though he left the inn and began to stagger towards his home. The gentle man paid his bill and returned back. The gentle man was not even thanked, even later.

At last, they reached his hut. It was at the farthest point from the inn. This hut was nearly ruined and devastated. The condition of the hut explained that they were indeed very poor and led a rather pathetic life. His wife used to clean dishes for others for some money. They had a small son of about six years old. The boy looked very helpless. His eyes were fixed upon his mother's face. He touched his mother's face and feet hoping she would wake up. But she laid there motionless. Never before had she done so. It was then he wailed and shouted until some nearby villagers approached him and consoled him. He looked very lean and thin. Till few hours ago, he was dependent upon his mother. She used to work hard all day to buy him bread. Even as a child, he could guess that his father was a good-for-nothing fellow. He did nothing except regularly attend the inn with the little money he earned from his little farm. The small boy had regularly witnessed quarrels between his parents but was unable to decipher the situation. Sometimes he wished he understood everything his parents were quarrelling about but he was limited in logical reasoning given to his immature childish brain.

As the crowd became larger, a neighbour said that the mother was sick due to overburden of work and diet inconsistency. She had no any financial support from her husband. She alone had to run the house. Even during her sick days, she went to work ignoring her weakness and fragile health conditions. She had her only son. She did not want to see him cry for food. She loved him very much. Her husband did not care a bit for and about his family. Every evening at about five p.m. he used to sell the vegetables from his farm and spend the money for his own luxury; simply discarding his family, pretending they did not exist. He was a burden, a more terrible thing than poverty.

With the very little money left in home and the little more the villagers donated, the last funeral rituals were carried out. All the time the small boy sluggishly crept besides his dead mother. It was one of the most terrible scenes to have ever been seen in the village. After the final rituals were completed, the villagers returned to their homes; it was already past midnight and the small boy was still unfed. He was hungry but now he didn't have his mother to whom he could cry for. His father lay

10

motionless on the floor and soon began to groan. But this small boy couldn't sleep as he was hungry and most of all he had missed his dear mother for good. His mother was his only source of food, love and affection.

The entire night he cried, longing for his mother; he desired for her touch, caress and loving goodnight kiss bestowed by a mother to her child. He reached for his father seeking a loving shelter but it was useless as his father was dreaming happily about the time he had spent in the inn with his contemporaries.

The next morning, the whole world woke up with a new radiant energy that the arrival of the sun had brought in but not his father. He slept till late. And this was not an unusual thing. It seemed the sun had forgotten to bring happiness in his hut, the boy could feel it. He did not know what to do. Helpless the small boy had no choice other than to cry. He was one of those hapless creatures that God created-just to be pitied upon.

The father finally woke up, he felt disturbed and was already in his vexed mood as if he had had a terrible nightmare. He scolded his son to keep quiet. The small boy found just the opposite to being with his mother and now that he was being abandoned, just by his father. His mother would cuddle her son and give something to eat. The small boy learned to hide pain from that very moment. But hiding the pain was simply inviting another greater pain. As a child he could not contain himself with the pain for long enough. He soon began to cry louder than before. This greatly irritated his father. The father stood on his feet and began to lash the boy. He scolded him this time more harshly in his volcanic voice loaded with anger and bitterness. Soon the boy found himself running out of the hut crying even louder and calling his mother. Kumar was what his mother called him.

Perhaps the Universe was blind to his pain and deaf to his sorrow. That could be why nobody came to help this poor little boy who was in a greater grief.

Kumar, the boy roamed all the time. But he was not a vagabond, but an orphan. The mother was dead and the father was a principled drunken fellow. The more he thought of it, the more tears would come in his eyes. Women from the village had pity on the boy. They gave him some food and a little milk. He consumed the food and milk with the humblest gratitude. He could not even express his thankfulness and appreciation through words but his shivering body did it.

His father still did not improve. He continued his usual practice. The son did not exist for him anymore. His son had lost a loving mother. He never tried to understand it. The small boy was destined to be lonely. Was it an act of God? It was a thing that shocked everyone. The boy was going through times beyond anyone's understanding and comprehension. Maybe only He understood. No one understood His inspiration behind it.

The boy remembered that his mother had presented him with a murali, a flute. He had seen his older brothers from the village playing a murali. He was drawn away by the melody that this miraculous instrument produced. It was then he had insistently forced his mother to get one for him. She was very happy to buy him the murali. She could not afford the grand piano but at least she would never refrain from buying an instrument so inexpensive. Holding it in his hand, the boy observed the holes on it and played with it. They were too large for him. It seemed as if his emaciated small fingers would slip in through the holes. But still he managed to produce some discordant tones. Sometimes his father used to quarrel with his wife for buying such a stupid toy and uselessly wasting the money. That was why whenever his father was around the vicinity, he did not even dare to touch his murali, the only gift from his mother.

The murali was the only token of memory for the boy that reminded him of his mother. He remembered the day when she has presented him with it; he even remembered the things she had told him. His memory was becoming more evocative and nostalgic. It was all he had –his memory. As he would look at the murali, he would remember everything, each and every moment he had spent with his mother. But constantly being aware of the thing that had gone forever did not do any good to the boy except it made him more vulnerable. The more he recollected his mother's memories, the much painful did life become to him. He was homeless though he had a small hut and a father to fall back on. He hated his father. He sometime secretly wished he had died instead of mother.

But wishes are wishes. His father was bad and unscrupulous for sure, now he started becoming worse and exhibited hostility towards his own son. For several days he would not come home while his son would be left uncared, unloved and untouched. He did not bother about his son. Perhaps, he too wanted his son to die. He did what he wanted to do. He started selling whatever he could find from his home so that he could get drunk and remain unaware of his surroundings.

The days were much terrible. His father was ruining his life. This little boy did not know what would come next. This made him helpless. One thing he did constantly was to play the murali, everywhere he went. He picked up another good habit. As the sun was about to set in his village, he would climb up the hillock, look up at the sky and remember his mother until tears would roll down his eyes and tremble on his bumpy chin. Then he would start playing the murali. As he played, he would look up at the vast collection of stars up high in the sky. He looked up for his mother anticipating that she might be somewhere there among the stars, constantly looking over and protecting her son from the whatever incoming danger. But as usual all he could see was the vast constellation of stars mocking down at him with pity.

Days were passing by with no one to stop it. Kumar was coming of age; it was time for him at attend a nursery school where he was supposed to develop and acquire the skills necessary to comprehend the fundamentals of life. All other boys of his age had already joined the nursery school, they had someone to take care of it and worry about them. But the little boy did not know what the school was for. He did not have any friends to move around with, to talk to and play with. 'Loneliness' was the name of this boy. Sometime there was not a single soul to talk to; and his only friends were the sweet memories of his mother, perhaps his solely intimate friend. In the uninterrupted boredom of his existence such memories were a genuine and cherished treasure for Kumar. It was for sure that both his boredom and misery were deathless.

And that intimacy pushed him to move on. He adored such memories very much. Such was the cruel choice of destiny.

One fine day, his mother's brother, Mama, came to visit him and his father. When he arrived the house was badly in a deserted state and no one was in except the dust and flies flying here and there. He was so perplexed to see the state the house was in. It was as if it had been discarded for good; kitchen utensils were untouched, in very dirty condition. He walked through the entire house with an unpleasant expression developing on his face. At last he stood with a dismal glance gazing at the floor.

He went to the neighbouring house and soon came to learn about the actuality of the events that had taken place recently. The neighbouring woman said regretfully with watery eyes,

"It should not happen, even to a sharp criminal. I can't stand to see that boy's pathetic condition but I am helpless." The woman described all the happenings that had taken place one by one and even pleaded with Mama to take the boy with him should he be concerned about him. Mama left the place in complete anger.

On hearing about the treatment done to the small boy, Mama got extremely angry and was raging and ranting with uncontrollable heartbeat against his chest. His face suddenly turned red like a heated rod. He returned to the house again and re-examined it; all he could find were the empty bottles that smelled of alcohol. The bed was in such a messed condition that little insects had already infested on it. Almost with no patience he waited outside the house. After about an hour the small boy appeared from the back of the house piping his murali. He looked broken and unfed for days. He was not even excited to see Mama waiting outside his house. Perhaps he had no any rational reason to be happy after his mother was gone.

Mama watched him fixedly as he approached with sadness lingering in his face and eyes, sometimes looking at Mama and sometimes just in random directions. He seemed to be having a hard time in recognizing the man in front of him.

With heavy heart Mama marched towards the boy, bent down on his knees and stared at the boy with an intense and sentimental look as if he had seen him for

15

the very first time. Slowly he moved his shivering hands towards the boy with blindness in his eyes. He gently, indeed very gently touched the boy with his hands, held him close and opened his mouth to ask him something. But depressed and deprived he could not even utter any sound whatsoever. He lowered his head down holding the boy in his hands, staring at the sodden earth.

Suddenly his meditation was interfered with an arrival of very strange and unclear sound-someone was heard approaching singing joyfully. Mama recomposed himself upon hearing the sound and waited. Mama knew it was him. In fact, it was his brother-in-law returning home after an evening spree and lavishness. He kept staggering and kept singing to himself. Still highly spirited he was unable to recognize the man. Finally he came to a complete stop while his body swaying from one direction to other, he was trying to concentrate upon this new character.

"H-h-h-heeeeey! At last you have come..." he stammered jabbing his forefinger into the man's left chest. Again he resumed his song with an air of restlessness.

The other man was so infuriated that he could not say a word. His piercing eyes were already radiating fire and anguish. He felt so disgusted that he found it useless to converse and reason with the irrational drunken man in his front. After all he was there and so he had to say something of the situation.

He started slowly.

"What have you done to yourself and to your own son?"

He wanted him to realize and see all the difficulties of his position, the hopelessness, the carelessness and the absurdity of it. Mama stood there with his stiff limbs waiting for some response.

But the boy's father nodded and looked at every possible direction except his eyes. He knew the eyes were expecting an answer from a father of a son whom he had abandoned for the love of his drinking passion.

"W... wh... at have I done and whooo... are you to question me?" he angrily retorted back spitting saliva from his mouth fitted inappropriately in his square and firm lantern shaped jaw.

The boy quickly took to his heels as he sensed the rising wrath of his father. He went into the hut and stood behind the door breathing heavily and with grave danger dancing over his face. He knew his father's anger was unleashed and would soon chase him.

Mama was no longer able to hold himself and shouted, "You have killed my sister and now you are after her son,"

Adding more anger to his volcanic voice.

"Why are you treating your own son in this manner?"

"Don't you feel any love for him?

Don't you have any love for him?

Don't you have any love for him?

Don't you have any love for him?"

He waited with his fist closed and with a questioning look in his troubled eyes.

This time he was expecting a solemn answer out of a drunken bastard even though he was out of his wits. But to his surprise he received nothing except stupidity and insanity. Not able to withstand any further after some time Mama decided to give up the dispute. He had now realized that no discussion was going to mend the

17

situation at hand, perhaps make it harsher and vulnerable.

He talked to his brother-in-law about it but the drunken one turned a deaf ear. Every line of reasoning was of no avail. They had a heated argumentation for some time. Kumar's father had already sold himself hopelessly to the devil and now he possessed no sense of appropriateness and aptness. He saw everyone through his liquor bottle so all the urbane and generous approach was to fail.

Without even considering any consideration for the little boy Mama left the hut boiling with anger. One could smell the anger and hear the echo even after he had left the place. Perhaps he would never have wanted to abandon the boy with a devil but his anger did not let him see what he had left behind. His anger tricked him.

Now again Kumar was left to his own fate. He watched as Mama left the place angrily, swearing to himself. Now his father's anger was already on the ground after having a heated conversation with his brother-in-law. He knew where to locate the boy. Very soon he got hold of his little helpless son and slapped him to quench his anger. He knew that his son would never fight back or demand for a reasonable answer as to the world expected from him.

The boy did not know anything but to run in order to defend himself from the ill and despicable treatment of his father into the nearby jungle of thick trees and horny bushes. He ran and ran, ran and ran, ran and ran clutching the murali in his tiny hand as strongly as he could. He just ran in all the directions that he could see and all the time he could hear his father's shrieks chasing him; they could take him over any moment so he had to run with no alternate left. Finally completely fatigued his limbs gave up and he crashed to the naked ground with no control over his body in agony. He hurt his left arm with bruises.

Now, as usual, he was all alone, discarded with loneliness as his only friend. He cried there for hours but no one was there in this whole world to hear the sorrowful and his silent screams. Maybe He heard but he choose to remain silent and witness the happenings. The gush of innocence, the pain and turbulence, even gods have terrible times to understand.

But how long could one remain in one state: the same principle applied to the boy. How long could he cry? How long could he feel deserted and naked? How long could he feel the pain and suffering? All have to end and it ended. When he came to his senses, he found himself protected among the thick jungle trees in the bamboo-brown forest. It was so green all around him he felt as if he was in a green leafy paradise. The forest was rather old and antiquated. He could hear the gentle breeze rumbling among the branches and making a buzzing sound. He looked towards the sky and saw the sky scraping trees just about to touch the sky. They looked so high and mighty; high than his pain, mightier than his father. He tried to move his body but felt a sharp pain that discouraged him to move and abruptly he gave up moving. He knew that all the trees and the leaves were staring at him liken a silent statue. Perhaps even the nature was unaccustomed to witness such agony.

That day Kumar cried for hours until it was dark and the stars began to twinkle up in the sky. It was now really dark around everywhere; the night insects began to make their grumbling noise. Then it was silent, real silent. Nothing prevailed around except the silence. Occasionally, grumbling of the insects. Then again terrible silent! The birds were all perhaps asleep.

The night began to hold a greater grip upon Kumar. Even the slightest sound magnified to great amplitude. The more darkness and silence prevailed the more the chillness increased. The boy Kumar did not know what to do except to close his eyes and think of his mother. He did not even know that someone called God existed somewhere, unknown; who we had to call upon in such difficult and coarse times. The boy was in fact never taught and advised about God. He knew just one god and she was now far away from him, seized forcefully from his life.

Out of chillness, he was shivering. He could hear the gentle movement of water somewhere flowing nearby. The creaking of the trees and the crackling of the leaves made him feel easy rather than the ear piercing silence. The crispy grass beneath him gave him a pleasant sensation but he was so afraid that he even did not dare to move his fingers. He was terrified even to exchange his breath lest someone might hear him. The constant ceaseless thought of his mother brought tears in his eyes and forced him to scream but this time he controlled himself. He had soon become aware of his helplessness and pathetic condition. He wondered if his father's unleashed anger was still there after his chase.

Kumar clutched the murali close to his small chest. The murali brought him near to his mother. Different types of thoughts struck his meek mind; suddenly out of nowhere he heard his mother voice calling him. He opened his eyes wide at once, and what he saw in front of him was nothing except darkness and silence mocking at him. Perhaps they were at fun ridiculing the little boy. He could hear their soft submissive laughter and timid whisperings among each other. Afraid, he closed his eyes, remained there motionless and did not even know when he went off to a deep slumber.

That night Kumar slept under a tree with all his limbs bent close to his body, and darkness and the forest were his only friends. He was safe. Perhaps God exists.

Next morning the chirpings of birds awoke him. He was surprised to find where he was. As soon as he thought of going back to his home he felt dismayed about his father and thought of his cruelty and barbarous act of violence and madness. Finally, he managed to get up on his feet and sluggishly began to walk through the forest, like an injured soldier in a battlefield. Deep inside he felt the jungle far better place than his home.

Sluggishly, he began to make his way towards his home. He was not aware of the directions to follow but the mountains guided him. Even though he had realized that he was lost in the wilderness but he felt good inside as if he had found the real mate for his life. For the first time he enjoyed the fantasies the forest had to share and the symphony all around. He found himself in a dazzlingly beautiful and wonderful world.

Late though he reached his little hut and found it empty, unwelcoming and unsympathetic as always. The look never changed. Now he noticed that almost everything that had belonged to his mother was gone. Only a broken chair and an unbalanced bed were left remaining in the room. The things just lay scattered here and there with no one to own it, with no one to clean it. The doors were open. Window even wide open, which undoubtedly indicated that his father was not in for the whole night; he must be on one of his night sprees.

Little boy Kumar had had his first night out alone so he was as hungry as a bear; he searched for something to eat but could not find anything. Under those circumstances, he could just weep and eventually cry but that would be worthless. He had just recently learnt that he should not cry anymore. He had made that important

21

revelation. He tried not to cry after that. In his early childhood, he had now already comprehended that crying would never bring him close to his mother or nor did it help him to escape from his father's brutality and madness. Suffering was inevitable and inescapable for him.

No matter how cruel, how unloving, he still had his father to fall back on after his mother. Somewhere in his heart he had some love and affection for his father, perhaps because of a child's instinct. That is why thoughts of his father filled his mind. He went wandering to the village never knowing why he went and where.

All the alcoholics are not bad in nature as his father was. Some of his father's friends were heavy alcoholics but they still went home even after getting drunk on their staggering feet. They undeniably shouted and kicked at their wives while they were intoxicated but certainly and fortunately loved them amply the very next morning and even regretted the previous night with all their hearts. Their helpless wives always forgave their husband for all the sufferings they had endured because of their husbands. One of such good alcoholics met the boy and asked in a high tone,

"Where are you up to this morning?"

The boy had nothing to say and a kind of redness suffused his face, he was perhaps overwhelmed by such a direct question. He stayed quiet, surrendering himself to the fetter-grey skies. Struck by the question he stood at complete motionless state binding his limbs close to his body.

"Where is your father?" someone asked.

The boy did not dare to look at the man. He resumed his state with chattering teeth and chilblained feet. He looked desireless, hopeless and now was completely a parent-less child. One of the villagers perhaps his father's friend took pity on him and gave him something to eat. He devoured the food like a hungry tiger. He ate the food like an inhabitant from a slum.

Later he inquired about his father letting them know that he had not come back home the last night. They did not reply anything, as they knew what type of man he was.

He was famous for his day drunkenness, irregular in paying off debts and had been a worthless, dissolute and deceitful rogue. He was the one who had seriously impoverished his family, no one else but he was responsible.

One of them just replied coldly,

"Boy, go you home now as your father is sure to return for his treasure."

The boy waddled back home and began to play his murali. But he could not concentrate on it for much longer. He discontinued blowing his murali as his unloved misery struck him. But what could he possibly do alone in his hut and alone in this world. He could not even scream nor could ask for love. So what could he do? Certainly desire for something big to happen; to find a friend. But who and why would anyone befriend a forlorn vagabond.

Suddenly his eye got fixed on a small pot. It was the same pot that was used by his mother to carry drinking water from the nearby well in the village. Kumar clearly remembered how his mother used to go to nearby well to get the water every day, while he followed and chased her. This was only the last thing left in the house that was directly attached to his mother and he was the sole recipient of that pot. That pot was what he had inherited

23

from his mother besides his murali. He at once realized that if his father possessed the pot he would trade in for his appetite for drinking and vulgarity. He decided to hide the pot and started looking around the safe place in the almost empty room. But his instincts aided him and he did it safely.

After some hours his father returned home and one could hear the tottering steps down the road. As he heard the footsteps of his father approaching nearer and nearer his heart began to pound faster and faster. His pathetic father slammed the door wide open making a loud cracking sound and stared at his little son. His poor son in return just sat there shivering not knowing what would happen next. Without even saying a word his father went to bed and soon dozed off, while the boy sat there in the corner of the room motionless and in eerie silence.

At evening his father woke up from his deep slumber. He seemed a bit relaxed and approachable; first he gazed at one corner of the room constantly, not even blinking or shaking his head. He was completely unaware that he also had a son to look after the demise of his wretched wife. Several moments passed in deathlike silence. His son finally broke the silence that had captured the hut so tightly.

He raised his soft immature voice,

"Pa, what happened last night?"

Perhaps he was afraid to complete the entire sentence; he just wanted to hint this father that his son was still in existence after the death of his wife who at least needed some care, love and affection. The child was anticipating some empathy from his father but his father simply sprang from his position and began to search the room for something he had suddenly realized about. He had already noticed the pot was missing the moment he woke up. He grumbled and suspected that his son might have hid it and shouted for the pot.

"Where is that pot I need to get some water?"

His son was speechless and stared with his small blinking eyes and shaking hands. He had never witnessed his father gone fetching water except his liquors. He knew his father was capable of the worst if not the good.

All of a sudden his dreadful and unloving father landed a harsh slap on his son's face that sent him straight running out of the house; galloping like a mad untamed horse. Little Kumar was horribly terrified to re-enter the house and eventually made his way towards the forest where he had spent the previous night. The jungle was now his second home after his mother had gone, never to return. He found himself alone there but better off without his father and his wrath that was so incomprehensible. He never understood why a mother always loves and a father always the way his own father was.

Kumar was alone again in the jungle, amongst the woods, with his murali and his beloved memories as his only friends. One moment he was striding gaily and the very next moment he was strolling. He seemed happy and content there with no one to be afraid of and nothing to expect of. He felt like a free child. Possibly he was the very first child to make such an important realization about his existence.

It was morning and the forest appeared fresh as if it had just recently been planted and the birds were chirping in all directions among the woods. The boy had no slippers, but that day he felt no pain, nor any uneasiness treading along the naked earth. A sublime relation had already begun to establish with the forest. It was the spring season at that time of the year; the forest had fabricated such colors even a mighty poet would find impossible to portray it in his words. The Amazon-green fields had expanded itself in all directions dominating over all the others; it was completely beyond any measurement. It was like one was amidst the music orchestra where the nature was conducting a grand symphony. The babbling of the brooks, the bumbling of bees and the chirring of grasshoppers did no doubt produce a never heard grand score, it was undoubtedly a soul comforting experience and one felt godlike. The boy felt peace and a tranquil within himself as if he was about to reunite with his lost mother. He completely forgot everything and he was in oneness with Him. The pleasant surroundings had dispelled his grief and he seemed installed in his new life.

So the rest of the day he spent making new acquaintances with the forest. He could not restrain himself from travelling where his feet took him; he had lost a total control over himself and felt like he was alive again after the departure of his mother. The balsamic sweetness of a flower really captivated the boy in its entirety; the exhaling of the winds galvanized him, again the puffing of the wind made him puff. This new vivid sensation intoxicated the boy that made him lavish, extravagant and exquisite.

Though he had not eaten anything in recent hours he did not feel any pangs of hunger. He was finally taken over by fatigue that made him dizzy and he never knew when he had slept for several hours until he was aroused abruptly by the howling of some forest animal. He found himself situated under a thick trunk of a huge tree. Despite the howling sound he felt protected and out of danger. Peacefully he glanced all around him; it was already midday and he was alone and desperately alone but he did not yearn for company. Perhaps he had already found company.

Kumar was at once attracted by the burbling and bouncing of a river that was thrumming through the vale. The little boy at once rose to his feet and followed the river that twisted through the thick forest skipping over the rocks and forcing its way against anything on its way. He ran and ran as agile as a monkey until he realized his run would never come to an end. He decided to rest and soon found himself taken over by hunger, severe hunger.

Life teaches everything to anyone. Hunger was one of the intense lessons the boy had to learn from life so he quickly mastered the art of finding edible food in the middle of the forest. At first he decided with his instincts.

Young bamboo shoots were the first thing he came across and he tried them and found the taste pleasant although he had never had that before. As he moved forward he found himself in the middle of multitude of giant trees with peaks up to twenty metres high forming a dense and well protected maze. Now he felt free to roam around like a deer as he had no responsibility to anyone and no one to fall back on. Moving even further he came across some papayas tree. He had a very good familiarity with the papayas and with some labour he acquired some of them and later enjoyed them.

Not realising he was already in the middle of the forest he was completely in a confused state about finding his way back to the village. The little boy used his best hunches and moved towards the direction targeting his village; the surrounding valley hillocks became his compass and scattered clouds his guide. He ambled along the jungle with quick and soft steps. After walking stiffly in a strolling fashion he became overcome by weariness. Finally he gave himself in to nature's lap and composed himself to sleep in the arms of the forest surrendering himself and all his being. He did not know anything about anything but now he knew everything about everything. Life was his real tutor who was destined to discipline him.

He spent that night there underneath thick pine tree in the same way as the proceeding night, unaware and unafraid of anything.

Next morning he woke up by the vocalizing of the birds but was utterly reluctant to go back home remembering his father's temper and bitter madness. So having nothing to do, he again began to roam randomly and carelessly just allowing his legs to wander about in all directions in the forest jungle with mighty thick trees all around him and bushy grass under his feet.

Wandering quite further he spotted a clear area where small seedlings were about to grow, just about to sprout up from the earth. Some of them were healthy but among them one at little distance was a little taller than others and seemed weak with fragile emaciated stems and tiny leaves. The boy went close to it and touched it with his gentle fingers, so tenderly making sure not to hurt it. For no reason he felt for the plant.

Like every other day, the day ended and the uninvited night approached smiling sympathetically at the boy from much further. Soon the boy managed to return to his home to face his father's torment and torture. He had almost figured out what was going to happen at home, he was boldly prepared, he rather forcefully prepared himself; He was prepared for every eventuality. Horrified he went in and found his father already deep in sleep, quite luxuriously. The boy really got anxious to see if the pot was still there or was already being consumed by his father. He tiptoed to the other room and reached the spot where he had hid the pot. He checked and a confident smile broke on his face as he found the pot safe and sound. He decided not to keep the pot inside the room anymore so he took it out at once and hid it beneath the pile of straw behind his house. Soon his widowed father woke up and remained silent as though he had made a revelation and wanted to share it with the world. With distracted attention he gazed at one corner of the room. Soon he saw his son. He made no sigh of affection or hatred upon seeing his own blood.

He asked abruptly, "What did you eat?"

The boy knew not a word to say in return and simply stared at him fixedly

"I asked you something!"

He stared back.

"Wait here, I will get something for us," the boy heard him saying so as he left the hut.

Soon he went out warning his son to stay in and not to leave the house. As his father went, the boy knew he would not be in for the night and felt somewhat joyful inside. The fear was gone. He had some inner peace but still with some curious hope he waited the return of his father with some food. The fear of his father was gone but his hunger of his stomach was still there, tormenting, troubling, and rising with each passing moments. But the man did not show up except through his ugly and loathsome thoughts.

Time passed and passed. The passing was so slow with nothing to do and no one to love and talk. His mind and hands were vacant, he found himself chasing ants just to give himself some occupation.

Alas and at last the boy was again all alone; loneliness caused more fear in him without any mercy.

Now that he was already hungry and alone he began to sob bitterly but there was no one to listen to him, hear his shrieks and come forward with a helping hand. Perhaps he was abandoned, left completely alone, in a complete state of desertion; even God seemed to have forgotten him. Suddenly out of the blue, something happened quite unexpectedly; the boy felt happy and he was hopeful. He mind served him the image of the seed that he had left behind the other night in the forest.

He pondered, "What might have happened to it, did it find its mother?"

The thought of the plant in the same miserable condition as himself, reluctantly made him stop weeping. He eyes brightened as if he was on a mission. He began to cheer up.

He marched his way back to the same spot from where he had left off the previous day leaving his small plant alone. On his way, he managed to pluck some strawberries and guava and ate them and for the rest of the hunger he satisfied with the clear water skipping over the rocks in the nearby flowing river. He drank deep and felt quenched and invigorating. Soon he increased his pace like a wild untamed horse and reached the place. It was half an hour run from his hut. He found the small plant still there, alone, unfed with its muddy leaves and lean stems with no other plant near to it and surrounded by clods of earth. The boy was undoubtedly sensitive to the plant as it resembled himself. He found it was something to cling to, to take care of and love. He took pity on it and sat near it. He found its tiny leaves drooping and stems fragile and delicate ready to break off even with the slightest of the wind passing by.

The boy thought, "Maybe it is hungry for it had lost his mother." He recalled his neighbours watering small plants in their garden. This made him think that water is the food of every plant. He quickly ran to the nearby river and brought a handful of water for the plant, although though his palm was so small it could not contain much water. He quickly remembered the hidden pot back in his hut and thought it would be a handy tool for this purpose and quickly rushed back home for the pot. At the beginning he was afraid in case his father was at home but as usual he found the hut was empty. He went back to the pile of straw and got his pot. On returning to the same spot in the jungle, he now used this pot to water the plant. He felt quite revived and satisfied.

Next day, he again visited the same place. As he was badly alone and at home he was terrified of his father, he began to feel safe in the forest for he had found a new friend, for he had found a new purpose, a new aim, a genial ambition to serve and be served. He felt a dire need to live and coexist with those woods, those shrubs and those rivers. There was no one to terrify him. He felt renewed with every passing moment with his newly discovered friend in the middle of the forest. Meekly he positioned himself near his friend, touched its gentle leaves and whispered, "Hi you, will you be my friend?"

The poor little lad again added stammering, "W... what is your name?"

His friend could not understand his speech and that could be why it replied nothing in return. Instead it stood quietly, trembling and shivering with every touch of the passing wind. Now the boy had found a grand vocation in his pathetically vacant and deserted life. He would care and tend the small plant every day by watering and clearing the space around it. He made sure that his little friend was protected, safe and not alone in the middle of the forest. The boy wanted his friend to feel that it was not abandoned there among the woods, left to die, to become extinct.

31

In fact, childishly, the boy had already started calling him *Sathi*.

His Sathi with every passing day was now getting healthier and stronger. The boy felt good and even more responsible. He was happy beyond any reasonable description and cried happy tears as he realized he had someone to fall back on and grieve with.

Kumar soon developed a good rapport friendship with his Sathi and with the surrounding jungle too that had witnessed the formation and the growth of this bizarre relationship.

For nine continuous days, the boy visited his Sathi. He felt deeply satisfied to be with his new friend whom he has named Sathi. Every day he went there to water it and talked to it as soon as his father made his way out of the house. He would sit there and talk to the little tree. He once asked, "Did you ever have a mother, I had mine once but now she is gone." And then he would remain there with no movement at all; he would just stare and stare at the loving earth beneath him that held those two friends so passionately.

When it was hot and humid, he was afraid the sun's heat might burn the leaves of his Sathi. With nothing better to devise he even protected it from sun's ray by blocking the light with his small tiny bare hands that in fact needed more protection than a mere tree in the middle of the forest. Mother Nature was there for the rest of the forest but not for him.

He was so innocent.

It seemed as if this new friend was only the reason that Kumar was alive and he was constructing his own mysterious world as the days started to pass by. He had a purity of purpose, but absence of reason behind doing all this. Perhaps he was too unprepared and untamed to ponder in terms of personnel benefits. He never allowed anyone to interfere in his world that was so pure and innocent.

This world he was creating was without confusion, sarcasm and exaggeration. He was taking his time as The Providence might have taken while he was creating our Universe and the distant galaxies.

As the day passed by the plant grew healthier. Sometime the kid would visit his friend twice or three times a day. He was in love, perhaps head over heels in love with his friend and always played his murali whenever he happened to be with his friend. Even at night he used to think of his friend and worry if some wild animals stepped it or consumed it. Sometimes he even gathered strength to go to his friend in the middle of the night, but the darkness outside would prevent him. He was still a kid to amass that courage and walk through the dark forest surrounded by fatal darkness.

There is one thing that cannot be interrupted in its course: time besides misery. So the time passed and passed, passed and passed without anyone noticing how swiftly it was slipping. His father was now already a highly esteemed alcoholic known all over the village for his genuine and authentic love for alcohol and even more for the genuine hatred for his own son.

Years passed by, and now the boy has already established his skills with murali playing. Among the woods and close to his friend he had realized his natural ability nature had bestowed on him, and had sharpened it thoroughly and perfectly though unintentionally and unknowingly. He just loved playing it and his discordant notes were now transforming into sweet melodies. Regularly, he spent hours and hours sitting by his friend and playing the murali. He simply played the murali with abandon. He had nowhere else to be and nothing else to do. His fingers were slowly becoming skillful avoiding the wrong notes while his supreme self was his tutor, tutoring him silently in the craftsmanship and the art of murali playing. His Sathi was not a plant anymore and had grown steadily. Now, no watering was necessary. It had even put on small branches and was on its way to becoming a strong, thick tree.

"The two friends are perfect matched to each other," the passersby simply would remark upon seeing them. It was undoubtedly a source of amazement and bewilderment for any normal being to see such a kind of friendship between the talking and the mute.

From the day the boy had known his friend, he spent all his time and energy for him. The boy talked to his tree friend, he said him everything as if the tree could comprehend everything he uttered. The tree in return stood silent, very silent, trying to understand his friend. It did in fact but never replied.

When the boy talked to it about the ill behaviour of his father, and the sad demise of his mother, Sathi just stood there motionless and soundless, ignoring the wind blowing, preventing its tiny leaves from moving so as not to dishearten its friend. Sathi knew he was the subject to be loved.

And when the boy was in his joyous mood, when he was gaily playing the murali the tree seemed happy and contributed by twisting and wriggling its branches to and fro along with the nearby passing wind. Perhaps this was how the tree appreciated Kumar, its only friend.

When the boy was happy, the tree spent its energy accompanying with the boy. They were perfect friends. Though they couldn't communicate in any language they were still the best of friends and never spent the day without seeing each other. They just felt pleasant to be in each other's company. They were sanctuary to each other.

On the other side' the boy's father was slowly getting worse. What can one expect after such a devoted lifelong passion given to drinking? His health had deteriorated to an incurable extent in that little village far away from the city .He was already an old man with a long dirty beard all over his wrinkled face. He eyes had sunk deep in those two eye sockets showing no compassion and passion for life. He had led a life without loving and being loved, which a human being should absolutely not abide by. He tortured his family and had annoyed the gods for sure. He had already done that sin and was a sinner and was sure to pay when he was gone for Judgement Day. Judgement Day awaits us all. Now he could not go drinking as before as his health was ruined and after a life of good splurge he had practically nothing to put on the counter to pay for his drink except his son, which he would agreeably and preferably do if society norms had not restricted him. He was man of such an infected character.

Years passed and year after year Kumar lived alone and miserable, confined in his own little kingdom. But he was happy.

The small boy was no longer a small boy; he had turned to a matured youth- a young man of nineteen with undying spirit and huge passion for his Sathi and his music.

Similarly, his friend Sathi had no longer small stems, now it had thick branches and a very strong grip on the earth. It has transformed itself to a tall deciduous leafy tree with its rough skin brown in color.

Kumar now had become a skilled musician equipped with a magical flute that could spin music of all generation and colors. The murali in his hands now sounded like a piano playing Beethoven. The melody sounded majestic, it created a fantastic effect among the listeners who happened to be there while he was playing his instrument. And on top of that the surrounding bamboo-brown forest reverberated the melody adding more energy and quality to its tone. The cracking of the bough and snapping of branches volunteered itself as a background to the murali music.

His friend, a fine tree, now didn't need any kind of help; it could extract its needs itself. With the arrival of spring it bore some fine fruit. Kumar was really happy to see his friend with plenty of fruit.

It seems as if he had almost forgotten his father and was no longer terrified of him as he was before, but still he respected him. Several times, he had made up his mind to abandon his home, but he could not because the last memories of his mother were so closely attached to the house, and he could never forget his mother. He still loved his mother so much. Although many things in his life had changed, the old pot in his life had never changed. The pot constantly reminded him of his loving mother. The old mother, with her caress, her soft touch and her nature. Her willingness to sacrifice everything for her son, her tendency to ignore pain and trouble for her family; she worked tirelessly and patiently. He regarded these memories as the treasure in his life. The only things of value in his life were his murali, his friend, his pot and the never fading lifelong memories of his mother that only existed in his memories.

Early in the morning he would go to the tree happily and climb on its branches .It was like oasis for him. The tree even became very careful, watchful all the time and held a friendly hand to his friend, always cautious that he would not fall off his branches. He climbed higher and

36

higher, while the tree helped him ascend much higher. The tree was now really happy to see his friend smile. He would relax on its branches and play music on his murali that echoed throughout the vale. For sure all the woods in the forest were accustomed to listen to his murali. They were his very first ever audience who would never grumble but ever willing to participate.

Now there was something very natural about his ability to play the murali. The music was really enchanting and was sure to mesmerize even the bees passing by. Even nature's music seemed dull as compared to his sweet melody. Every note he produced was a wonder. The villagers passing by halted for some time to listen to his murali and could not restrain themselves from admiring the youth and his instrument. Some who had seen the world around and read would not hesitate to compare him with Orpheus who lived in the land of Thrace. Everyone from adolescent to old just agreed with his music. The animals and the birds loved his music. The doves hovered in the air so as not to miss even a slightest of the note produced by his murali. It seemed as if the surrounding nature would stop then and there to listen to him, and most of all, nobody dared to intervene in the melody. He brought to life everything that was music, indeed he was music himself.

While Kumar played the gentle wind blew to add harmony to his tone like in a grand orchestra. And surprisingly, beetles would join in to provide a drum-like sound and sensation. It seemed as everything in that vicinity approved of his sweet music and was always willing to contribute it. Some of the local musicians, who passed the way, were jealous to hear him play so beautifully. They knew that such skill was hard to acquire without much diligence. His passion was strong, unreasonably strong.

Kumar once said to his friend, "Had my mother been alive to hear her son play," he added with tears in his eyes, "she would be so proud of me."

Listening to his friend, the tree listened passionately, full of emotions and agreed. Normally, when they talked to each other the villagers passing by felt confused and left without saying a word. This was something unfathomable for their understanding.

But now everything was so normal to them. Anyone who saw them felt they were really communicating; the tree was also able to respond to him and his queries. He was in fact able to commune with the tree.

Chapter Two

Evil dies and Virtue saved

As usual, one day Kumar was poised in one of his majestic positions among the branches and playing his flute. His eyes were completely closed and he was immersed, emotionally engaged in his playing mood. He did not hear somebody calling his name again and again until he felt interrupted and opened his eyes. He saw a villager standing quite desperately and using all his means to attract Kumar's attention.

In his hoarse voice he was yelling, "Come down... come down..." He seemed to be struggling to say something more but he was unable to complete his sentence because of his irritation and confusion.

Kumar climbed down searching for any kind of gesture in every corner of his face but could not guess the reason for his awkward behaviour. After a very brief moment of time had fled the villager recomposed himself and panicked-

"Kumar your father is no more, he died last night on his way home."

Stunned, Kumar quickly changed from his highly elevated musical mood and rushed back to his home. He did not know what to do. After all, the man who had deceased was his seed giving father, the person whom his mother had once loved before he turned out to be a worthless creature. Kumar ran as fast he his feet could run and reached home in no time.

Some of the villagers had gathered already. At home, he saw his father lay there dead. He was gone for good. It was quite sure. Tears filled Kumar's little eyes. Kumar tried not to weep and tried to remain steady on his grounds. Though he was not happy, deep in him, he knew this death was good for both – his father and him – a death for good.

Villagers and his father's friends carried away the corpse for the last rituals. No one present there seemed to be sad for this death. They all knew it was for good and for better. Kumar simply followed the procession and he completed the last rituals that were required of a son of a deceased father. He cremated his father's dead body and even every thought and memory of him.

Now needless to say, he became completely lonely in the world. His house was void except for an old bed and a broken chair. There was nothing that could make him feel that it was his home, the very place where he had taken birth. The home was gone. For him the hut was never a home it was just a dwelling. He did not like the place. He abhorred the very thought of it, every essence of it. The very walls now reflected abhorrence. Soon as he felt extremely lonely, he rushed back to his friend in the jungle; the place where he truly belonged and where he had his real home, his real identity and now perhaps a new introduction. But still every evening he returned back to the same hut for some shelter. As days passed by he began some maintenance of the hut with some little aid from his neighbours. After some quick fix the hut resembled a place where a human could at least reside. Now it was almost a residence. Kumar now dwelt there all alone but still the devastating sudden memory of his father sometimes still struck him violently and gave him nightmares.

His old friends back in the village had grown up into fine matured men and already in some profession. In that remote rural village the schools were not advanced enough to prepare their students as future man of science and entrepreneurs. So money was always the only primary need. So many had already left their village to earn money for their poor parents and family. It was not a desire but, necessary that all those boys were bound to leave the village to straighten themselves and their family financially. They all believed so immensely that more money will invite enhanced lifestyles and better lifestyle.

He had a friend named Ghale. One day Ghale's father approached Kumar and asked quite friendly, "So my son, what you have thought of doing ahead now? You know life must go smoothly and it is not convenient to get through life without money."

Kumar knew not a word to say at that point while Ghale's father was expecting some word in return. Kumar looked blank in his eyes with one of his peculiar expressions.

Looking surprised his friend's father added," I am sure you know what I am trying to come at."

Kumar helplessly nodded, "Yes"

"See, you are like my own son, so I am here to advise you. If you need any of my assistance then don't hesitate to come see me."

41

Just as he was about to leave he unanticipatedly looked back at Kumar and poured his heart out.

"I can't lie but I have spent a good number of splendid years with your father, but please do not think I am accountable for any of your miseries. I always warned your father about all the shortcomings but he was a complete wretch. Look son, I don't say that I did not drink, I drank, but I knew when to stop but your father would just keep going on and on."

With a final shrug of his shoulder he said, "There was no stopping for him."

Then he abruptly rolled out and left Kumar alone.

Kumar was indeed worried about his life too. He was a poor man but was deep and wise inside.

His future looked broken. He had no money, no education and above all no proper guidance. In fact he had nothing to be responsible for and responsible of. He had no business to take care of, nor any family inheritance to guard against. There was nothing that belonged to him except his miseries and pathetic childhood and coming uncertain manhood. He got incompetent and desperate.

Every evening he visited the small local market to sell his little vegetables produced in his little farm and tried to earn his living. He had to walk several miles to sell them and it was all very tiring and not of much profit but for a single person that income was enough to just get by. Kumar was already really tired of all this travelling. He was just so anxious to find new means out of the situation. But things were not of much help no matter what he did and how hard he managed. He found himself at the same place where he had started off.

It was one sunny afternoon. Kumar was sitting underneath the tree and was in his thoughtful state. He was worried and he did not know what he was looking for, exactly what he was searching for. He knew something had to be changed as quickly as possible, but he knew not where and how to start. He had a master plan to accomplish but he was all alone so very badly alone. All he had was a mute friend to talk to. In complete restlessness he was just aiming his eyes at whatever it could aim. It was then he suddenly noticed something new, something just about to take birth on one of those branches. Kumar was at first unable to identify what it was: the little things on the branches looked half-flower and half-bud and they were slowly changing in colour, shape and size. They were beautiful. He was really excited to see them as he had never viewed such beauties on his tree.

Kumar then realized his Sathi was now ready to give fruits! He quickly surveyed the other tree around and found the same change in many of them. It was the time, the season for the trees to give though they have never asked for anything. They just know to give, give and give.

In no time, there appeared lots of them.

Kumar had an idea. "I can sell them to get good money in return and eventually make a good life."

Days passed, so did the weeks. Kumar kept on watching the change in his Sathi. There was a complete change – a metamorphosis.

There were now ripe fruits. They were now hanging on the branches everywhere!

The Sathi was indeed very happy to see the smile upon Kumar's face. In fact Kumar was the only friend the tree had and Kumar had saved him.

Kumar plucked down as many fruits as he could. They were many for him to start counting. He was very happy and his mighty heart full of joy. At last he seemed to find peace and seemed in perfect harmony with nature and with God.

Soon he borrowed some sacks and a cart from one his friend, filled the sacks with all the fruits he could and went to the nearby market with eagerness in heart to make a handsome return out of it. He arrived at the marketplace and quickly was able to find himself a place to sit down and begin his new business.

His fruits were really the best. They looked fresh, ripe and special. Every passerby would look and stop and at last buy a handful of them. Kumar managed to sell almost all of them with his Lady Luck residing by his side. He filled up his pocket with cash and returned back to his Sathi and thanked him and showed him all the cash he had collected.

He thanked him from his heart and said,

"Thank you Sathi for letting me pick your fruits and sell them." He now started imagining good times ahead of him just with some recently collected paper money. But let's ask ourselves – "Can this paper money buy us all the things we ever pine for?"

After some momentarily silent he said as if there was someone else listening to him, "Look how much money I have earned by selling your fruits."

Sathi stood there erect and proud of himself; proud because he has helped his friend when he was in the lurch – helped him during his bad times. There was already a sensual complacency between them – a perfect friendship was already to be seen between a human being and a tree – it was just a matter of time before they perfected it. It was yet to be seen.

That season Sathi produced plenty of fruit and happily handed it over to Kumar. Everyday Kumar went to his friend and everyday he went to the nearby market and sold everything he had received from his friend. He went to see his friend every day from sheer force of habit.

Kumar's life was getting better, accomplished and fulfilled. He had not had the faintest notion that one day he would earn so much. He repaired his old hut. Now the ceilings and walls were much stronger and solid than before and also the room was also well equipped and furnished than ever. He seemed to live a life of a king with no worries.

One day he came to his friend and said, "I wish my mother was alive to see this day.

He cried as he said this. Tears started rolling down his cheeks. His face bathed in tears as the old fond memories of this mother came tumbling by.

"She would be so happy to see her son earning money I would give her so much happiness with this money but now what I am to do alone with this money while my needs are so limited in this little village?"

He sighed and looked upon the heavens perhaps waiting for an answer. But there are some answers that time will reveal at the right time and with proper ceremony.

Sathi stood perfectly silent and responded to the moods of Kumar. Sathi listened and reacted to Kumar as if he had followed everything spoken. The sign made by Sathi made Kumar a little relaxed.

Kumar sat under the shade of the tree and soon dropped off. He slept there like many other nights.

At the end of the season he had already managed to earn a good deal of money. Some of his well-wishers advised him even to start a business.

45

He was somewhat bewildered about what to do with all those money. He had never played with such matter before; all he knew was his friend, his music and his pathetic little solitary life.

He thought for days.

Finally he decided to open a small grocery store in the village. And he did it with help of his friends. That is what friends are for, to help and be needed when in hard times.

With a little surplus effort from here and there the grocery store was finally launched and even inaugurated with the great enthusiasm the villagers could ever contribute. Everyone came to see the store being opened the first day and wished Kumar good luck. This store was rather small, but well decorated and flashy, though it didn't contain much varieties but the sale was good. It was just opening up and the villagers were helping him a lot.

Kumar was a good youth with a warm and pure heart so the customers poured to his shop to support his venture. His business prospered like a rocket across the skies.

Slowly he began to earn more and more money.

The money he had earned did not satisfy him much. Not that he was greedy but was missing the companionship of his Sathi. Now he had to devote more and more time to this store thus he had meagre time for his Sathi, but he never missed to see him every evening after he was done for the day. The evenings were the most appropriate time for him as the weather was much better at the time of sunset and gave Kumar more inspiration to play his music better watching the setting sun.

Kumar had such a vivid and genuine sense of originality that he was easily inspired by everything he could see though his senses. He could even compose watching the happiness of the birds and could even compose much better watching the separating clouds. Kumar could just pour all this feelings, his tenderness and his intuition for the entities he could see all around him in his music; such was his musicianship. He was a rational musician and wanted to capture all he could perceive; he knew Nature was expressing itself in all its entirety each and every passing moment. The fools are bewildered upon the totality and expressiveness of the Nature while the sagacious simply bow and appreciate.

Whole days he would sit in his shop waiting for his valued customers. For some he would merrily play some old folk tunes in his murali and that made them visit his store more often without any compulsion and obligation but with a sweet surrender; with a kind of urge that drove them there at that store just for reasons of attendance, responsiveness, sympathy and appreciation. Kumar preferred to be busy and most of the day he laboured quite in effort but he never fizzled to see his friend at the end of the day. It was like an everyday vacation for him.

Every evening unerringly at five he would close his shop and tramp his way through the forest to his beloved Sathi. He would tell Sathi everything that had happened during the day, about the items he had sold and the different funny and bizarre conversations he had had with his customers. Sathi would feel really glad and enthusiastic about this. Some of the events Kumar would shout and tell, just to let the surroundings trees listen to it. He exhibited remarkable modesty, faithfulness and decorum even to the woods in the forest.

Time went on.

47

Kumar had the same routine for the entire year.

On top of that every evening Kumar would sit on one of the tree's branch and play his murali making the entire surrounding musical and privileged. There would be no mistake, no misapprehension from his Murali, no shortage of notes that would let the forest sad and alone. They all had him and he had them all.

The fruits offered by his Sathi assisted him to enhance his economic condition to the next level. He was getting well off with many things a poor villager can pine for. Many times he bought new clothes for himself and showed to his Sathi and even asked how he looked. "I can't judge, can you tell me does it look on me?"

The tree on such occasion would just gesture to manifest its approval.

Even heaven has its rainy days. The seasons would change and Sathi would stop offering his fruits. Kumar never thought of sowing another plants and earning huge amount of money. He loved Sathi. There could be no other tree like his Sathi. Kumar was true to his Sathi and was not into money multiplication occupation. He knew that one could never amass enough to relish upon. So he never tried to search for happiness in material possession. He calmly agreed to whatever came in by the grace of God and his hard effort. He showed no resistance and reluctance on God's way.

Kumar was determined not to leave his Sathi and make new friends for more money.

Needless to say his business was running much better than before and most of all he was at one with his friend.

At times when he felt isolated and alone, he would shut his shop and rush to his Sathi; his friend would always be ready to accept him no matter what. Sathi would open his arms wide and welcome him. Kumar would feel like a King on his throne when he was on one of those branches, so strong he could always rely on them.

One particular year brought a terrible disease. A terrible thing started to take place that made Kumar feel miserable. A terrible disease had spread widely in the village. And soon it started to kill trees mercilessly. A flower may die unnoticed but a tree cannot just perish just like a flower. It catches everyone's' attraction. Bark would become brittle and fall off just like that and in no time the tree would finally die off, lean and naked like a carcass. The trees were all sick and infected by some unknown fatal disease and it was hard to find an expert to identify the disease attached with those trees in that remote part of the village. Hardly a human disease detecting doctor was available.

Many good trees in that village had already died. They all looked starved and gnarly with their leaves turning to pale from green. They all had one surprising characteristics; they all looked shaven, bunched and drooping. Some were about to die anytime soon. Viewed from a distance one would have a reflection of a huge skeleton leaning on one side and ready to collapse even by the slightest kick of wind. Kumar knew that only some good and strong trees were about to survive the disease.

On learning this, Kumar got tremendously worried and checked his beloved Sathi for any effect due to the disease. But so far he could not find any such. For some days Sathi looked in perfect health not exhibiting any symptoms that could have happened due to the disease. But as days rolled by Kumar started getting more and more agitated and finally he was more than being apprehensive. But all of a sudden one day he saw the terrible disease had already started consuming his Sathi as he could see the premature symptoms. As his mind was uneasy he summoned his friends from the village. They could not help him. The disease was very powerful and had started to work on Sathi.

Kumar wept while his soul howled like a mad angry animal. He couldn't possibly do anything except wait and anticipate. He thought of nothing except his friend. Now it had been four days that he had not opened his store so his regular customers began to get concerned about Kumar.

They visited him in the forest where they found Kumar weeping painfully underneath the tree.

"My boy what devil has taken over, why and what you have been doing here?" exclaimed one.

Kumar tried to conceal his pain and tears but they were easily visible to anyone. His face reflected his inner pain and there was no way he could obscure it. Soon he burst into a fit of sobbing.

"I... I was..." Bitterly he started sobbing before he could complete his sentence.

"Oh no, no, please don't panic like that. You are a good boy and believe me God is there to take care of his good fellows," an old man joined in.

Someone then added, "God can't be that irresponsible; he just can't fabricate something and leave it uncared, be inattentive to it while it is in misery," They all did their best to commiserate with Kumar and tried to console him but Kumar was deeply and profoundly immersed in grief. Later the visitors left Kumar and persuaded him to return home and continue with his store and keep his health. Even after several moments they left, Kumar remained, stationary to his posture and kept gazing at the farthest corner of the forest without even a blink in his sad dispirited eyes. He thought that he was finished without his Sathi. The tree was the last relation left for Kumar after his mother and beastly father. Kumar had lots of acquaintances but just one friend and that was also about to perish in front of his eyes.

Kumar did not know what to do next. Questions hovered in his mind, "Should I also miss my only friend. Why? Why do all terrible things happen to me?" Perhaps he was waiting for an answer from Providence but mysteriously, sometimes He chooses to maintain his silence.

Tears were the only answers he had.

His Sathi was getting diseased day by day.

Passersby showed pity on him. They too were very well accustomed with the affection Kumar had for the tree. For two days he did not move an inch from the place. What he did was he just sat on the thickest branch of Sathi and kept praying for the heavens for his Sathi's quick recovery. His grief even made him forget to play his music. Nothing seemed to interest him except that his friend was slowly and silently dying.

His Sathi's branches were his playing ground; Sathi's fruits had saved his fate. Sathi was everything for him, his father, mother, brother and now a friend. He had exhibited perfect friendship and proved to be trustworthy. Several things came in his mind that made him more discomposed and utterly pathetic. He kept on crying and crying until his eyes gave way and could no longer cry. Even they had surrendered and they were unable to express such terrible pain.

Sathi too seemed upset to see his friend in such a terrible condition. But Sathi was already fragile that it could not even respond to the lovely wind passing by nor

51

did it stretch its arms to invite the birds hovering around. Any passersby could realize the gloominess of the place all at once. The silence that prevailed seemed to be getting gloomier and deeply maddening every day.

Villagers knew that the year was appalling for their trees and other herbs and shrubs. They too had lost their trees. For some the trees were the only means of livelihood. But for Kumar it was more than a tree. Villagers had already decided to plant another trees as the alternate source of income. But for Kumar losing Sathi was like losing his entire source of happiness. Villagers were busy, they did not have much time to think about the plants and trees all the time. But for Kumar he had no work so dear than looking after his Sathi. In other words a fragment of him was dying.

Days passed by. He did not care about the shop and it was left unattended for days and weeks. He just visited his home to take some hours sleep and eat something enough just to get by.

Some of the trees just died while some fortunate ones began to show signs of recovery. That day too Kumar was sitting under the tree. He reached for his murali and began to fill it with air. Kumar played and played until he could play no more. Perhaps his soul was too weary to entertain as it had always done. All the time he played tears rolled fiercely from his eyes. But the tone touched everyone's heart and it was not a mere sentimental tune; it was much more than that as everyone and everything, including trees and birds turned serene and sad. This made the surrounding even more mournful and depressing.

Trees were falling mercilessly all around. Their roots up in the air! Branches, stems laid on the ground scattered here and there. It was a real scene of tragic moment. Many trees were uttering their last farewell words to the air, birds and to the skies. Alas, there was no evident sign of renovation with Sathi. The windy wind also decelerated itself as not to jiggle the diseased trees. The wind passed swiftly just gently whispering to them, "Good bye, my friends."

Often Kumar would play his murali. He believed that his music could cure Sathi. He would sweat and panic as he noticed the condition around. He would hang close to the trunk and wish for his Sathi's long life. But nothing satisfied his grief.

It seemed as if the entire world had abruptly come to a sudden stop, all of a sudden, without any warning. Everything was so passive and undisturbed. Insects stopped making any noise; they too must have realized how serious the time was. They too did not wish to make the listener more wearisome. Kumar knew that even his murali could not lessen the pain but he intensely played and played incessantly. The time had become pain itself with no one to heal it, with no remedy.

As he played his murali, Kumar discerned that one single funeral procession of thousands of families was taking place and a single musician was playing his tribute to all the lost souls and the musician himself was dying, dying after playing too long and too hard. He goggled at the sky that night sitting calm, motionless under the tree. His knees bent close to his chest. Slowly he was dying inside. His smile on his face was gone for good.

It was already past midnight and he was still there with his Sathi. The moon shone as usual surrounded by the stars far and wide. And the sweet smell of the dark forest was wafted along by the sluggish breeze. He searched the sky for his mother for he had heard that good people remain as star in the sky after they die. Although he could not find her, he kept on searching and eventually dropped off to sleep along with the moon on its first quarter.

Next morning he awoke with the chirping sound the lively birds made. He did not know why but there was a sense of easiness and trust in the air. He felt a little drifted away from his pain of yesterday. He at once felt enthusiastic about nothing but there was something he could sense. He automatically felt the sweetness in the air and gentleness of the wind. Soon he got depressed on seeing his friend. He was sorry inside thinking that he could not help his friend who was slowly dying. Many a times he felt guilty of himself. Suddenly a few birds came and began to circle the tree happily. He never knew the reason why. But what he saw on the branches made him jump out of sheer happiness. Kumar saw there was a small zone on the tree where butterflies were circling around and for which the birds seemed happy for. He soon climbed up the tree and found a few new small leaves about to sprout in the world. He came closer, anxious to look at it. As he came closer he could not believe with his eyes what he could see. He went nearer to see it and was so joyful. Voluntarily a beatific smile lingered on his face. He at once comprehended that his friend was slowly recovering from the fatal disease. He touched the small leaves gently, they were whispering some words which were hardly audible.

Soon he disembarked from the tree and rushed back to the villagers and invited them to see what had happened. All the villagers were so eager to see what had happened. Many of them rushed to the forest to examine Sathi.

One of them spoke out, "Your Sathi is getting healthier and is almost out of danger."

But one elderly wise man from the village suggested that, still the danger was not over and said,

"My boy Kumar, watch the plant for three more days. Notice each and every change that takes place in it. You should not leave the tree just like that. Maybe your friend is spared,"

This made Kumar even more impatient and restless than ever before. He had not been to his shop and home for many days now, but still he was not willing to return back. He knew he was home. He prayed to all the gods he knew for the well-being and prosperous health of his friend

The first day passed, the new leaves grew in size and number indicating the confident signs of improvement. Kumar was very contented then and said,

"My friend, don't worry, you are getting well, soon you will have all green leaves all over you like you were once before," and laughed gently.

"And then you will be Mr. Green again,"

"The whole world will call you Mr. Green,"

He kept on shouting like a lunatic just out from a lunatic asylum. Kumar was too restless to gather himself.

The disease had caused all the green leaves to fall off. He saw all those scattered leaves, now already dry and dark, said to himself, "The black and dark days are gone forever, thank you God,"

"I knew you would listen to me... you had to,"

The second day too passed. It ushered in great signs of recovery. Kumar was so elated that he could not stop himself from running all across the village and informing every single person he came across. The villagers loved Kumar very much and they all equally participated in this happiness. They wished him good luck and said this to be a real miracle done by God. Only a few trees had survived the deadly disease and Sathi happened to be one of the fortunate ones.

That day too Kumar visited his home briefly as usual just to look around. He did not bother about his shop being in a complete abandoned state for the past couple of weeks. He knew his attendance with Sathi was of prime importance. He carried some food with him and returned back to the forest to his Sathi. On his way, he would take out his murali and begin to play with great enthusiasm. This enthusiasm was overwhelming and at the advanced stage. He did not feel like stopping playing it. He went on playing and playing this sweet and melodious music; this music had become his new theme of his new life. His fingers were getting perfect enough to produce the kind of note he wanted to describe his happiness, his integral emotion he had within himself. The music enlightened the surrounding and every soul that it hit upon. The sound of this murali music travelled all the way through the distance deep forest and produced a wonderfully majestic effect. Some villagers who had seen enough of the world remembered Maestro *Hariparsad Chaurasia* as they listen to murali of Kumar.

Finally, the third day brought more leaves on the branches of Sathi. Sathi was getting better and better every moment. Soon Kumar found himself running all over the village with openness in his heart as if he had unbolted the enigma of the Universe and wanted to share with the world. He asked everyone he encountered to come and see the changes in Sathi. They came, surprisingly they all came. They checked, examined and they assured Kumar that his Sathi was fine now. Many of them reexamined the tree and found that it was now completely invulnerable and remarked that it will be bearing fruits in the coming few months.

It was nothing but news of sheer joy and ecstasy to Kumar.

Kumar jumped with happiness, tears in his eyes, he could not prevent himself from playing his murali as a means of expressing his newly found tranquility and peace of mind and more importantly as a reunion with his friend.

"Yes, time for good music," shrieked one of the villager.

"Yes, yes," quickly added the rest of them.

Then, as usual Kumar briskly climbed on one of the top branches and started. His music enchanted the multitude.

The villagers listened to his murali intensely and were full of emotion. They knew that he was not to be disturbed while he was playing. Some even appreciated him and said that, "Son, it is all due to your music, your friend is fine. "Your music restored life in your tree."

He felt pleased and highly gratified.

Days passed, so did the weeks and undoubtedly the months. Why and who could stop it?

Sathi was completely fine. The fatal disease had gone now and it was back with its bushy leaves and strong branches ready to face every uproarious wind that came on its way.

The following season, Sathi gave a lot more fruit than expected, much more than it had given earlier. Kumar was so happy that he could not constrain himself from laughing. As a matter of fact that very season he managed to earn a lot of money and had some money accumulated aside for any further rainy days. Now content in heart he started giving his attention to his store again but this time he multiplied his store with all the cash he had collected. He decorated his store to make it look more fancy and appealing and also furnished his little hut. He felt more complete.

But no matter what he did he never completely forgot about his Sathi, it was like a background thought process that was always initiated and active all through the day as long as his senses were alive.

That's why he would visit him every day after closing his store. He would sit for hours, and return back when it was nearly dark.

Someday, he would close his shop early and spend times with his dearest friend. He became more attached with the tree just not to contrive the empty hours but out of a forceful compulsion that had become so irresistible. He would climb on the top of the tree and sing and play his murali. The love he shared with the tree was just enough not to remind him of his deceased mother. It fulfilled him and gave him a strong sense of being in love in his solitary world.

Kumar now had transformed to a fully-grown youth with long equine pleasing face, broad chest with great muscles, strong hands and feet. His trimmed short hair gave him the perfect look along with his bristly eyebrows and defined cheekbones. And on top of these attributes he always had a fruity laugh hanging on his petal soft lips that perfectly was in harmony with his aggressive look and bass voice. He was undeniably the charming hero in that little village who was sculpted by God himself. He was undeniably the most handsome and gamesome in the village. His slender and trim figure attracted everyone.

The story of this young boy was now everywhere: a boy with an irresistible look and unalloyed love for music. His flair for music was known wide to the people in the neighbouring villages. The villagers from nearby villages talked about Kumar's ability and some would even envy while the girls would always be eager to behold him. After all he was formed in such a handsome manner; he was simply inviting and was the cynosure of all eyes.

Chapter Three

Settled Down

Now it happened that a young girl in the nearby village often took her sheep to graze in nearby woods. It was not just her but the trend of life for most of the girls of her age at that village. There is nothing more one can expect out of life in the village. It seems there is nothing else to do, but always the same thing to do over and over without any variations. But the nature of sameness never seems to overwhelm the villagers as we can hear sometimes city dwellers complaining, "Oh my life has become terribly boredom with the same task to complete for each and every single day." Perhaps nature also does not engage in something noble and new every day. She has been doing the same task since the dawn came into existence-morning-noon-evening-night and start all over again. There are some patterns that have been laid down for all creatures and plants in this world to which everyone and everything must calmly and submissively give into without any expression of dissatisfaction. Perhaps there is nothing more we would be able to do even if we desire not to follow the pattern, except face unexpected consequences and sometimes even humiliations. Desiring or being without desire is just the two alternatives that we can have but following the grand pattern laid down is our main recourse. We just have to join the stampede and be a part of it.

So this village girl was not an ordinary girl except she had an ordinary life – she was full of life and vigour. She would graze sheep, take care of her family that composed of her parents and a little brother, do almost all the cooking and cleaning chores of the house and in her spare time tended the sheep. What an extraordinary but still uncomplicated life where one did nothing but still did everything – where one's accomplishment at the end of a day would just be exactly the same as of yesterdays. Her father was a local labourer while her mother was a mother, and her brother was the eye of the entire household who had no responsibilities but he was the permanent responsibility of the house where everything emerged and ended on his satisfaction and dissatisfaction. Such was her family-simple yet loving.

She would let her sheep freely wander often times and in the mean time she would just listen to the birds singing or sometimes chat with her fellow friend. Now and then she would run after butterflies, sometimes would sing some folk songs and sometimes even respond to the whispers from the forest.

Needless to say that she was a girl with an elegant beauty. She had long brown hair that was so silky and smooth. During the day when the sun was high, the reflection on her hair made the surroundings even brighter. At night the light emitted by the moon was a perfect match to her beauty. Her radial face glowed white and her beautifully placed rows of teeth were of inescapable beauty. When she smiled, hardly anything in the world was comparable to it. Every creation of nature readily seemed to give up in front of her smile.

Similarly, her eyes, big and dark with carefully designed eyelashes made her even more beautiful. No words could catch the beauty that her dainty nose and lips exposed. Her beauty was nothing but was the despair of every other young lass in the village.

She had a slender queenly figure with a chalice waist, long limbs and flawless glowing complexion. Her unblemished skin was white as snow. The most dazzling part of her body was her eyes – they shone in brilliance no matter what time of day one looked at. Her elliptical shaped, symmetrical eyebrows with walnut shaped eyes were by no means worth comparing with anything. She glowed like a night lamp amid the darkness when she smiled revealing her bleach-white teeth. And every youth in that small village was enchanted by her angelic smile followed by a soft and soothing weak voice yet so full of innocence and simplicity. She was highly a sophisticated creature and at the same time dear as a deer.

She was called Phul Maya. A poet would utterly fail to depict her with his ink on a small piece of paper. Her traits were countless and certainly inexpressible in words.

Like every young girl, sometimes she even fancied a young prince coming on a white elephant, surrounded by his mighty soldiers to take her to his distance palace on an isolated majestic island. She fancied that the water around her island would be overwhelmed by dolphins and she would sing and amuse herself in their company. But the fact was she was just a beauty with her grazing sheep in the woods.

One fine day, she was out with her sheep. The cool breeze was blowing and the day was really friendly in every manner. On that breezy day she was sitting and chasing the butterflies like every other day when she heard soft yet relaxing music coming from a distant place. It came from quite a distance, perhaps from the woods. She at once was attracted by the melody and its timbre. The vibrations lured her all at once and she felt captivated-the temptation was strong and she was too fragile to resist. She had never heard such a melodious music before. She was surprised and bedazzled at the same time. She wondered who could have played so wonderfully. Her entire attention was attracted towards the melody as she knew no one that could perform so fantastically. The day ended.

Next day again she went to graze her sheep following her regular rhythm. She arrived at the same place where she had heard that music the other day but that day she heard none though she was intently waiting. With no amusements and pleasing the day too passed and she returned home with her sheep in the evening. At evening, she asked one of her friend about the music and her friend introduced Kumar as the music player from the adjoining village. Her friend even managed to add some words about his charms and his debonair look. Now Phul Maya was even more yearning to see the boy and listen to his music from a close distance where not a single note was to be slipped. Phul Maya was not trained nor was she well versed in music but music served itself like a hunger unfolds itself to a hungry man-one should not learn to be hungry.

Days quickly moved on showing no resistance. It never hesitates to move from one day to other, does it?

Every day she would hear the melody at the same time with the same love, same scattered attentiveness and eagerness. The breeze brought the melody to her and she would wait for the time for the breeze to come in.

The melody was such an ear pleasing one that no one could resist paying attention to it even if one wanted to.

It just captured one's mind and soul. Even the breeze loved to carry it wherever it went. Phul Maya too did not want to miss this melody even for a single day. So one day she decided to follow the melody hoping to meet the player, meet the author of such a divine and inspirational music. Her first attempt was futile. She adventured the forest till dusk but she had no idea where the melody was coming from. The following day she came early and went up to the spot where she had been the previous evening and waited patiently, waited patiently for the music to be heard again. In no time, the melody resounded the entire valley. She now had a hint which direction to take. She quickened her pace and found herself in another village where she had a very few acquaintances. She followed the music and soon she found herself amid the strange woods staring at her vaguely. With slow pace she toddled along the grass making some crispy sound underneath her foot. Almost like a magic she found herself in a clear area surrounded by thick brown forest. Now she was very close to the place where the music was coming from. With her eyes wide open she marched towards its direction and found herself in his presence-Kumar was there playing his murali with his eyes closed. She stepped further, and encountered the beautiful magician sitting under the tree holding his wonderful murali to his lips and weaving a very mesmerizing music.

She went a little close and stood there without even uttering a word, without even shaking her body. She was feeling little nervous as this was a new place and she was facing a complete stranger so charming and captivating. Without letting him know about her presence, she just stood there and listened intensely. He too was so engrossed that he did not even notice a complete stranger standing just behind him – the sole human listener of his music.

Quite some time later, Kumar felt something was shuddering behind him, and looked back and to his surprise saw a young girl all alone by herself covered with shyness and giving a coy smile. She was in her first flush of youth and voluptuously beautiful and mesmerizing; she was a beautiful maiden that Kumar had ever laid his eyes on.

Kumar could not believe his eyes for he had never seen such a dazzling foreign beauty before. He glanced at her hair and could not believe that any one could have such a long, dark, shining and pleasant hair. Her face perfectly shaped. They were meant to caste spell bound as it were. Her eyes were deep and wide and he knew that there were answers hidden to all the complex questions one faced in the world. He couldn't stop himself staring in and into her eyes. He said to himself - She is a vestal virgin.

She, in return, was not less attracted. She too had found something mysterious in his eyes that still had to yield so much. She too kept on looking them for a long time accompanied by silence until a gust of wind dared to interrupt it. She felt ashamed and lowered her eyes with a lovely smile hovering cowardly around her lips.

He said to himself, "Never have I seen anyone so beautiful in my whole life."

Finally he broke out and asked, hardly giving himself any time to compose himself, "W... hat! Who are you?" in a stammering tone.

She was speechless and finally replied in her tensed state.

"Phul Maya," and ended up abruptly not even asking his name in return and waiting for the next moment. She seemed apprehensive.

Again Kumar said with hollowness in his voice, "I have never seen you in these parts, I guess you are new to this place,"

She replied quickly this time,

"Yeah, I … I am from your neighbouring village, I live there."

Kumar added agitatedly, "And what made you come here, do you have some friends or relatives here in this village?"

He thought himself of many different things regarding the beauty of this girl and realized that her name should be Laila or Juliet for she was so beauty.

After a short pause she answered briefly, "Y… yes,"

He questioned,

"Who are your friends? Maybe I know them."

She was completely at sixes and sevens not knowing what to answer. She rightly realized that she was in a miserable condition with those little lies so she abruptly turned back and ran towards her own village, without even saying a word to him. She shied and ran and ran until she found herself at the place where she had started.

Kumar too was completely confused. She was already out of sight before he could stop her and ask any thing.

He smiled to himself, "Is this all a dream, am I day dreaming or real?" But he was truly fascinated by her persona.

How could one not be directed to her sweet voice and looks? Kumar fell in love at first sight, unquestionably. He got vexed with himself for not asking her real identification or any further details. He even admitted to Sathi that he liked the girl he met just a few hours ago, the tree as before responded in such gesture which only the two of them understood.

Saying goodbye to Sathi he returned home for the day.

Back in his hut, he was all at unrest; with constant thought of her, her melodious voice kept on striking his eardrums again and again. All the time, he tried to remember her fair maiden face, her lips and everything his eyes had struck upon the moment. At night he tried to sleep but could not sleep. The coming of this girl had completely changed his life. He constantly kept on rewinding the brief moments shared with her that were so firmly captivated in the fractions of his mind. Perhaps all those recurring thought gave him some inner peace.

On the other side, Phul Maya was still not ready to believe the person she had met in the forest. She had never ever seen a man with such imposing appearance in her village. She just kept pondering again and again – How could anyone be so handsome, well-proportioned and as talented as well? His handsomeness had completely overcome her. She recalled the questions he had put to her and laughed to herself at her foolishness. She summoned her mother and presented everything to her as it had happened in the forest. Both the mother and daughter laughed.

The next day also, she decided to go there but was full of nervousness and shyness as she thought about the answers to the questions he had asked to her. So she waited for evening. By this time she had known that he only played in the evenings. She let the sheep graze on their own and waited for the sun to set, rather patiently.

She said to herself, "Shall I tell him the truth?"

"If I tell him the truth, then will he take it positively or think it the other way?"

Finally, after a long conflict with herself, she decided to tell the truth, and waited for the evening to arrive even more impatiently than before.

Kumar, in his shop got worried and of course he got tensed, thinking,

"Will I be able to see her again? If yes, then how and when? Maybe I asked more than I should…"

Such random thoughts kept lingering in his mind and made him more restless.

With such questions he passed his day and soon when he was done with the store he went to his Sathi's place. He climbed the branches, the tree readily accepted his friend and helped him get to the top, his usual place. He began playing his music with the same artist in him. He played and played. Suddenly he felt a look and opened his eyes and looked around. And to his disbelief she was there looking at him with a pleasing glance and questioning eyes. His eyes met her eyes like never before. He stopped playing. He could not believe it. It was the same shape of beauty that he was pining to see. He got down the tree quite nervous and there she was standing with an evergreen smile mixed partially with fear and shyness. They both exchanged their greetings.

Not knowing how to start Kumar at once got over excited and asked,

"Why did you run away all at once yesterday?"

Not even waiting for her answer he added further,

"What was the matter?"

Phul Maya flushed red with fear and anxiety. She was ignorant and did not know how to acknowledge it. So she admitted that she had lied to him. She told him everything, the real thing. She told him that it was the music that had drawn her close to that tree from her village. Soon they were acquainted and this acquaintance turned to a fluent and an amiable conversation. Both seemed agreeable, hospitable and easygoing.

The very first day he introduced her to his Sathi. At first, she could not believe it. She tried to be convinced but could not persuade her consciousness. It was something far too inconceivable for her to come across: *a fact that a tree and a man can become good friends*. On top of that they understood each other perfectly and could even commune.

Kumar told her everything about Sathi and how Sathi had helped him when he was in a crucial moment in life. He recalled the childhood days of his own and the first time he had met Sathi, how it helped him, and all the minute details. Phul Maya listened attentively like a good student. She could read the very truth of their relationship in every word Kumar said. She realized that relationship had survived over the years till this day.

Phul Maya was quite amazed to learn all his secrets and the life he had led so far. She desperately listened to every detail with a complete silence and dedication making sure not to interrupt him. At first everything that he said to her was enigmatic, whatever she heard and learned from Kumar was quite exceptionally new, unheard, unfelt and hard to embrace that such relationship also ever exist in the world. She had heard many evil things – people tending to kill and destroy one another to satisfy their own lust and vanity. She had heard the stories of the best of friends turning to become the worst enemies; she had heard tales of two brothers quarrelling and expressing disagreement over a small piece of land and some sum of money. But here what she saw was nothing except pure love, trust and harmony.

69

There was no place for sarcasms, exaggerations and deception. There was no need for one to lie or hide something from one another. Everything was as clear as the blue sky.

Gradually, the days passed by. So did months.

Phul Maya and Kumar were getting much closer as they started see each other with undisturbed regularity. Not every day, but she came to see Kumar twice a week whenever possible. Everything must and has to change so how could their relationship remain unaffected. So naturally in a slow and gradual manner it began to emit sweet fragrance of love which was slowly spreading to the surroundings of which the forest has already known. The breeze carried with it. They tried to conceal this newly formed connection, even with themselves. Now it had become a part of her life to listen to the music and stories of Kumar's childhood. Many a times Kumar would just be repeating the same lines again and again but she never got annoyed listening to them, and Kumar never in fact got tired of speaking at length about his past no matter how degraded it had been. He was proud to speak that the tree had nourished his soul. She had realized that his childhood was a complete pain, a misery, a sorrowful episode which had now happily ended. She looked at his Sathi and for the first time she felt something for it. She felt a rush in her blood, a deep and profound sensation that she had never experienced before. She felt the tree had responded to her, she could not explain how but she felt it, it was strange though. Gently Sathi moved its branches to and fro conveying her that she was always welcome in their world. Now, she knew that everything Kumar had said was true as the Sun. Once she even visited his shop and helped him arrange the shop properly, so that customers would buy more stuff.

Some evenings, Kumar would go with her up to her village. He liked her very much and wanted her to be safe and happy. Many villagers had noticed them walking together and had already started talking about their relationship. Such friendships cannot be kept hidden from the parts where people are less occupied; people generally sense something new very quickly. And they did.

One day Kumar was in his shop when his childhood friend, Ghale, came in out of blue one fine afternoon. Ghale very enthusiastically asked about the girl Kumar was seen walking with for several evenings.

"No, it is nothing, she is just a girl from the nearby village," reluctantly replied Kumar.

But Ghale quickly was able to decipher his reluctant nature and jumped to the conclusion.

"I know everything," Ghale said openly, looking right into his eyes. Confidence was all over him.

Finally Kumar did not hide anything. He pleaded to Ghale to keep that to himself.

He said, "Yes, I like her." Ghale was more than happy for his friend. He knew at last Kumar had found someone to love and be loved. He was exhilarated.

The following day, Kumar closed his shop at his usual time and went to Sathi's place. To his surprise, Phul Maya was already there. He came close to her and asked, "Why so early today?"

She smiled and replied, "Just to surprise you."

Phul Maya stayed calm and said nothing, but he understood everything. Between the two lovers only the silence could be heard distinctly. Finally Kumar disturbed the silence and asked, "So how are the sheep?"

Phul Maya gave a sarcastic look and answered wryly, "As fine as can be."

"I guess they are happy grazing."

As they were talking a flock of birds hovered above the tree for some time and sat on the branches; a sweet chorus resounded through the valley. As soon as Kumar saw this, he took out his murali and wove a tune so elegant, so majestic that the entire forest came to life all at once. The gentle wind blew at that instant adding more melody to it. Kumar kept playing incessantly. Phul Maya was now breathless, completely mesmerized, not being able to withdraw her eyes from him and not even permitting her senses to migrate elsewhere. Soon she looked around and found that a group of audience had already crowded there. They were the local villagers passing by. The music went on and on and he was so much absorbed, nothing could disturb him – such was his passion. He was completely in a world of his own. She noticed him as he played with his fingers, his lips as they made the Murali alive. It was so enchanting and glittering. Finally, the music ended and it was followed by a small applause. The crowd requested him to play some more. He then began like a real musician who could do everything but not play his murali. Soon he would be tireless and busy as a bee.

"Why don't you go to the town and play there. I am sure you will make good money there," one from his audience commented.

"Yes, he is right." added the other immediately.

Kumar could say nothing to these volunteered proposals but just, "One day I will."

Soon his small audience went away approving him with one more round of applause. He gently bent his head low and expressed his thanks. As a matter of fact he never gave a serious thought about going to town and using his talent to earn money. He never thought of it in terms of money, he played because he simply liked it and was fond of it. Many had even suggested him to go to the big town and join a band but he had never thought of it seriously and thought it nothing but a joke.

Once, even Phul Maya had suggested him to enhance his musical talents, but Kumar was so naive he could not understand the success story behind music. He did nothing but ignored. For him, performing on his murali was a very personal mater. He did not call himself a talent. Murali for him was the best way of expressing his soul. Nature taught him to play and he thought it his responsibility to entertain Nature now rather than audience for trifle of money. There were many other ways to earn money.

Phul Maya and Kumar were more than best friends now; they were lovers, full time lovers. But lovers are not always free. Neither were they. Phul Maya's father heard about her daughter's involvement with a boy who was a musical in nature from the neighbouring village and whose best friend was a tree. Her father talked to Phul Maya.

"Phul, I have been listening to something about you lately."

"A… About what?" she stammered.

Further, he asked her many questions.

But the daughter was no less clever. Most of the time she tried to be silent rather than replying something. Speechless, she stood in front of her father with her head bowed down in agreement. Her father and mother understood everything. After all, they had also passed through the same age and time. She was afraid that if her father knew all the truths she would be in hot water.

Phul Maya decided to let him know about her affair through her mother. The plan worked. A mother is first and foremost the best friend a daughter can have to share her feelings, especially related to love and marriage.

At first, the father was really infuriated but when he came to know about the well-natured manners of the boy from the villagers, he somewhat cooled down. But this did not completely alleviate his curiosity. Personally, he decided to meet Kumar. In this, his daughter helped him. A father has a right to see who his daughter is dating even in that remote village.

Phul Maya went directly to Kumar and told him everything not even missing out a word and said that her father was longing to see him.

Kumar could not respond to it, was in complete bewilderment, and replied, "See Phul Maya, I think I will need some time to think of all this."

Phul Maya did not know what to do. She was confused. On one hand, there was her father she could not betray and there was her sweet lover whom she did not want to hurt on the other.

Soon Phul Maya returned back home promising to return the following day.

Kumar could not sleep well that night. He had never experienced such circumstances before in his life; he was alone with Sathi and was happy and seemed animated in many ways.

He thought of different things over and over, he considered and reconsidered, he was trying to reach a decision but every time he found himself lost and utterly at miserable condition.

In his mind, the past moments flashed, the moments shared with her, her gentle smile and friendly behaviour that showed sign of prospering. He loved her, but was scared to carry the responsibility.

Early next morning he could wait no longer and rushed to Phul Maya's village to meet her father. He was just not having enough confidence to face her father. And finally after many attempts he succeeded in overcoming his fear and went inside her home.

No sooner had Phul Maya heard him, she rushed out in the yard. Soon her mother arranged the meeting between Kumar and his would be father-in-law. Her mother liked Kumar as soon as she saw her. How could anyone remain without liking him?

Phul Maya's father asked Kumar about his life and all the things related to his life. As a father he had to be sure that his daughter would be in safe hands. He knew that his daughter could not do anything wrong being in love with Kumar. He was confident that his daughter loved Kumar so he must be a righteous man for her. He knew Phul Maya could never be wrong in her judgements. So after a long conversion both the parties reached a conclusion.

They were to be married. Very soon, without much delay.

Phul Maya's father liked Kumar and thought that her beloved daughter would have a good future with this boy even though he played the murali and had only one friend.

The news made everyone happy. Happiness was in the air. Phul Maya was probably the happiest one. She was overpowered by sheer happiness that made her even more blissful. She felt blessed and now she had matrimonial glint in her eyes.

They got married in a nearby temple as both the parties were substantially not very rich.

Her father invited almost everybody that he was acquainted to and from the village. The visitors congratulated the newly married couple and wished for their everlasting and eternal happiness. From the boy's village, very few people came since the boy was alone in this world. But still he managed to collect some of his best friends and elders. People danced and made merry. And the guests in the party got more excited as the bridegroom played his murali. For the whole day and night guests kept on celebrating the wedding party and everyone wished it would never end. The local musicians arrived and started to accompany the murali music. The music was magnificent. Although all the music played was not amplified, still it was no less than an orchestra. The rhythms and the intervals played were perfect and every note was played so gracefully. The music romanticized the people and all the attendants began clapping in unison. Local villagers and other major nearby musicians were completely taken by the boy's ability on hitting perfect notes on the murali. Later on Kumar played many famous music pieces by popular contemporary and ancient musicians. This made others realize that he was the best of all of them. His musical talent was outstanding and astounded other musician.

Finally after many hours rejoicing, the ceremony was over and the invited guests started walking off to their respective destination; completely elated and they blessed the couples as they moved on.

Phul Maya's parents bid the newly married bride and bridegroom farewell. Both the parents had tears in their eyes and promised to see them on suitable occasion. Her mother shed tears and sobbed a lot as her darling daughter was going out of her hands. She just burst into a fit of sobbing. She just could not stop sobbing and was rather hopeless. Just in time, some of her relatives convinced her to gather some courage and speak farewell words that eventually encouraged her to cast a gentle smile on her face. Seeing her beloved mother's face, Phul Maya too could not help crying and after a moment she hugged her mother with thick streams of tears flowing from her eyes. Her eyes welled up as well.

Kumar was the one who handled the situation and separated Phul Maya from her mother who now had realized that it was a complete idiotic to cry like that on such moments.

Phul Maya's parent left them with lots and lots of blessings.

After everybody had left the party, Kumar went to his hut and found Phul Maya waiting for him on his newly arranged bed. Only a candle was lit at the farthest corner of room and that dimly lit the room. Phul Maya's bright face reflected the entire room. There was no need for another source of light.

He reached close to her and found her even more prepossessing than ever before. Her glowing skin, her arched eyebrows, her delicate ears, her long and slender fingernails made her all look more alluring and that made Kumar feel even more romantic. Phul Maya felt the same way.

Gently he touched her hands and her cheeks. Phul Maya hesitated with shame and moved his hands away, but actually gesturing to him that she loved that touch of his. He then kissed on her red lips which were now wide open and welcoming. Their tongues met like fireballs and they made sweet love throughout the night. It was after all their first night together, ever.

Next morning, while Kumar was still in bed, Phul Maya had already woken up and completed all the household tasks. She prepared two cups of tea and went to Kumar. Kumar abruptly woke up by the tingling sound of the bangles Phul Maya had worn and put out his hand to get hold of the cup.

"You got up so early! Why?" asked Kumar.

Still ashamed to face Kumar directly she responded looking slightly in another direction,

"A good housewife should always get up before the rest of the house, which is what my mother has taught me."

"Oh yes! Then your mother has taught you all the good deeds that an excellent housewife should possess, right?"

"Yes," said Phul Maya.

"Then I still guess that your mother did not teach you everything because she did not teach you something rather important,"

"What?"

"Hm, she didn't teach you that a wife should invariably kiss her beloved husband every morning before serving tea."

Flushed with shame she could do nothing other than run to the kitchen. After all, this was just her first morning of her married life. Kumar chased her to the kitchen like a hungry predator after his prey. He ran his hands around her chalice shaped waist and kissed her gently on her neck. She soon managed to release herself from his iron-like hands and replied, gasping for breath,

"See this is not proper time for this. I think you will have to wait till evening."

But Kumar began to approach her, but she had already suspected the incoming danger, slipped quickly through the little gap, grasped the shop's key and went directly towards the shop. Kumar in return gave up his attempts and followed her. Both of them spent morning in the shop rearranging the stuff while Kumar instructed her about the groceries and their respective prices. But it was Phul Maya effort and ideas that gave the shop a much better appearance than before. Otherwise everything was placed out of order and showed completely indication that Kumar had handled the shop roughly and carelessly.

"This is how a good shop needs to be set up if you expect customers."

"Yes, I have made a very important realization, your highness, and thanks for that comment," replied Kumar with a sheepish smile.

Then Phul Maya went indoors to prepare lunch. Sweet fragrance emitted from the house and sent powerful signals that something very delicious was being prepared.

Not only Kumar but even the neighbours could smell that.

In no time, she invited Kumar for lunch, the first lunch that she had cooked for him. In fact he had already waited patiently and he was hungry to eat the food prepared by his wife. He leapt off from his sitting position, rushed into the house and landed directly in the kitchen. He could not believe his eyes at what he saw; an array of his favourite dishes was in front of him and his mouth watered.

"How, how on earth did you come to know about my favourites, dear?"

"Well, my dear, you see, my mother, actually taught me that an excellent housewife should know everything about the likes and dislikes of her husband," she remarked in a jocular mood.

"Hmm, I see," fervently remarked Kumar.

He quickly devoured his lunch for he had not eaten such delicious food in his entire life. He ate like a glutton.

Kumar was accustomed to feed on whatever was available to him.

But Phul Maya was really skilled on cooking things. She was a perfect cook. The kitchen for her was like what the murali was for him. She knew how and when to mix spices with foods. She knew the exact time they should be poured and diluted.

Both of them enjoyed the supreme dish with little conversations in the middle.

He even inquired about the techniques she had applied but she said, "Look Kumar, everybody has their own part, so concentrate on yours, and let me concentrate on mine."

Kumar highly appreciated her wisdom and from then afterwards he never asked for the recipe. He now had her to do the cooking for good.

He ate his portion, appreciating the food all the times.

Chapter Four

She Comes

Kumar and Phul Maya had an important routine to follow with each coming day. They visited Sathi in the evenings at about five almost every day after closing the store as usual.

In no time since Kumar and Phul Maya married, Sathi was already a member of their family. Not only Kumar and Phul Maya but Sathi too was glad to form part of this family. Sathi, standing firm on his place was always elated to see them approaching towards him hand in hand.

Every evening, the couple would arrive at Sathi's place in the woods; it was just the only place they really longed to be. Sathi would move its branches as they approached towards it as a gesture of warm and affectionate welcome. Sathi always wanted them to know how much he loved their arrivals and hated their departures. Phul Maya and Kumar understood Sathi's feelings. Often they would laugh, joke and make merry. It was at such moments that Kumar would take out his murali with great love and care and play it. Many a time, Phul Maya would dance even though she just only knew how to shake her slender body in the name of dancing. Sathi was probably the happiest being to watch it, to observe it with all its passion. The strong wind seemed to unite them and make them inseparable.

Time kept on moving with its own grace.

Kumar and Phul Maya lived happier and happier than ever before. It was one of those times when Kumar comprehended the meaning of true and unconditional love; what it was like being in love with another human and to bestow love in return. Now he would never be apprehensive like the way he had been all his past life. Now he had an angel by his side guiding him through the way.

Now their small shop reasonably in good shape and made a satisfactory amount of money for the couple. Both were polite to their customers and always attentive. Both of them took care, exceedingly good care of the shop. Kumar wanted the business to flourish, so did his beloved wife. He wanted his family to be rich in money now. It was for the first time Kumar had ever pined for the wealth. Perhaps he was getting accustomed to the fact that money played a very vital role for one to prosper if not spiritually then at least materially. He knew he had to keep his wife happy and satisfied and for that all he needed was money except his unsurmountable love. Phul Maya was also turning out to a very good and efficient housewife and loved preparing delicious food simply to make her hubby happy. She knew her husband had never been loved and fed before.

As the days rolled by she could feel that Kumar wanted to be rich as he started talking more about money. She understood his wishes and gave into it and tried to help in all the ways she could devise of. Kumar had discerned that they were living a poor and unhealthy life in that little village but Phul Maya's support made him feel easier and much comfortable. He always counted on Phul Maya to come and deliver some nice soothing words to him during the times he felt down and out. After all she had inherited the traits of an angel. Her talks and thoughts always had a galvanizing effect on Kumar and made him ever assiduous and gallant.

Needless to say Sathi also bestowed them with a plenty of good fruit that year since it had regained good health after the epidemic. It was like all the prosperities and good luck had come to Kumar since he united with Phul Maya. The fruit was sweet and full of fragrance. With the sale of the fruit Kumar and Phul Maya made a deal of money which they saved for rainy days.

One fine evening in the forest, Phul Maya said to Kumar, "Kumar, why don't we buy ourselves a piece of land, it may be of good help in bad times"

Kumar, as always, welcomed her every idea and made up his mind to buy a good piece of land without putting any further consideration upon the subject matter; Kumar knew that his wife would not entertain any immoderate ideas. She was the thinker and he was the doer. Soon after that both went to their neighbour and expressed their interest in buying a piece of land.

The neighbour was a good man and loved them. He was more than happy to inquire about a piece of land for this new couple.

Luckily just a few yards away from their door they bought a piece of land that they could call theirs with pride and distinguished ownership. Kumar and Phul Maya were the happiest couple now – such is the power of money or the possession of its equivalent – can turn grief to bliss. They thought that it was God's desire for them to buy the land. They thanked God and Sathi and in spite of everything they never stopped thanking and paying their homage.

Kumar thought, "What would have happened if I was not married to Phul Maya? Probably I would have ruined my life in some gutter in the farthest corner of this village," he thought himself.

Sometimes he would give a piercing look at the sky and say out loud, "God, you have a plan for everyone, I know you have healthy plans for me."

Kumar thought that he knew the secret, perhaps every secret He had.

Kumar and Phul Maya sauntered along to Sathi's place. They were very elated to tell the news that they had bought a piece of land to Sathi. They tried to explain the very importance of the land. They thanked Sathi again and again. It was mainly by the sale of the fruit that allowed them to buy the land as the savings from the store were not enough for the land.

Phul Maya closed her eyes and thanked the tree,

"It was all done by your mercy, and I know you will always continue to protect us in the way you have always protected Kumar all these years. I know we can always rely on you, through the thick and thin of life."

On hearing this, Sathi felt proud and tried to explain that it was nothing great, it was just his duty to help his only intimate close friend.

That evening too, soon Kumar took out his murali and played the happiest, the sweetest and the melodious music. Phul Maya laid her head on his shoulder making sure not to miss even a sixteenth note out from his wonderful magical instrument. Sathi felt how happy Kumar was becoming. It too almost cried with joy. It seemed like Kumar was never grief-stricken. Kumar gathered all his strength and vitality from this friend.

Kumar ploughed the land while Phul Maya watched in contentment. He ploughed to make her happy and she watched to make him happy so eventually they were in an infinite loop that never relinquished. It was just the relentless love that was so strong in the family of three. Kumar wanted the land to be fertile. He was a determined man with lots of patience and energy. Every morning, about five o'clock he would leave his house and plough the field for three to four hours. Nonetheless, tired and exhausted, Kumar would be very happy as soon as he saw Phul Maya waiting for him with a gentle smile on her glorious face that never ceased to exist. It was for the first time that he realized that he was doing more than just surviving; he lived his life with full compassion and vigor. As she touched him his exhaustion would disappear and again he would be filled with vitality and enthusiasm for the rest of the day. They spent the entire day in the shop and formulate new plans to make their life happier and richer and perhaps better. Kumar was rest assured that his wife knew the maths behind it.

It seemed that good luck was always with them. The very first year, a good harvest was cut and soon he went to the nearby market to sell the harvest that returned him a very handsome sum of money.

The couple was indeed extremely delighted to see such money all at once. They prayed and thanked God for this for they knew it was only Him who had witnessed their sorrow and pain and thus finally brought good luck to them. They approached Sathi and shared every bit of news.

They were busy. Kumar was so industrious that nothing seemed to stop him. He seemed invincible and he looked so enthusiastic, brave and daring that even the threatening thunder would roll off from far distance before encountering him.

Seasons rolled in and out like every other year.

They and Sathi were the happiest souls in the land.

Every evening, Kumar and Phul Maya would visit Sathi. They would spend some time very happily forgetting the daily routine matter of life and get immersed in the world of peace, harmony and music.

Each of them was very sensitive to each other's pain and shortcoming. Never at any time did they even think of hurting each other with their deeds or any rude actions that was completely unreasonable. Their friendship bond with each other was very strong and the relationship they shared was very especial and mysterious.

Sometimes at night if the thunder cried out loud and angrily, Kumar and Phul Maya would be extremely petrified in case anything bad should have occurred to their friend. Next morning they would rush to Sathi's place without even opening up the store. Seeing them with fear and pain, Sathi would open its arms from a distance. All their imaginings would melt into thin air. Their tensions that had accumulated so far would fade away like a melting snow under the bright sun. Sathi would welcome them and all three of them would spend some time in complete silence embracing each other. Love was the greatest source of happiness, no one needed to tell them.

The following year Phul Maya became pregnant.

They were much happier than ever before. So they started to make all the preparations for the new comer with the energy they had. Phul Maya's parents helped them a lot.

On fine day, she gave birth to a little daughter.

They named their baby Champa.

Champa looked very extraordinary. Everyone said so. She was incredibly beautiful, even for a newly born infant. She had large black eyes that exactly resembled the eyes of her mother. Her lips and chin was a perfect match with her father. She had long straight fingers constructed so beautiful; everyone from the village came to see the child. They would find themselves completely amazed and astonished to say even a word.

Many whispered, "Oh God! She is charming, cute and beautiful."

Kumar was happy above happiness to find his beloved Phul Maya and daughter both in a sound healthy state and his daughter so beautiful that he even did not have enough words to praise her. He just kept staring at his wife and his daughter and tried to find a match between them. And every time he thought he found some match he rushed to say it to Sathi. People in the village and around visited Kumar's family to see his daughter while her parents nursed both the mother and her child.

They all congratulated Kumar on this happy occasion.

Some would say, "You know Kumar, you are the luckiest father in the whole world for having such a healthy and beautiful child."

While others would say to Phul Maya, "Phul Maya, you must be so lucky to give birth to such a darling baby."

Champa was just so bright just like a midday sun.

Kumar's Uncle, Mama came by when he heard the news. Along with him came some of his distant relatives who managed to show up at such occasions. They had brought some simple gifts as well. Every one of them was very delighted to see Phul Maya and her daughter in perfect health. For Phul Maya's parents, Champa was their first granddaughter and apple of their eye. This was a matter for them all to be proud: they were happy for their daughter's family. They seemed to have an everlasting ecstasy. Phul Maya's father hugged Kumar and threw a small party for the villagers. It was a custom among the villagers on such occasions.

Phul Maya's mother and some of her relatives managed with the clothing for mother and her child. In fact, she knew the every detail of how a newly born child should be clothed. She tried to her best to impart her knowledge regarding everything related to child caring cases. She seemed so busy all the times nursing her Phul Maya, and her grandchild, Champa.

Kumar gradually returned to his everyday activities. He now needed money more than before. Before they were only two. But now Champa had made them a complete family. Kumar would often think of additional expenses he had to bear. He decided to work even harder than before. There was a limit, but the family's needs are boundless. He found himself working late at night just for the sake of earning more and more money to make his family happy and satisfied. It was as if he was money making machine who had to spit out money in a routine fashion to run his household in an agreeable manner.

Two months later, Phul Maya's parents left them after they were sure both the mother and child were in a good health. Phul Maya's mother prepared a lot of good stuffs to eat for Phul Maya that they considered might help her to grow healthy soon.

Kumar thanked them for this; that was all he could do. In fact, he loved his father-in-law and mother-in-law and without their assistance he would have been completely disoriented and perplexed about the methodology to nurse a mother and her child. He returned many thanks to them and expressed his deepest gratitude for them with all the words he had in mind.

His mother-in-law constantly said to him, "See Kumar, still it is not the right time for Phul Maya to get off her bed and prepare to work. I guess she still needs a complete rest for two to three weeks more," she added in a motherly tone.

She further remarked, "Real care should be taken to nurse and feed the mother and child regularly, otherwise a careless diet might cause malnutrition both to the baby and her mother,"

Kumar's father-in-law joined in,

"Oh, yes, yes, our Kumar is smart enough to take care of his wife and daughter, you do not need to remind him of these pretty simple things."

They finally returned to their own village, blessing the couple and their newly-born granddaughter with hearts full of hope.

Weeks passed ever rapidly than before challenging Kumar and making him realize the titanic responsibility he had to deal with.

Phul Maya was restored to her health and strength. She was alive and kicking again in her kitchen. Soon she made their small hut habitable complaining about all the mess Kumar had created all the time she was in bed.

"I can't understand why you can't even learn to keep a house," she would sometimes fire at him, expecting some response from Kumar then again fire back at him against the response he would make.

But Kumar was wise enough to maintain his quietude and soundlessness at such extenuating circumstances.

One sunny evening, Champa, Kumar and Phul Maya went to Sathi who welcomed the new member warmly with great eagerness. It was happy enough to see this new little friend and jerked its branches back and forth just to gesticulate that it was so happy to meet this new small friend. Kumar and his wife understood the gestures and translated it themselves to a more wonderful meaning.

Kumar took out his wonderful murali and climbed to the top of the braches that readily accepted him while Phul Maya remain seated under the tree comforting herself and the child. Soon he was on with his gentle melody, harmonizing at several intervals. He even named his piece 'To the child so bright' and he said that it would be one of his finest played musical pieces. He played, the entire forest could feel the impassioned rhythm, the throb and the urgency of the music. The silent wind volunteered itself to the music while the soundless sound of the tumbling river had already joined, into the clearly distinguished rolling of the drums, the depth of the cello, the deep-toned voila all singing as one; in oneness to please the new baby.

This music score was indeed better by far than the rest of his pieces where any keen listener could identify the depth of his musical inclination while the musically ignorant could enjoy the tone, timbre and the sweetness present in the melody. This was truly his masterpiece, perhaps his Ninth symphony. The scale degree and the intervals were perfect and to this composition he had even added the diminished intervals while the other time he was perfecting his counterpoints. There was just a need of someone who could copy his music down on a piece of paper. The whole environment was enchanted and the air was filled with music. The legato then finally played the most vital role of all. The smooth and connected style in which one tone led to another was wonderful. It made the listener think he was in the middle of a great ocean with thousands of dolphins flying over and diving deep into the waters again. At other moments, his staccato made them feel that they were on a bumpy pony disturbed by the discordant noise made by pony's hooves. He created various moments. Every now and then the murali music grew stronger, rhythmic and passionate. The forest was one, united in one just to serve, perhaps the Supreme.

Days passed sometimes easily and sometime uneasily.

Needless to say, change is the steady nature of the world!

For many it is not a surprise that things do change. But for some it is the most crucial part of his life. Some wise people believe that every change can have divergent effects on each one of us. Learned ones often know that in a course of time an immensely wealthy person can turn to a vagabond and die worthless in some unknown street as a penniless vagrant. A great scholar can turn into a fool. A man of prestige, education and knowledge may be forced to exile and be a subject to hatred as a result of his thoughts and actions among his men. A nation proud of its history may turn poor. Many say that even a dull and weak student once can turn into a great genius like the greatest scientist, philosopher, thinker and musician the world has ever seen. The world is full of several examples; we just need the intelligence to interpret, admire and fathom its unfathomable depths.

No major change did affect or cause any harm to Kumar's family. By God's grace and Kumar's honesty, dedication and faithfulness things went extremely well in a smooth, uninterrupted manner. Sometimes, Champa would be ill but soon she would be fine. Luck was with them all the time, but time was still to come so who could tell for how long! It is not to be forgotten that unhappiness ends and happiness begins and vice versa.

Kumar's family lived in a peaceful and undisturbed manner. It was neither a rich nor poor family; just a happy family. Everyone thought about it. People thought every new day brought nothing except joy and happiness to Kumar's family. Now that with the arrival of his daughter Kumar's jollity knew no bounds.

"My daughter is the most, and the most, and the most, and the most, and the very, very most, and the very, very, very most beautiful child in the world," he would go on and on, holding her in his arms all the times. He never grew tired of it. Sometimes Champa would cry and cry all through the night keeping the house awake. Both the couple would invent instant ways to pacify the child but she would soon start again grumbling and shrieking. But all was nothing but fun to Kumar and his wife.

Phul Maya was now completely a mature woman, and she looked even more beautiful than ever. The local women turned jealous of her and her family's prospects. Similarly, local village men got irritated with their wives whenever they happened to see Phul Maya for they complained that their wives were not as beautiful as Phul Maya, in fact they were incomparable. Every youth stared at her. Their eyes would try to read some secrets hidden in Phul Maya's body. They thought that her bosom that was shaped so gracefully and beautifully must have some hidden truths in it. Her movements were always majestic and full of grace. Sometimes she went to her parent's home to stay with them for some weeks along with Champa and everyone would comment on Phul Maya saying, "You have turned out into such a beautiful woman. What is your secret, tell us?"

Some of her friends would say, "Oh! I guess that her husband certainly dotes on her too much. That is why she is so very captivating,"

Phul Maya's maternal uncle, her dearest uncle came to see her and Champa with bag full of eatables. He fondled and kissed Champa and took her in his arms saying, "Hey you, what is your name, tell me, what is your name?"

Champa cried. She did not know her name yet. Uncle got scared and handed her back to Phul Maya instantly. Everyone laughed. Thus, Phul Maya's days in her parents' home passed in complete luxury. She did not have to do any work, no cooking, no dishwashing; she ate delicious food and took rest all day. Days passed without any noise. But it was too quick.

Back home Kumar was alone, he was extremely anxious to meet his family but at the same time he was having a hell of a time on their absence. . He tried to manage the store, house and the kitchen at the same time but never succeeded and was always with a worn out pathetic expression lingering on his face. He had now completely registered in his mind that he was fallible when it mattered with housekeeping.

One night he sat pathetically in one corner of his hut glancing at the mess scattered all over the floor.

"Had my wife been here she would have kept the place as clean as a garden," He felt disheartened counting the days of her arrival. Even his prudence came of no use this time and found himself in a quandary. He had agreed to disagree with his kitchen that eyed him from all the corners as he set about cooking his pathetic recipe with the rattling of the utensils and spilling of water all over.

Now ever than before he coveted to see his daughter's face more than his wife's. This time he was in deep trouble because he had to do all the cooking stuff by himself. As he was so poor at cooking things, now he was completely disappointed eating the same food over and over again that was always unpalatable and always tasted terrible. Sometime his neighbour's daughter would come and help him to cook. Those times were good for Kumar but for the next time it would all again be the same. He was a real bumpkin when it was required of him to clean the house or do some cooking.

He went to visit Sathi. Sathi was also in his youth days with its branches and trunks so strong and healthy. Kumar went running and jumped on Sathi's branches. Sathi too extended its branches making sure not to let him fall. It was also glad to have Kumar's company. His murali's music made Sathi lively and happy.

Kumar started, "You know, I am so alone without my Phul Maya and my daughter. What could they be doing now? Are they even thinking about me?"

Kumar put his head on one of the branches and began to think himself.

Sathi also was not very happy that day, it had wanted Phul Maya and Champa to come along. It too was now accustomed to hear the yelling, screams and crying of Champa, and sometimes it laughed to itself seeing Kumar and Phul Maya trying to make Champa quiet. Many times it had seen Champa not stopping until Kumar played his murali to make her quiet.

Finally the day arrived. It was now time for them to return back to Kumar. Being said, that implied that the vacation was over for Phul Maya.

"I wish I could stay more," calmly said Phul with passion in her voice.

Both her parents' eyes welled up while her brother stood beside her all the time simply gazing attentively at Champa.

"We also wish that, but you have your own home to take care of now and Kumar must be waiting for you," retorted her father not looking in her eyes.

Her mother could not even say a word. She kept holding and hugging the baby at all the time. She never wanted to detach herself from the baby. Final goodbyes were made and she returned home. Her brother saw her off.

So Phul Maya and daughter returned home. Kumar was not expecting them at that hour. In that little remote village there was no mobile phone service so message conveyance was out of question. That very hour, Kumar was sitting in his small shop wondering what to do. . He wanted to close the shop. But did not know what he would do after. He wanted to be busy but being in the shop did not make him feel good. He wished them to come-Were Phul Maya and Champa here it would be so fine.

All of a sudden, they were there in front of him.

He could not believe his eyes. He thought he was indulged in day dreaming. At last he saw Phul Maya in the yard, holding Champa in her hand.

He looked at Champa. She cracked a smile as soon as she saw her father and went to his arms directly.

Kumar began kissing her all over her face with his eyes full of tears.

Seeing this Phul Maya could not hold on and embraced Kumar and whispered, "Oh Kumar it was such a dreadful time living without you, now I promise I will never leave you alone again even for single moment."

Kumar replied with animal like anxiety in his eyes, "Phul Maya, I was so lost and alone without the two of you but now you are back, everything will be okay."

"Yes, I know," responded Phul Maya.

Soon, they went inside the hut, that day Kumar closed the store a little earlier than usual. They fed Champa and she went to sleep. When Phul Maya was about to leave the room to get something to eat, Kumar pulled her vigorously to him and began to kiss her lips intensely. Soon Phul Maya was too was out of control full of emotion and excitement. They had not made love for several weeks. Soon both of them plunged into the ocean of lust and love. They made love several times.

Kumar whispered, "Phul Maya, you feel so new and fresh,"

Phul Maya responded in a fragile voice, "This is because we have not made love for several weeks, so everything seems new and fresh to you."

Both of them laughed for a while and then finally slept with nothing for dinner except love. That is why it is said, 'Love will keep us all alive at all times'.

Next morning Kumar said as soon as he woke up,

"Phul Maya, my stomach is so hungry since it has been weeks I ate some good and tasty food, I am starving you know."

Phul Maya was disturbed to hear this and remarked, "What do you mean 'weeks'? Have you not eaten anything from the day I left for my parents' home?"

"Every day I ate, but the taste of my cooked food was so terrible that I could hardly consume anything of it. I am hungry for the good food that you make," Kumar admitted fervently.

Phul Maya responded, "See Kumar, everything in this world is classified and everyone else falls under this classification. The God has chosen a fate for everyone and anyone who attempts to outlaw the rule is certain to face misery."

She said it in her deep philosophical voice. Kumar did not know she could get into so much of seriousness. It was something like seeing a new facet of a coin. Kumar was not able to comprehend what she said.

Suddenly she changed the topic and said wittingly,

"Like you did, God has destined you to be a musician but you tried your hands on cookery so your stomach was never full and satisfied."

Both of them laughed.

Phul Maya, a fastidious housewife, proceeded with all her agility and started cooking while Kumar sat there watching her refined movements. The way she moved her hands and fingers, the way she pinched the exact amount of salt and other peppers, the way she stirred the handle of the spoon made Kumar gaze in bewilderment. That day Kumar realized that cooking food was not as simple as he had thought. It was indeed an art that had to be mastered.

He did not even try to learn to cook when he recalled what Phul Maya had once said in her same old serious accent, "It is not that everyone can learn everything or anything if he tries; his hands have to be gifted and that gift is not granted by any teacher but only by the God at the time of his birth, and if he is lucky enough God bestows him with many gifts like he did to Leonardo da Vinci."

Chapter Five

And He Comes

Days begin to melt even more quickly without anyone noticing it. Kumar got even busier than ever in his life and now Champa was already five years old. The family welcomed every joyous moments as they approached with all their heart and personality.

Champa has already begun attending the nearby local school. Kumar was probably the happiest man in the village as he was free from all the unnecessary desires of lust and greediness and had a principle that God would provide him with all the necessities in the meantime. He disliked the idea of acquisition and avarice. He had bought Champa a small satchel and school uniform. His best moments to treasure would be to watch his beloved daughter going to school in her tiny uniform. He would touch her with love and care as every day he took her to school with great fondness. Likewise, his wife, Phul Maya, would go to school in the late afternoon to collect Champa. This was their regular routine. Besides that, they visited Sathi and sat underneath. Champa was always the busiest one. She would talk about her everyday experiences with her new friends, teachers and the new world she was in. Kumar would listen attentively to his daughter's words as he himself did not have such an experience. He never had the privilege of going to school in his life. He had always desperately wished of going to school and taking lessons among friends and teachers.

Kumar's childhood was a complete misery. He often tried to disclose happy moments hidden in his childhood days but only pain and sorrow would cloud over his mind. Someone had deliberately seized happiness from my life- he sometimes would philosophize. No friends, no teachers, no birthday celebrations but a cruel, merciless father. His childhood privileges were completely taken away from him; most of all his mother's love and affection. He calmed himself thinking all this as his fate and nobody was responsible for that. God had planned it, so nobody else could change it.

Sometime Champa would babble to her father to play some melodies for her. "Papa play me. No, no not that. H...m, yes, yes, this. Okay."

Kumar would be more than happy to play his murali for her. He wanted to provide all kinds of happiness that a father could. Champa was growing stronger and clever compared with her peers. She had even learnt to climb the branches of Sathi with a little assistance and jump from one branch to branch swiftly like a monkey. Sathi too made arrangements not to let her fall in every way it could. So in this manner Champa would frolic about the branches. When the season came Sathi gave them abundant amounts of fruit. Now that the family needs were little more advanced than before instead of selling all the fruit they kept a little for them and sold the rest in the nearby market. More often they also distributed some among their neighbours.

Everyone would say in their fruity voice, "Never eaten such a delicious one."

Time moved. Who could stop it? Two more years passed just like that.

Phul Maya was again pregnant and carrying a second baby. This time she gave birth to a boy. The boy was no less beautiful then his elder sister, Champa.

"The family with one son and one daughter is the happiest one. "What a small, peaceful, blessed family," the denizens remarked scrutinizing; some out of jealousy and some with their true heart.

Everyone remarked this again and again. The new born baby was the talk of the village.

Close relatives visited Phul Maya and her family as before. There were plenty of presents for mother and her child now.

Champa was the happiest girl in the world. She had now a new brother and a new friend to play with.

Soon a ritual was conducted, and it was announced that the child's name should start with M.

After much consideration they named the child boy Manoj.

Champa constantly called him by the name "Manos", "Manos", and so on.

These children were born to poor parents but they looked beautiful with their dazzling looks. Rich parents wanted to have babies like them because they take for granted that whatever they should acquire should be irresistibly charming and no less beautiful.

Relatives and guests visited and departed.

Before leaving them, Phul Maya's mother said, "Why don't all of you come over to our village for a little change?"

Kumar replied, "Yes, indeed, a very good idea, we'll think about it when Phul Maya is fully recovered."

Saying the last farewell words the old parents left for their village.

In no time, Phul Maya was in sound health and was back to her regular household errands. Kumar set himself busy with his shop. All four of them would visit Sathi quite very often.

In a matter of few days Manoj too got acquainted to Sathi. Sathi could not say anything but expressed its deepest joy that only Kumar and Phul Maya could understand; the inaudible voice. They could already feel Sathi's vibration; experience the emotion, its earnest feelings, Sathi's gestures sometimes were a perfect communication to their thoughts, ecstasy, agony and pain.

Wise men know this world is full of miracles. Human beings talk to each other. It is nothing new. Animals can communicate with each other. This too does not surprise us. Wise men tell us that there is mystic side of reality and plants and trees also talk to each other as well as to human beings. Ordinary human beings may not believe it. Simply, they cannot decipher the mystical side of reality. Many cannot even conceive it. For many of us we are firm on the idea that the human species is the one and only one capable of performing any action and reaction. How dull we are! We simply ignore such discussions because we lack the power to venture into complicated yet interesting ideas. Wise men like Socrates, Plato and Tagore among others believed and did probably experience such mystical sides of reality. Perhaps they were able to fathom the puzzle. On the contrary, ordinary people feel rather insulted if they are asked to decipher the language of a speaking tree or a fish in the pond. For such people trees and fish can never express anything and are nothing but mere poor pathetic expressionless creatures.

Oh, things are getting complicated, are they not?

The simple thing is that Champa was growing, full of curiosity.

Little by little, she was learning to decipher what Sathi would say to her. She was already familiar with the idea that to become able to understand the things Sathi was saying to her, she had to learn to open the ears of the soul, and the two ears on each side of her head were not adequate for this. She thought that she was gradually gaining the power to understand Sathi's emotions, which were pure without any deceptions, untruthfulness and avarice and never had to live life seeking absolution.

Time passed.

Kumar and Phul Maya were becoming familiar with the other side of family life. Everything around them changed and nothing remained the same. Their children were also growing up. With all the ongoing growth the expenses and expenditures of the house were also bound to increase. So the urgency of saving money was necessary as anything else. Guests visited occasionally. The old hut had already become a small home; a sweet home where four loving souls dwelt.

Manoj and Champa were fond of playing as every other children of their age. They loved playing in the beautiful garden in front of their home which Kumar had so artistically decorated. Almost every day they would spend some time together in the garden jumping and smelling the flowers of all kinds. Manoj was the one who frisked a lot.

They sang and chatted a lot. Perhaps singing and music was in their blood.

Kumar loved to spend all of his spare time with his family. In fact, he did not want his children to ever feel deserted. Kumar and Phul Maya tried their best to provide every kind of attention and support to their children. Phul Maya was the keeper of good morals, the centre of the family and her ideals were intact.

Kumar did not want his children to live the same kind of life that he had to go through years back. He wanted them to enjoy and lead a blissful life without any agony and sufferings.

Sometime, Kumar would come across some orphans in the village and he would almost cry. He would say to himself, "If he had better parents then he would not probably be here, in this place, this pathetic wretched condition." Sometimes, he would feel very disturbed especially when a terrific question would strike him.

"Who is to blame for the child's destiny? Father? Mother? Grandparents? Children themselves? Or. Gods?" A stream of unusual queries would drum his mind calling for an absolute answer.

But unfortunately he would never have any answers.

And unlimited inquiries which had not any clear answers would keep on spearing him.

Should a child's birth be taken as result of his or her own will or is he or she forced to take a birth to lead a pathetic life?

Does this universe register that a baby is born?

Who then decides a baby's so-called destiny if it exists?

Is destiny simply like a game of lottery so that whoever is lucky enough gets great fortunes?

Who decides which children are to be born to rich parents or poor parents?

Why was I born into a poor family?

Why did my mother die so young?

Why did my father behave the way he behaved to me?

Who stopped him from being good a person?

Was my birth a mistake that I did?

Often such intricate questions hovered in his head making it really difficult to find a complete resolution.

Every time he tried to answer them he found them getting more convoluted.

Sometimes he would talk about such riddle-like questions to his villager friends. They too would add more questions. They also believed that there is something planned ahead of every person's birth.

They also shared some similar questions to him.

"Why does a child die young?"

"Should disease be responsible, or God?"

"Why does a particular person die young while another lives for years and years with good health and blissful fortune?"

Addressing brightly one elderly answered, "Brother, Kumar our fate is predestined before or at the time of our birth. Everything is a set up and we, the poor human beings, do nothing except pretend to live our lives. We cry on our failures and throw huge parties over our success and the events; the success and the failure are also predefined. God, and nature has already calculated exactly everything for everyone. All of us get our share as a result of his calculations. And the things we call success, failure, happiness, agony, pain, fortune are the characteristic features of our share provided by God. Some of us are lucky enough to get provided with excellent shares like an erudite mathematical mind or a musical mind like that of Mozart. And on sharp contrast some of us are unlucky enough because God has provided us with nothing except incapability and misfortunes,"

Sometimes Kumar believed them. Other times he believed that no one knows about the mystery of life and we are all bound to live in this darkness and uncertainty.

Kumar, to forget all these terrible questions, would ask to himself,

"Why did not He equip me with the fingers of the great musician of the world?"

"Why did not he provide me with the brains of a great scientist?"

He pondered and asked, "Were all the great minds, which the world knows, born great or did they achieve such greatness and erudition?"

Champa's teachers, and many educated persons he knew and respected, mentioned all kinds of great people.

"Sir Isaac Newton, Mozart and Bertrand Russell. Were they born great?"

"Should we call them lucky for achieving what they managed to achieve?"

"Why cannot every one become successful?"

Kumar would reach a hasty conclusion that probably individuals with a higher mental capability and power can comprehend the matter perfectly.

Kumar did not only think about big things but he concentrated on things which were very simple and urgent and also part of everyday life. He philosophized about the world around him with his unlimited inquisitiveness.

The small piece of land they had purchased was now beginning to produce some very good harvests. These harvests they used to sell in the nearby market and receive a fairly good sum of money. This money was solely expended for household activities and for the better education of the two children. These two children, actually never lacked any basic needs. Champa was wise enough not to demand things out of her parents' reach. She had inherited certain intellectual qualities from her mother. At her age she had realized how difficult it was to earn money and she had clearly witnessed the troubled days. So she never complained about anything like her brother. Manoj was still too small to comprehend the matter at hand. He just acted according to his senses.

Champa was now six and was admitted to a school. It was a local village school. And all the villagers' kids went to the same local school.

Kumar was never satisfied about his daughter going to this school. Actually he had realized that the school was a primary school with very little facilities for a child for proper development. The school did not have any singing, dancing and sports classes. These things were not part of the school curriculum. Also, he was not happy that teachers did not do anything about music and mystical side of life. Kumar wanted teachers to behave like great persons so that their students would learn goods things in a matter of few years' time. He thought the teachers were just arrogant and condescending.

Phul Maya, like her husband too wanted their kids to get exposure to arts from the beginning and wanted them to have collegiate life later in their youth. Both of them had realized the importance of the arts. Their friendship with Sathi had made them wiser. They wanted their children to be good human beings and they believed the study of arts would instill such goodness in them.

Kumar and Champa visited their neighbours and inquired about better education. Their poor neighbours were very happy that their children were taught to learn formulae and derivations. Their kids were studying hard and getting good scores in the exam. They were very satisfied that they were securing good positions in the class so what else they needed?

"Do your children know how to appreciate music?"

"Do they teach such things in the school?"

Kumar and Phul Maya wanted to know everything about the school education system.

Many parents declared to them that they wanted their kids to be 'an engineer' or 'a doctor' or may be 'a veteran lawyer'.

Kumar and Phul Maya, on the other hand, wanted their children to be good individuals above the rest of the credentials one could later achieve in life-great persons who could understand the sayings of trees and birds and read the pain in others' souls.

They did not want their children to work hard just to grab good money termed 'salary' at the end of the month. Why should they work for hours every day if it only meant money in reward? They talked about it; they talked about the purpose of life.

What Kumar and Phul Maya believed was really genuine.

These days no one bothers to interpret the chirping of birds or the whistle of a dolphin. Our connection to this earth and its habitats is disconnected. We are restricted to our families and ourselves. Many people argue they want to live an independent life, they abandon even their mothers and fathers, leave them uncared for and sometimes they die old and grey in some care home. We victimize birds and other animals to demonstrate our mastery at shooting. We lock up and abuse poor wild animals inside a cage just to entertain our yielding senses. So, there is one vital question to every human being on this earth.

"Is this the reason why God created earth and all the living beings?"

The reason why we are living under such circumstances is clear as if in a mirror. It is due to our untamed greed of accumulating money. Ample money reflects sufficient luxury and we do not care how the money comes and how we earn it. We just need it, no matter how. We have the notion,

"Earn it all the possible ways you can and just forget the rest." It is the stupidity that speaks.

And it is for sure that if such disposition exits inside every one of us then finally one day the earth is going to crack and judgement day will confront us. On account of a new Earth let the Pandora's Box remain closed. The Garden of Eden will be there but there will not be any Eve there to out pass God's order.

Kumar and Phul Maya wanted good things to happen to this world, and to their children, even they were poor and not educated.

They were very happy that their kids were brilliant and had a flair for learning. They never had to be told to study. They hoped that as the days passed, both of the children would turn out to be silent and serious. Most of the time they would be on with their studies, and in their spare time they would play and frolic around. Champa was always a full time mentor of her little brother, Manoj.

Champa would help her mother with the stuff like gardening, cooking and other household activities with all the might she had.

The entire four members seemed perfectly satisfied with each other; they never quarreled or complained about each other. They stayed in the bosom of the family.

Time helped the family a lot to nourish themselves and they grew more efficient as time passed. Now Champa was at grade four, while her little brother at grade one. She was excellent in literature, but rather weak in biology. She complained, "Oh God, help me to memorize all this awful stuff,"

Manoj was best in logic among all the students in class and every teacher admired Manoj for his outstanding talent and witty remarks.

But Champa was not so good at working out her mathematical problems, but her literature was good.

Even the teachers were surprised that she wrote in such an elegant style.

No one had to teach her how to write an essay on issues like: Environment, Preservation of Wild Animals and Plants.

Champa was a down-to-earth type of girl with very little to say, exactly like her mother. She was the one with meek and gentle spirit.

Like the proverb says, 'Morning shows the day'. Both the kids exhibited incredible performance. Their grades surpassed all the others.

Many local guardians would say,

"Oh! Laborious kids they are."

Champa and Manoj understood nature, God and most of all pain and sorrow of others. This made them different from others. Most of all they were telepathic like their parents.

In no time Manoj scored top grades in his first grade.

So did Champa, she was never to be left behind.

Kumar was extremely happy. He bought him a nylon-stringed guitar. He wanted his son to be a great musician.

Manoj played it the way he could.

It was just a dull disagreeing noise.

Kumar soon started teaching him the basics of music. Soon, within a couple of month he started well off with his guitar.

Kumar wished his son to grasp the theory and with lots and lots of practice and begin to play arpeggio. He wished a great guitar teacher would come and help to play him. But in that remote village the guitar teacher was out of question. He wanted to hear him play guitar the way a true maestro does.

"Kumar, you know, your son has inherited your musical talent and I guess one day he will turn out to be a maestro classical guitarist if he continues with this enthusiasm," his friends would repeat often.

Many a times Kumar would see his son's fingers plucking guitar strings and he wished that his son learnt to pluck them neatly and smoothly.

"If only my son played like great masters one day," Kumar just desired.

Kumar had great hope.

That's why he would take his son to party or gathering in the village.

Kumar and his son always loved to perform their compositions. Manoj would look with great awe as he saw his father playing his murali with such a great passion and with such authority of expression. One particular show he got so drawn into by his father's playing that he started plucking strings to accompany the murali. Audiences were surprised to see the father and the son doing so. They knew the son was going to be a great musician. No doubt Kumar's performance was incredible.

The local villagers remarked among themselves, "Kumar now should train his son so that this village will have a great musician in the days to come,"

Often times, the family would visit Sathi and play their music. Kumar would be up on the trees and Manoj would pluck. They would change their position. Kumar often watched Manoj getting engrossed in playing his guitar. Kumar could feel that Manoj was absolutely not aware that he was about to fall off the branch he was sitting on. Kumar never stopped feeling proud both of his children.

Manoj was a novice and undeniably he had miles to go ahead. He needed to learn to make a balance between life and meditation and so on.

Sathi would watch this silently and approve of it. It expressed its ecstasy by swaying its branches heavily but nevertheless exuding a warm and smooth gust of wind. Kumar and Manoj would play even more joyfully and create more playful notes than before. This made Kumar recall his childhood days he used to spend underneath Sathi blowing air into the murali but making rather discordant sounds but still Sathi seemed to praise him and encourage him to practise more and more. All these vivid recollections made his heart heavy with pain. He thought of his mother and his cruel father. How harsh was his father to his mother! He almost cried.

Whenever he recollected all his past, he experienced nothing but pangs of pain that ultimately made his eyes watery.

Time and again, he would make a strong vow to himself that he would never let his family go through

111

any misery like he had undergone. He vowed to give them happiness in every possible way he could. He stood firmly by the thought he would always be a good father, a good husband and above all a very good teacher, indeed. As a result of his teachings his children had turned out to be very good and efficient students.

Phul Maya was very happy to see Champa carrying all kinds of books. Kumar and Phul Maya decided not to overburden Champa with household works. They wanted her to concentrate on her studies that she was carrying out on her own. Champa loved to read books with beautiful stories and drawings. Champa wanted to read all kinds of books and she loved stories. She wished to grow fast and read all the famous writers.

One day she saw her teacher was holding a book. In the cover of the book, she saw the words *Fathers and Sons* and 'Ivan Turganev'. She realized how uneducated she was and what hard work she needed to do to educate herself. That particular day she stayed at the school library for long and soon realized that her school library was not big enough. She wanted to get hold of all books, no matter what subject matter they dealt with. Many of her friends were surprised to see that Champa could stay at the library for hours with acute concentration. They were even surprised to notice that though Champa did not talk much but when she made an argument no one would dare to disagree.

Chapter Six

After all Money Matters

Kumar was extremely gratified to see the performance of his children. Both of them were doing excellent at school. Soon they excelled above every other kid in their locality, both in studies and extra activities. Teachers would come to their small hut and say, "Indeed your children's performance is outstanding."

Phul Maya was probably the happiest mother in the universe and who would not be?

But somewhere deep inside his heart Kumar felt that the school his children were being sent to was not good enough for them. He could feel that the school lacked creativities to open opportunities to their students. Many parents were just simply happy that their children could memorize mathematical formula, poems and chant. They were exceedingly fond of the teachers who made students memorize everything dictated no matter whether they understood or not but they could not understand that the teachers were mercenary.

Kumar personally knew the class teacher of Champa. A middle-aged person with large and liquid eyes. He was only good at shouting at students. Kumar could feel that the class teacher himself was confused about several things. He looked unhappy and was not creative at all. He did not want to talk about anything beyond the textbook. Kumar was very sad for this man acting as a class teacher but what could he do about it while the rest of the villagers seemed so content. He dropped the issue among the villagers as he found it quite contentious.

Kumar wanted his children to master over the knowledge that they were comfortable at. Often Manoj and Champa complained about the rude behavior of their class teacher and others. Kumar tried not to pay serious attention to them because there were no alternatives, no other possible substitution. He abhorred the way teachers made their students go through all kinds of punishment for not finishing their assignments on time. Manoj and Champa never had to go through such reprimands; they had a sharp mind and great promising parents. Many parents he knew would simply look on helplessly at their children coming home with stripes on their back and sometimes with swollen cheeks. Many of them indeed believed that the school was doing very well by punishing the kids. Kumar wanted to take them to school and complain the principal. But Kumar knew that the principal was as nonsensical and insensitive as the class teachers were. Moreover, there was no alternative. But he wanted good times to come and he knew that radical changes were impossible to happen in his life as well as in his community living under those pathetic circumstances.

As days passed on, Kumar and his wife realized that they were not in any better condition than they were before. They still had to work very hard and the land they had purchased only rewarded them once in a year or so: the land did not help them a lot and the land was very small in size to produce anything substantial. The money they received by selling the fruit provided by Sathi was just not sufficient to meet the requirements of the family. The children's books and school fees had to be paid along with the daily needs of the house. And all expenses are self-expanding in nature.

But Phul Maya never complained anything about this to her husband. She knew that her sacrifice would undoubtedly bring good fortune to her family. She readily let go of her wishes and womanly desires in order to make her children happy. She never ever wanted to turn down her children regarding their small wishes. She longed for a very happy family and for that it seemed she was ready to pay any cost.

Kumar knew everything about his wife and children but still he was helpless; he did not have any extra source of income. The income he generated from the small shop was getting inadequate day by day. He thought real hard but did not get any clues about how to be richer. He would sometime think,

"I think it is much better to talk about with Phul Maya, she might have better ideas."

But soon after some self-consultation he would give up the idea; he was afraid the very notion of money might sadden her. Sometimes it can bring chaos to a sensitive being. Every night terrible questions would hover over his head. He would get vexed and depressed but there was nothing he could do at that point.

He desired to send his children to a private English medium sized boarding school at some other city. For this, he needed more money. He wanted his children to be a successful with a promising career. And he had finely observed that for all the refinements and luxurious in life there was a vital need of more money. It was evident that money had made his life poor and now money could engage his life with better prospects and bring great relish.

He would think about such a terrible side of reality. Every night he would doze off with such wondrous things in his mind.

Too much is too much.

One fine morning, Kumar lumbered to the jungle and found himself lurching. He walked fast and arrived to his Sathi's place. He disclosed all the problems he was facing with sadness in his unusually jarring voice and asked for any way out of it. He asked himself and Sathi,

"Is there not any other possible way to earn more?"

"Will my family's poor economic condition always be the same?"

"Will my children never be able to attend a good English Boarding school?"

"Will my wife never get good opportunities to put on jewellery and look pretty?" and so on.

He put many such intricate queries to his intimate friend, Sathi.

To all his questions Sathi did nothing except maintain the morning silence with perfect motionlessness. It looked as if Sathi was looking somewhere else, simply hearing but not listening to Kumar.

Sathi in fact knew that his friend was undergoing a critical time and needed to be consoled. Sathi could detect the desperation in his voice.

Suddenly, Kumar heard a kind of gentle whisper in his ear and he was dead sure it was his one and only friend talking to him.

The winds in the tree had responded to him.

He was sure of it.

He looked at Sathi with his loving eyes searching for an answer but on that day he could not see it.

On his way back home Kumar saw an elderly woman with a missing leg. She was accompanied by her son, probably helping her to wade and to trudge along the way.

As Kumar watched, an inner voice that only his heart could hear spoke gently. The voice perhaps contained the answers to all of his questions.

This brought massive relief in his heart.

Kumar went back to his old hut. His family was anxious, because he had left the house early in the morning without informing anyone.

His children started complaining. But his wife, Phul Maya, was terribly angry for his awful behaviour. Soon after everything had settled down, his daughter approached him and embraced him and asked,

"Dad, what's wrong with you, is there anything about us that has made to bother you so much; you seem very much depressed, don't you?"

Without giving a second thought Kumar let her know that he wanted more money so that he could send his children to better school. He even philosophized about the diversity of life, its variations, its diversifications, its eerie complexities that one must bear in his life and many more. His daughter, as wise as a Solomon, already was grave, silent, and listening attentively to his words. She wanted to learn everything that was troubling her father. She wanted to learn more about the philosophy of life and nature of human civilization. She was grave and silent and uttered nothing as her father spoke with great wisdom and unflinching concentration. She did not wish to interrupt her father's thought, she just watched him revealing all the secrets from his heart that had burdened him.

Next day she came close to her father and said,

"Dad, I have tried to find answers to many of your doubts in this small piece of essay that I found in the library of my school, please, I will read it for you; it might help you,"

Kumar could not believe his daughter could read essays.

"The title of the essay that I am going to read," she said was, "'All the world is a Stage.'"

She read:

"All the world is a stage.

As Shakespeare has said,

'All the world is a stage.' It seems to me, true, and not only to me but also to anyone who thinks it in my way. Indeed, this massive world is nothing but a single stage that is decorated and staged so beautifully as well as being full of fantastic characters.

Let's take an instance where we are watching a short drama of span of three or four hours, maybe even longer or shorter, it does not matter. We all have a notion and strong experience of what a proper drama is like. It comprises a stage finely decorated, along with some actors clad in costumes to suit the respective characters they are playing. A director and of course a dramatist. The actors are anxious about their performance; anxious in the sense of how would they act. They constantly think, 'Will I be admired and appreciated by the spectators? Would they prove this by applause?' And infinitely many more insoluble questions and doubts emerging in their minds.

In a drama every actor is given a character he must follow. In the beginning the director informs them about the things, the scenes which take place. The director informs them about the things all the actors must strictly follow; things like what he ought to say or how he ought to act. He is strictly forbidden not to play or act in any other way. If he tries or even thinks of going against the director, he is dead sure to meet a horrible consequence.

Does not this prove and clarify so clearly that he is born before he is born?

Likewise, we are all human beings, the supreme of all the creations created by Him and are nothing but a minute character of a drama literally in a worldly drama. A director is there who directs. The only difference between this stage and an ordinary drama is that in the ordinary drama each character knows how he is going to end; which way the story will go or all the lines he ought to speak. Quite contrary to this, in the worldly drama the poor characters do not know what he must do the very next moment. He even does not have a slightest of notion of where he goes and what he does. In fact, I think this is or may be the only reason that makes this drama interesting. All the characters are extremely aggressive to reveal secrets about themselves or others. Like in a drama, if a character becomes rich or he gets married to a king's daughter, he is not glad at all, as he seems to be. In reality only a phoney smile lingers on his face. The reason is, he has sound knowledge that everything is soon going to be over and he must hand everything over to someone behind the stage and quit the stage, just in the same way as he had entered the stage. All he does is simply comes in, utters magnificent dialogue written by others and returns back as soon as his part in the drama is accomplished. He does not have a right to act according to his will.

So, cannot we contemplate our life as a stage and everyone has their own part and everyone not sure which way to go, just abandoning our life in some luck or some other sources. Have not we come in this earth as naked as a wild desert and return empty handed to where we came from, abandoning all the accumulations and heavenly achievements.

If we ponder over our existence and our identity suddenly some questions knock our brain. 'Who are we? What are we doing here? What am I to do? Really, is this the place we belong to? Are we the real actors and leading a role and thus bearing a misconception of living a life? If this is true, then are not we all disillusioned of living a life? Is somebody watching us all the time, without even a slight hunch of being watched?'

Briefly, it can be put that our life and our future is predestined. Our destiny is waiting for us. We could never change our role in this drama. He has already written everything for everyone. He will never let us know our forthcoming time. We as poor as robbers can only dare to predict and act accordingly. But sooner or later we are sure to confront our fate, predestined.

Let us again put this entire baffling situation in other way. A child is born. And then the other child is born. The first child is born to a sophisticated rich dynasty and the other to an awfully poor breed. Now it is almost sure that the child born to the rich dynasty will prosper, surrounded by all the luxuries of life, but tragically, on the other hand the poor child will live and die like vagabond. Now who is to blame for this severe partiality and indiscrimination?

What did he do that he was born there and what did the other do that he was thrown over to the poor hands. The answer is as easy and simple as ABC, yes. He again wrote the life of both the child and finally confirmed to throw them to this stage as a prince and a ragamuffin vagabond. Now I think it all depends on his

120

mood to choose the destiny for those two children or maybe he decided their fate just by tossing a coin up in the air. The one with the heads a… and so on. The rich prince steps in foreign land to study while the poor lad sits under a leaking ceiling; calling it a school.

Lastly, thinking philosophically we may depict life as 'useless and a meaningless span of time' as some great old thinkers of late ancient days have thought. On the other hand we may go against this mind blowing weird ideas about life and try our best to live our life as we believe it.

But I suggest don't play against the rule. He is constantly supervising you and your action. Finally when the show is over you can imagine the way you are going to be treated by Him?"

At first Kumar just could not believe his eyes and his mind. Most of the words were a completely new and anew to him. He did not care about who wrote it but the way his daughter had narrated it seemed as if they were meant only for him. He was also happy that the art of reading of his daughter was just extraordinary. He never knew that his little pet daughter could read texts which were loaded with serious themes of life with such expression. It was incredible. Many a time, Kumar had to obstruct her in the middle to decipher certain sentences and the logic behind it. He was just too proud of his daughter selflessly and aimlessly. He talked about this to Phul Maya but she was helpless. She could hardly understand the point he was trying to make.

Now Kumar lived in a village where going away to the cities to earn money was an established practice. Kumar had not only heard about this practice, he had in fact seen many of his childhood friends go away for years. He had seen them sending remittances back to their family. Many would stay for five years in the cities and some for unknown years. Kumar never liked the idea of doing so. He wanted to stand firm and rise from the very place where he belonged to. He was a family man and had chosen his family over money.

Talk about the devil, the devil comes. Kumar was thinking about his friends that morning and one of his childhood friends, Ghale, came out of the blue and talked to him.

"What are you doing these days, Kumar"?

Kumar replied, "Oh! I run a shop. You know that. Anyway I'm preparing a list about the stuff to be bought for the shop you see?"

Bluntly, Ghale replied, "People like you just intend to spend their lives anyhow."

He further added, "How far can you get with this small shop of yours and that little piece of land, my dear friend, now that you have another mouth to feed?"

He attacked Kumar viciously with that question.

"Don't you ever want to see more money, see a great deal of money, touch it, smell it and even make love to it?

"See our Hari, that poor teacher. Three years back he resigned his teaching post in the school and went to the city and when he came back he was changed in everything, and I know why he changed, it was because of the wealth he had amassed during his stay in the city,"

To all this Kumar maintained his dignified position and looked engrossed in his work but he was keenly aware of all the words Ghale said. He inwardly agreed to it.

Ghale reached to a conclusion, "So, my friend, money changes everything and …"

As the conversation was going on, Phul Maya came from inside with two glasses of tea in her hand and said,

"You look so anxious today, what is the deal, are you fine, Ghale *dai*?"

The neighbour just nodded his head and murmured some quick words to himself as if he knew some of the secrets to life.

Finally he broke out good-humouredly, "*Bhauju*, why don't you encourage Kumar to earn more money and live properly?"

Phul Maya though, had not understood everything; she finally managed to speak out,

"Ghale dai, nowadays I'm really too much upset due to many reasons and one of the reasons happens to be related to Kumar. He does not seem to be happy with his life."

She said everything in a single breath.

Kumar remained in his old position, a surly look visiting his face, thinking too hard and too deep, holding the tea glass in his hand. Suddenly, he seemed to wake up from a deep trance and broke a pitiful smile looking at Ghale. After that for about two hours, Ghale, Kumar and Phul Maya had a hot discussion. Eventually, when everything was over Ghale went back to his home.

Phul Maya approached Kumar and said,

"Please, Kumar do not think too much, time heals every pain in life you know."

At once Kumar retorted, "Does time gives us money just by sitting idle? Does time heal the dire necessity that money can fulfill?"

Now Phul Maya was completely speechless. But somewhere inside of her she was exalted that her husband had sensed that money was needed for a smooth execution of a family life.

The day passed.

But the night seemed much longer, denser and not inviting. Both of them could not sleep. The war had broken out in that tranquil family. Now a peaceful coexistence with the money was required. They thought over different issues. Kumar was completely at sixes and sevens about whether he should leave his village and go to the city in order to earn money. The money temptation was too strong for him and it was convincing. On the other hand, Phul Maya was pondering how to pacify her husband and bring him to rest from all his callous thoughts.

Night marched by.

The following evening Kumar went to Sathi's place, wept and sobbed, like an infant to his mother. He complained about not being a responsible father – a father not fulfilling his family desires and needs. He presented the entire scenario to Sathi who listened, attentively.

Sathi replied, "See friend, I'm always ready to help you. You can take as much fruit as you wish from me but despite that I cannot help you in any other ways."

Sathi further added, "My friend, I will never be able to produce money and that is the only thing you humans want."

Kumar sat there just silently crumpled up against the trunk of Sathi and resting his head. Sathi tried to console his friend taking sympathy on him. Actually, Sathi had never seen his friend so sad and so gloomy over all these years of friendship. He was always happy and the degree of happiness was even multiplied with the advent of Phul Maya in his life and later on with his beloved children.

Days passed but the fire in Kumar's heart was not to be quenched so easily.

Kumar was extremely depressed about his life and his living standards.

One morning he woke up and he seemed perfect and full of happiness. The sorrow that had lingered upon his face for the past weeks seemed to fade away all at once. He smiled like a baby who knows nothing about the riddles of the world and relies upon his parents for his needs. Upon seeing Phul Maya he said joyfully,

"Good morning, darling, is not the tea ready yet, and are the kids up or still in bed?"

It was quite strange to see the mood shift in her husband.

Phul Maya felt a little relief when she saw her husband so happy all at once and gave a deep sigh. It was like a miracle. She went to the other room and informed the kids all about their father in modest faith. The kids at once kissed their father and requested him to play some wonderful melody since it had been weeks he played anything enchanting for the family.

They asked, "Papa don't you think today is a wonderful morning and definitely calls for a song, so why don't you play something to cheer us all up?"

Excited enough, Kumar pulled his murali from underneath his pillow and started to pipe it until the next masterpiece was born.

Phul Maya announced herself with a tray with two cups of tea and two glasses of milk. Soon, they enjoyed the melody over the tea. Sometime later when the kids went to school, Phul Maya went close to her husband and sat down.

Kumar said, "Phul Maya, you know why I am so happy today. It seems that I have found the answers to all the questions I was looking for such a long time that had really got on my nerves,"

The long duality had ended and he was at peace with himself. Now he was refused to be frightened as he did before.

Phul Maya diminished her voice and asked softly, "What ...What is it?"

Kumar replied, "Now I am not lingering anymore and spending the rest of my life just thinking. The thing is, I have decided to leave the village and go to a better place to earn lots and lots of money. And when I return we all will have a joyful life and our children can get admitted to better schools and you can wear better clothes and jewellery."

Kumar added with enthusiasm,

"Just look for yourself. The blouse you are wearing is three years old, the slippers on your feet are about to tear but you are still using them"

He went on with nonchalant look in his serene eyes,

"So, see for the furtherance of our family I have decided that I must leave this village for some time." He spoke as if he was all at once driven by a demon.

Hearing this Phul Maya's eyes was wide open and she began to sob without even uttering a word or so. She was afraid of something but was not clear of it.

Kumar seemed nervous though he looked self-assured and assertive a little while ago. Perhaps he could not see the woman's tears.

He retorted blindly, "See Phul Maya I don't know why you cry. Just try to understand that we cannot continue to exist under such circumstances. As you

126

know the little piece of land is not enough for four of us. And most importantly we need more money for the better education of our children."

He desperately wanted his children to attend posh schools.

He cried, "I know how you feel but please do not make me weak by your tears, you know I love you and cannot tolerate to see tears welled up in your eyes like that."

After much endeavor she managed to gather herself enough strength to speak up and finally said with humility, "Okay, with whom are you going?"

"Ghale," he instantly responded. Perhaps he had already decided all his actions.

She remained in her pose for a few moments as if she had turned stationary all of a sudden of some evil wicked curse. She gently sobbed but Kumar could not even say a word. He knew how she felt inside. He could feel her emotion personally.

That was the longest day in and of their life and it ended finally. It had to end.

In the evening the two children hustled into the hut and found their parents upset. Well, the son was not quick to decipher the situation but Champa quickly found out and promptly calculated the scene. Not to disturb their parents, she took her brother to the other room. It was as if Champa was powerfully anointed by the Holy Spirit to understand the matter at hand so precisely and so accurately.

At about six o'clock, Phul Maya summoned her children from the kitchen for dinner and soon everyone gathered; Phul Maya served her family. Throughout the dinner time the only one who never stopped chatting way the son Manoj. He constantly kept talking and taking despite many objections Champa made. Once or twice, Kumar even got annoyed but his son never understood the crux of the matter.

After dinner everyone retired to bed. That day Phul Maya went to bed a little early than the others. In the other room, Champa kept pondering on not being able to reach a conclusion. She tried to find out what had really made their parents so upset. She thought what could be the reason. She even asked herself,

"Maybe I have made some mistakes."

She was still too young to fathom that her parents were going through a misfortune that had to be accepted with joy, resignation and humility.

Chapter Seven

The Departure

Kumar crept into the bed as silently as a snake, making sure not to disturb Phul Maya. He covered himself with the blanket and threw a passionate look at Phul Maya with tears welling in his eyes.

All the past days flashed in and out of his memory. He recalled everything from the day they had first met till that very moment and became very nostalgic. He was in no time taken over by powerful evocative times. He was indeed very much astonished to find he had each and every past moments of their past lives stored in his memory for good, knowingly or unknowingly. He touched her meek face that looked so obedient even while she slept, as gently as a feather; soon she woke up to find Kumar staring at her with his full attention and began to cry submissively but nothing could stop her. She hugged Kumar and kissed him violently all over his face as lovers do on their first meeting. They embraced each other like never they were never going detach no matter what.

Kumar said as if he was hesitating, "See Phul Maya, it is high time we earn money. For this I must go to the city as soon as possible otherwise I am sure that the love of you and our children will enchain me."

Phul Maya stared at him reproachfully as if she had an ocean of things to say.

Kumar continued, "Today again I talked with Ghale and he even had similar things in mind. And see here, I am not the first to leave the village and go somewhere else."

Holding Phul Maya's doomed face he said, "Just remember Hari, the teacher, and also the others who left this village for some time; in a matter of a few years of struggle they have completely changed their life and their living standards have gone up. I have heard that Hari is now going to admit his daughter to an English Medium school next year."

He further attempted to convince her.

"See when those children come back after completing their studies, they will automatically become better. They will adopt a modern life style and will never have to bother about living here in this poor condition. A proper educated man also can bring good changes in society."

Phul Maya cried and replied,

"Listen, Kumar, your words are true and to some extent exactly right but how can I live…"

Then she stopped abruptly, no longer being able to go on. She was a very affectionate creature but very delicate at the same time.

Kumar found himself in a voiceless state, dropped his head back on his pillow and without being aware went off to a deep sleep.

The following day the children also knew about their father's plan. Kumar noticed that everything was the same all around his vicinity. The sun was the same, the little birds chirped the same melody in the nearby jungle, farmers lazily going to their field, small kids gamboling with their wheels, the blue sky above looked the same. Kumar realized that the rest of the world looked the same except his small hut. He looked at his wife and children painfully. They were in pain and sorrow. He could hear their bleeding soul.

He did not have the impulse to open the shop that day so the shop remained closed. He did not want to work at all with all the vivid random thoughts penetrating his mind. Phul Maya looked very sad and dismayed. Kumar blamed himself for all this and he was ready to go through any suffering if that could bring prosperity, peace and happiness in their lives. All he wanted was to harmonize the family but that harmony was not feasible with the little money they had, more was required as a matter of extreme importance. He just cared for his family and out of despondency instead of looking towards their appealing faces he looked sternly at the horizon.

Ghale arrived in the early morning. They wanted to make plans.

He looked very happy, he was more than happy; 'exuberant' could be used as the perfect word to demonstrate his happiness.

Euphorically he said, "Namaste! The most perfect couple I have ever seen."

He sat near to Kumar and said, grasping both of his hands tightly, "So Kumar, is everything planned and ready, are you surely going with me?"

As Phul Maya entered the room Ghale said hurriedly looking towards her,

"Now Phul Maya sister's rainy days are about come to an end. Soon you will have all the accumulations as that of Hari's wife, you will see to that."

Phul Maya did not reply and gave a loathsome look facing in the other direction. She uttered forcefully, "Wait, I will get tea for you," and rushed to the kitchen.

Kumar certainly knew that his wife would not be able to bear the moment he leaves home.

Ghale sensed the repugnant look in their eyes but ignored it. He did not want to spoil the purpose he was there for. He quite intelligently explained about the different prospects and opportunities in different cities but Kumar sarcastically requested him not to talk about the issue in front of his family. Ghale understood that and did not talk about it. Ghale seemed more curious to leave the village so he was more outspoken on this matter than Kumar. But Kumar was also well aware that it was an unhealthy choice to continue living with such uncertainty about the future.

Soon Phul Maya came from inside with two cups of tea falsifying a smile over her sympathetic face. To some degree she succeeded in her falsification but Kumar could discern the reproduction. They talked on different matters.

The tea was over and during that discourse the plans were compiled. They made plans to leave the village and go to a city where jobs were easily available in abundance. During the conversation, Kumar showed signs of discouragement and discontentment but Ghale then would try his best to cheer him up and provide some friendly advice.

Later that evening Kumar sluggishly walked towards Sathi's place and sat underneath its huge trunk and leaned weakly against it. Tears rolled from his eyes in a

132

violent manner. This was the first time ever he was compelled to make a decision against his determination. The Sathi could feel his pain and agony but there was not any way to help his friend. As Kumar's family grew, the money received by selling the fruit was not of much use. So Sathi felt real sorry for this. It could feel the pain Kumar was going through; it felt his sentiments. It tried to relieve him from his pain by supplying a gentle gust of wind over his head but it seemed that Kumar would never come out from the pain of leaving his family.

After staying there for about an hour or so he returned back to his own hut and boldly informed everyone about the date of his departure that night. There was no other way except facing the inevitable.

Silence prevailed the following days.

The following night, Kumar played his murali just to entertain his family but the music failed to bring joy to their faces. Even the notes seemed weary as if they were coming from a dying flute.

Kumar glanced up at the sky so full with stars. The stars winked at him slyly. The shimmering and glimmering moon shone with its fullness in the lonely sky that illuminated the entire environment. He looked at the full moon and questioned himself,

"Have I made the right decision? Will my leaving the village bring real happiness, prosperity and some wealth in my family?"

His grief had become major and minor at the same time. Kumar felt deluded and felt utterly useless.

Suddenly he felt a loving touch on his shoulder and he knew it could only be Phul Maya. She sat beside him and rested her head against his shoulder. He held her close to him and embraced her. He felt like crying but he controlled his emotion realizing he was a man who was never meant to weep.

The couple were joined by their daughter, who was as wise as her mother; she knew just how to act under such circumstances. Phul Maya and Kumar were not surprised to see their daughter at that hour. They knew that she understood each and every moment that has passed and was passing – the pain her mother was going through and the sorrow of her father as well. Her eyes welled up to see the disaster that had befallen their parents. She thought it wise not to say a word. So she maintained her silence. All three of them watched the stars up in the sky with sheer helplessness. A thick cloud swallowed the moon. It was the worst thing to see. Soon they went back home and retired to bed. Both Kumar and Phul Maya could not sleep, but finally tiring soon dozed off.

Early, next morning Phul Maya woke up, took a bath and quickly got busy in her daily household activities. Both the children, after having a glass of milk began to study their lessons. Kumar opened his shop and waited for his customers, but his heart was surely not into it. Something was tormenting him. He knew what, and that torment was as bad as a torture.

Phul Maya approached him with a fresh smile on her face, trying to conceal her pain, and sympathized.

"Kumar, I know you sure would like to do some shopping before you leave; like get yourself a pair of trousers and a warm coat."

She further said, "Oh, yes and what about the shoes, the pair you have deserves to be thrown, so get yourself a new pair of socks and shoes."

Kumar, with a pitiful smile on his face and nodded,

"Yes, I think you are right, I was also thinking the same."

In the afternoon both of them visited the nearby village market and bought trousers, shirts and shoes. In the market place, they met friends and neighbours. Almost everyone inquired of him.

"Kumar, is it true that you are moving to the city?"

Kumar agreed, "Yes, but not only me, Ghale is accompanying me."

They wished him good luck.

The next evening he went to the jungle with his family. Kumar knew he was surely going to miss them for a long time to come. Sathi welcomed them. Soon the children climbed up Sathi while Kumar and Phul Maya sat underneath it. Kumar took out his murali and began to weave the magic. He played the same melody that had first attracted Phul Maya towards him. Every note was the same. Even the intervals and the rests were perfect. She listened to the melody intensely making sure not to miss a note. This made her feel like crying, but she stopped herself because she surely did not want to spoil the wonderful evening. The children soon got engrossed in their own methods and gymnastics. They were in perfect harmony with their friend. From time to time Sathi swayed its branches to provide more entertainment to the kids but making sure not to let them fall off. Sathi had even realized the gloominess in the melody. It knew everything that was going on. It was not just an imitation of empathy but it actually comprehended it. It was sorry for himself because there was just not any way to help Kumar. Saying goodbye for the day they returned back to the village.

Kumar's heart was in panic, the countdown for the departure had already started. Now only six days were

135

left, so he decided to live and just live each and every moment with his family. He spent more and more time with them not really paying much attention to other matters.

Upon hearing about Kumar's trip the next day Phul Maya's father and mother came to visit Kumar. When they were informed that he was leaving the village, firstly they were shocked, but upon learning the circumstances they felt a little relieved. The poor have no choice except to join the stampede that targeted the wealth.

Kumar's mother-in-law was not satisfied with the decision Kumar had made. She even thought of suggesting that to Kumar but Phul Maya stopped her.

She said, "Mother, now everything has been decided, so let us not disturb it."

Soon the days passed like minutes. The rolling of each day multiplied the family bond to an unsurmountable degree.

"Tomorrow he will be gone," thought Phul Maya and cried to herself.

The day before Kumar left, the kids did not go to school as they knew they would miss their father for a long time to come. Relatives and neighbours came to see Kumar and the elderly people suggested to him the various things he had to take care of in the city. Ram's uncle, the neighbour, even handed him the address of his cousin and said Kumar was to visit him if anything unexpected cropped up. All the villagers helped the family in their own individual way and conduct. Soon the visitors left and the family was left alone as before with no one to talk to. There was not much to hear and say amongst themselves. Kumar panicked, he repented for not having gone to see his friend. The very thought of his friend made him cry. He consoled himself. It is unmanly behavior to cry like a baby.

It was eight o'clock in the evening and the next morning at four they were to start for the city. Kumar said to himself, "Should I not see my friend before I leave? Is it, and would it be fair to leave without seeing him? How in the world can I be so mean and selfish?"

It was ten o'clock and he could not sleep. Thoughts of his friend encountered him again and again. Within a fraction of time he recalled everything from the day he had first met, the murali days with never-ending long conversations with Phul Maya under the branches of his Sathi. How Sathi had helped him when he was in his bad days and needed money. He felt from deep inside as if Sathi was calling him. Now he could not sleep at all. He felt like a man who had realized his sudden death was sure to come waiting for him round the corner.

Night was falling.

He said to himself, "If I go away without seeing my friend then nobody in the world could save me from being cursed. This is inhumane and a sign of insanity to act this way – perhaps a complete sign of negligence, selfishness and ignorance." He repeated this to himself in a soft murmur.

He changed his position but nothing worked. He heard the calling so clearly and distinctly. He glanced towards Phul Maya; she was asleep with her hand resting on his left chest and shoulder. He felt in his heart a severe ache. He just did not know what to do and how to deal with it.

Not able to resist the urge, he rose up from his bed as silently as he could and went to see his children. They were fast asleep; seeing their face made his eyes full of tears. He watched them for a long time remembering all the joyful and happy times they had spent together. At one corner of the room he saw his father-in-law and mother-in-law who treated Kumar like their own son.

This reminded Kumar of his own mother. He at once recollected that he had saved some of her belongings from his father. He then went to the kitchen and opened the old box. The box was already rusted and mostly covered with spider's web. In the course of time he had almost forgotten about that hidden treasure that solely belonged to him, and no one else would be interested in its acquisition except his long dead ignoble, unworthy, contemptible, vile, mean and sordid father. Perhaps all the summarization of adjectives did not even suffice to criticize the traits of his father. He was beyond condemnation. His father had in every means disgraced himself luminously and luxuriously.

He took out the old pot from the box that reminded him of his mother. He at once remembered all the days he had shared with his dear mother. He recalled each and every moment and every drop of pure love that his mother had for him. He even remembered the day when his mother had given him the murali and kissed it. Kumar was amazed to find everything so fresh and new again. He was within moments taken back to his own childhood days where almost everything flashed back into his mind like they were presently taking place. He recalled how the first time he had met his friend and his gentle heart gave way and wept. Now it was almost too difficult for him to tolerate without seeing his friend.

He opened the door as slowly as possible making sure not to make even the sound of two colliding feathers. He then glanced all around him; everywhere complete silence and dead darkness prevailed. Not a single source of light was to be seen except the glittering of the stars. At that hour of the night even the streets slept. No buzzing sound of the marketplace, no human voice, or even dogs barking were audible. For one second his heart was filled with terror, but his love for his friend was insurmountable, he could not stop at any cost. He then began to run directly towards the jungle while all his fear melted like snow under a blazing arrogant sun. None but the Sathi heard his footsteps and Sathi at once recognized him as no one but his own little friend. Resting his head on Sathi he began to sob like a baby and soon began to cry and howl like a wounded wolf in the dead of the night. Sathi tried to make him stop but nothing helped. Sathi even knew that the next morning he was about to leave. But it was really proud of his friend. It was extremely happy to see his friend at that hour of the night. Both of them knew how much they adored and loved one another. Kumar uttered nothing but remained quiet. Sometimes silence can be the best way to communicate.

He was trying to act sly but Sathi could smell the desperation and could hear his heart screaming apologies. It too in return remained silent and still as possible, just not to disturb the prevailing mood. The entire jungle witnessed that at that dead hour of the night. The jungle was wide awake. Sathi gently moved its branches not even making the slightest noise at all; just like a dog wagging his tail in front of his crying master just to please him. Tears rolled from Kumar's eyes and fell on the tree – he was longing, pleading to God. It even felt it and knew that his friend was crying. Their long and deep friendship was about to end, at least for the time being. How could they live without seeing one another? How could Kumar withstand the pressure of not being able to see his beloved ones? Could he sit still without touching his Sathi? How would he pass his days and weeks and months without his family and his friend? Perhaps it was sure to be a torture!

There were just so many such questions and there was no one to answer except the mighty God, who was not talkative at all. It is wished that sometime He would speak up not to prove his existence but to show that He is living with us.

Both of them remained motionless for about half an hour. They felt very close to each other like never before. They spoke a lot of things but it was not audible. Kumar cried and shouted like a wild bear but it was never heard. Silence proliferated everywhere and darkness spilled itself on every possible corner of the forest.

He tried again and again to explain his exigent need to depart to the city but he was at a complete loss to explain the matter to his friend. Sometimes Kumar really wished that his friend could talk to him like a real person but it was such a pity that it could not talk. But no matter what he was full of pride.

Kumar recovered from his trance-like state and looked all round him. Several hours had elapsed before he knew he had gone into a deep slumber. He guessed that it was already midnight and he should be moving back to his home. But he still wanted to stay there longer with his friend. He did not want to depart at all. But Sathi, his friend said, "Kumar, now you have to go back to your family, they might get worried to find you absent. Never worry about your family, I will help them with all the effort I have in me; just think of returning back as soon as your work is done. Just think that you are needed here."

Kumar could clearly hear these words. The words were so different and clear. He heard with his own ears.

He felt an immense urge to cry but he controlled himself. He thought that now was the time to be strong. Unwillingly though, he left his friend. The thick branches and the green leaves were clearly visible in the moonlight. He embraced Sathi for the last time and bid him bye, perhaps goodbye; who knows for how long.

He moved on but he turned back many a times. Sathi moved its branches slowly gesturing him goodbye, gesturing him good luck for his future and certainly for prosperity. Kumar was almost at a very far distance from it but he did not stop turning back to see his friend standing there, just like ever before.

Soon he reached his hut and slowly opened the door and found nothing disturbed. So he gave a last look to his children and moved to his room where he found Phul Maya sleeping in the same position as he had left. She was not even aware that Kumar had gone missing.

He thanked God.

He pulled the blanket over him and soon went to sleep. In the night he dreamt of many things.

Whispers of a dream were all over his head and soul.

Next morning Phul Maya woke up early and quickly made something to eat for her husband who was to depart that morning. Kumar too woke up early. Quickly he took a bath and dressed himself with a sad erratic look hanging over his face all the time. He seemed lost to himself, quite lost, completely lost. Soon after, everyone woke up and were ready to say good bye to Kumar. His children just sat and remained close to their dad not knowing how to act. Kumar looked at Champa, she looked very sad and perhaps she was the saddest of all. He could feel that her heart was at unease. He was telepathic.

Needless to say, Kumar also could feel the pain that Phul Maya was going through. Any moment she could start weeping. Kumar knew that she was just at the point of explosion.

His mother-in-law said, "Phul, it is not a good thing to cry when someone is leaving for foreign lands, especially the women of the house."

"Yes, that might bring bad luck," continued her father softly.

Those words could hardly pacify Phul Maya who was already surrounded by unappeasable sadness. She kept looking at Kumar with tearful eyes. By this time Manoj had already understood that his father was leaving the village and going to the city to earn money.

Innocently, he requested, "Ba, bring me lots and lots of chocolates when you come back, will you?"

Kumar could say nothing except nod his head.

Breakfast was ready. Kumar started having it and his eye welled up. He did not know how to conceal it.

No one uttered a single word except Manoj. He chattered all the time, incessantly. Soon again the hut was quiet as mice.

Champa was grave and silent until the time the breakfast was over. She knew the situation that she was surrounded with.

Phul Maya prepared tea for them.

Over tea, Kumar's father-in-law gave him many useful suggestions about city life. Kumar listened attentively like a very good student with keen interest and enthusiasm. A few villagers gathered to see them off to the city. They were all nice villagers.

Ghale rushed in and asked Kumar to hurry.

"Let's get going now, Kumar, otherwise we will be late for the first bus," he said ghastly as he moved in.

Ghale's family had also followed him up to Kumar's house and someone in the crowd said Ghale's mother could not even face him leaving his home.

But despite all this Ghale looked unaffected. He knew it was rather a difficult choice but had to be done for the betterment of the family. It was like an unavoidable conscription for those villagers.

Kumar got up and glanced at his family. Both the children came running to their father with tears rolling down their eyes. Phul Maya's mother took care of them and made every possible attempt to make them stop crying. Phul Maya's eyes were already swollen. For her it was such a painful task but she managed to operate like a gallant woman. She endured it.

Kumar picked up his luggage and walked out while his family followed him silently like in a procession. Phul Maya could not help weeping and sobbing all the time.

Phul Maya whispered, "Kumar, please do not forget to write …"

She began to cry violently with greater loudness as if someone had deceased.

Kumar consoled her, he softly said, "I promise I will write you every week, you really do not need to worry about anything at all, you just keep the house and stay with the family."

In the middle Ghale shouted,

"*Bhauju*, my dear sister-in-law, you don't have to worry about Kumar, now he is in safe hands. He is in Ghale's hand; you better know this." Ghale shouted this to lessen the pain and just to let them feel relaxed and moreover to distract their attraction.

Both Phul Maya, his father-in-law along with mother-in-law bid him good bye and wished him success in his life. He gave his last hug to his children but could not even utter a word. He was too weak emotionally.

No matter what pain Kumar was going through he knew Phul Maya, his beloved wife, an innocent and adorable creature with unsurpassed skills as a wife and a mother would keep the house in her bosom and never ever let the children go astray. She would work miracles to run the house in a well-managed fashion with her acute intelligence.

He was confident, in fact very confident.

Kumar did not dare to look back either.

He was leaving his village for the first time in his life.

He knew that many people were looking at him. He could feel their compassionately afflicted look piercing him. His eyes were already weeping heavily.

After a half hour walk they reached the bus stop. Kumar did not speak much that morning. He looked at Ghale, a very talkative person, who looked serious and taciturn most of the time. Kumar believed that Ghale too was thinking deeply and passionately about his family and his future.

Kumar asked himself, "Am I right or wrong?"

He just felt something within him reacting,

"Don't you dare right or wrong."

Then again, there was silence, except indistinct chattering from the early morning people.

But he consoled himself. "It is all in God's will. Maybe he had thought a very good character out of me. He must know I have a family."

Ghale paid the bus fare and he cheered Kumar up,

"Brother, this is our destiny, to leave our loved ones. Destiny is what directs us and destiny knows what we are destined for, otherwise we are nothing on our own."

Kumar simply maintained his still disposition. He had walked into oblivion.

Finally the bus departed the station.

Chapter Eight

Men at Work

From time to time Ghale cut jokes and very ridiculous tales. Kumar just broke into a gentle smile while the fellow passengers laughed and cheered at every cunning joke he passed. The gathering daylight was slowly making the day clear, bright and friendlier. Out of the bus window one could see the swiftly passing houses that were made of mud, brick and some of stone. The acceleration of the bus made the outside view like a linked blurred photographs; one could just see the glimpse of everything that passed the window before it vanished in obscurity. The greenish trees just appeared like a green scattered paints by a novice painter on a scrambled piece of paper. Kumar was just beginning to enjoy the outside when all of a sudden sadness honored him with its presence and this time more forcefully and brutally. He looked around him to find Ghale completely engrossed entertaining the fellow passengers. All those strangely unfamiliar faces engendered appetency to meet his family all at once. This was perhaps the ever first time he had been out of his tiny village without his family. He panicked with extreme desire; soon he

146

consoled reminding himself of the grandeur purpose of this mission-a promising good future for the family. But Kumar looked altogether disheartened with death dancing in his heart.

Just to keep himself away from all the remembrances he focused his attention towards Ghale hoping that his jokes would cheer him up and subside his sadness to some extent. Kumar knew with certainty that Ghale was just acting up and trying to forget the pain; he thought those silly jokes and laughs would kill the giant pain lurking inside of him. How silly!

One of the passengers complimented, "Friends, this is the only joke that has made me laugh. It is one of the best jokes ever."

But Kumar knew that Ghale too was despondent inside and he was only professing that he was happy. He too missed the same way as Kumar was missing his family. Everyone loves ones family for sure. Kumar could already hear those silent screams and uproars from his heart and soul. It was a pathetic way to lead a life but one had to. That is why someone has said so righteously,' beggars can't be choosers'.

The destination was at a great distance and the bus made some stops at small hotels. The passengers ate and changed. After nearly a twelve hour long bus ride, they reached the city. The first introduction to the city was chaotic. People hustling and rustling all the way in every direction, the loud and ugly noises of the car and shrieks of the bus conductors, the polluted air, hard to breath. For the first timers the city life presents itself as a rough kid playing with his toys amongst the other rough kids in a muddy grassless ground.

Finally the bus halted, Kumar and Ghale disembarked with their mouths gaping and wide open frantic eyes trying to adjust to this new weird world. They looked all around and saw signs of the lodges and hotels.

"Where are we!" exclaimed Ghale frantically.

"This is where we were headed for," replied Kumar whimsically.

"Now what and where should we go?" questioned Ghale in his breathy voice.

"Let's find a lodge first and then we will see," answered Kumar although he was no less bewildered than Ghale.

"All right."

Both the friends after many visits to the different lodges managed to find a cheap lodge to stay for the night. They needed a shelter and they found one. The lodge was in utterly bad shape and needed immediate maintenance; the roof from one side had given its way and it was perilous but the rent was inexpensive, rather it was very cheap compared to the other lodges at vicinity. Later they had a stale meal that was greasy at the lodge and lodged themselves in a room already occupied by spiders, mosquitoes and other ants roaming here and there. Those occupants seemed like old inhabitants of that room and behaved alarmed when the room was opened for the new temporary tenants. Some of the ants even momentarily stared at them before hiding themselves wherever they could while the spiders managed to place themselves in their secluded places and began staring at them.

The very first day ended swiftly without their knowing, they were too exhausted to go outside and find some work, so they remained in the lodge and took some rest. Both the pals were too overwhelmed by this new city life they had just been strangely introduced to.

They conversed a little in that hotel room and went to sleep overcome by fatigue. Ghale was so tired that he did not even utter a word before going to bed. It was then ten o'clock in the evening. The outsiders could be still heard conversing.

Kumar thought about his family and Sathi in the jungle. His eyes shed with tears as he recalled everything. He pondered, "My Phul Maya might be thinking about me at this moment, and Champa might be staring at the corner of the wall and thinking about me too, while my little son should be fast sleep."

He tried but could not sleep. Various thought visited his mind on and off. Sometimes the thoughts were positive and the very next time they were negative. He cast his glance on Ghale; he was already half dead. He did not even feel mosquitoes sucking blood out of him.

His Sathi in the jungle might be alone remembering nothing but his friend.

The next day at about seven o'clock in the morning they set out in search of work after a light breakfast that composed of a big glass of tea and a couple of scrambled eggs.

For Kumar, the night had been a nightmare, he just could not sleep and kept constantly changing his position He dreamt of all the happiest moments of his life he had spent with his family and Sathi in the jungle. Alas, now all that he possessed were the dreams and memories to cherish.

They kept loitering in streets wondering at the malls and array of shops along both the sides of the streets overwhelmed with automobiles and rickshaws. The rattling of human voices was gruesome and that, mixed with the constant honking of the cars, made the place full of noise and chaos. The people with mobiles in their hands talking without stopping, the black smoke coming from the vehicles, the ladies with a nice hairdo crossing the streets with bags hanging on their shoulder. All these new introductions made Kumar and Ghale bewildered and made them do nothing but stare and stare at every new thing they stumbled upon.

Now finding the work in the city was the next major problem.

Both Kumar and Ghale were completely virgin to the city life and style, so they did not have any knowledge about where to go to search for jobs and how to contact people. The two naive men were badly confused and perplexed with no good sense of what was to happen next. So the entire day they roamed the streets with much luxury of their foot and just did not know where to go and how to apply for a job. They were just so new and original to the city life. So after a long and tiresome day they returned back to their lodge and retired to bed hopelessly. The men seemed so full of confusions that they seem to have nothing to say much.

The next morning they went out again in their search. They were faced with disappointments wherever they went. Perhaps they were too slow or did not know how to start the interesting conversation or be a promising appealing job hunters.

Every shop owner, the *Sahuji*, they approached, simply rejected them saying, "No work," without even looking at them.

They were the harshest sounds Kumar had ever heard in his life. Back in the village he was not accustomed to such a life. He felt strange to be treated that way but he maintained himself with a dignified motive.

"It seems we are out of luck in this city," cried Ghale giving a sharp penetrating look at Kumar.

"I know, but we must keep looking, I know we will find something soon," replied Kumar assuredly.

"Yeah…" retorted Ghale with losing confidence.

Later that night while they were in bed they briefly had some conversation of trifle importance. Kumar said he remembered his village and his family but Ghale remained silent. In fact Ghale was also undergoing the same pain as Kumar was going through. But Ghale hid his emotions. Now a more intense problem was before them and the sweet remembrance of their village certainly provided them some comfort but did not make them strong enough for this selfish world in to which they had just recently landed.

After many hopeless attempts to go to bed, Kumar got up and took his murali and went to the roof of the hotel. It was a full moon night with brilliantly shining stars. He sat down on the roof and stretched his entire body and relaxed. He watched the billions and billions of stars that were scattered up in the sky. The sky looked the same. He tried to find some stars that he had seen from his village but here they looked different and unfriendly. So to amuse himself he took his murali and played his favourite. He played with not much interest and declining heart. Soon he was overpowered by the boredom of the night and the surroundings also seemed indifferent to his music. Kumar felt rejected and alone under the sky; perhaps he had lost his faith. Abruptly he quit playing and stared into the infiniteness of the sky and heard himself asking, "What about my family at his point? Perhaps Phul Maya must have done the cooking with sluggish movements and desirous heart. She might have been uninterested in anything after I left and probably favoured a solitary life appearing like a recluse."

"My daughter, Champa knows what is going on. Her sophisticated understanding will motivate the entire family to grow and survive during my absence."

This massively broke his heart and discomforted him; he continued to stay silent and motionless until he was overpowered by fatigue. Then he then went down to his room and finally dozed off.

A few days passed.

Kumar and Ghale looked like vagabond.

They did all they could do but nothing ever helped them.

One of these nights Ghale was just loitering in the lodge. The lodge owner came to him; he was a jolly man with his unshaven face, large round shoulders and strangely long hands with pointed fingers. He asked him various questions about their background. Ghale replied to everything, plainly with his full intelligence not knowing the reason being asked.

At last he asked in a friendly manner, "Where do you work?"

"Nowhere," was the straight answer.

Ghale then added, "We are in search of work... if you could provide us some work then it would be so kind of you"

But upon the request made by Ghale, the owner responded with nothing and went gallantly down the stairs as if he heard nothing. Both the men remained stunned at this peculiar deportment.

Ghale was astonished by the way he acted all of a sudden. Then after, Ghale went back to his room. Kumar was as usual in his position.

"See Ghale… we are finished now."

Kumar cast his glance over Ghale just for a few seconds and without even saying a single word he began to stare at the rough walls that surrounded them like a prison.

"Come on, Kumar, what's wrong with you, you look really messed up and…?"

Before Ghale ended his words Kumar interrupted and said harshly, "You say what's wrong, what's wrong with me? Do you consider anything good has happened to us all this week?"

In the same fit of anger Kumar further said, "Is this the reason why we have come here, abandoning all our loved ones back in that village, you, you…?"

Kumar suddenly terminated his words and remained calm trying to control his anger and words. Ghale just could not believe this abrupt change in Kumar's behavior. He had always regarded Kumar as his intimate friend and a real hard working honest man.

After that Ghale did not dare to speak to Kumar. He clutched his bed and slept.

The night passed. It was a cruel night. It did not bother to listen to the pain and chaos of the people under its shadow. The next morning Kumar felt a little ashamed for his rude foolish behavior. He felt remorse.

"I should not have spoken to Ghale in such a rude and ill manner."

He looked for Ghale but he was not there in the room. He waited for some time. Kumar did not know what and how to talk to Ghale after all that had happened. After half an hour, Ghale returned back to the room and found Kumar sitting in his bed. Ghale still felt a little nervous talking to Kumar.

Kumar, on the other hand, was ashamed to face Ghale and finally after gathering much strength Kumar started up. "Ghale, I am really sorry, I did not mean to scold you. I know you can better understand what I am going through." After a brief pause he added, "I cannot understand what happened to me last night, all of a sudden I felt like…"

Ghale was happy that they had made up again. He knew that Kumar was very honest and the humblest creature.

"Okay, Kumar, now stop all this rubbish action and reaction, the past is what we left behind so let's prepare for the job."

Putting on a philosophical mood he said, "No matter what the consequences may be, the past can never be summoned back again by any means and if there is any way then please tell me. I promise I will change all the matters at hand myself, perhaps I don't even need God's help in this matter."

This was a real chance for Kumar to escape so he managed to remain silent for a moment. There prevailed a perfect silence when finally the virgin silence was broken by a gentle tapping on the door.

It was no one other than the lodge owner. Ghale welcomed him with a warm smile upon his face even though he was still astonished by his last visit.

The owner said coming straight to business, "You people are looking for work, right?"

Both of them nodded excitedly.

"A friend of mine is looking for some men who are interested, hardworking, and trustworthy and most of all, punctual at work. Think about it."

Kumar instantly questioned,

"What is the work?"

The Owner cleared his throat and clarified.

"Well, the work is to keep the shop. Your work would be to prepare the items demanded by the customer and hand it over to them and prepare a final bill, so you understand it is like salesman's job."

Ghale asked energetically without any further consideration.

"And the salary?"

The Owner guessed.

"I think he should give you around twenty five hundred rupees a month. Is that okay?"

Kumar in no time replied, "Yes, yes too good, you see we are now ready to do any sort of work under these circumstances."

Kumar further said politely and smoothly, "It is your greatness and mercy of you approaching us with these jobs at these conditions, anyway thank you a lot."

Ghale added too, "Yes, thanks, thanks a lot, thanks,"

With the air of relief and contentment the owner asked, "Well then, can I inform my friend that he has found the people he is looking for?"

Ghale was a little confused, he asked, "We are two of us, so who will work, Kumar or me?"

The owner replied, "Oh, don't worry at all, my friend is a rich merchant, he has multiple shops in the nearby market. So you both will be employed in different shops."

Ghale put his problem, "All is fine but what about accommodation. We cannot stay in this lodge and pay like this, soon we are sure to finish our money."

155

"Do not worry, everything will be managed, just wait and see," said the owner and went away.

But before he went out of the room, he told them to be ready at eight o'clock in the morning the following day.

This news made both Kumar and Ghale extremely thrilled and jubilant. They laughed without any restraint. Both of them decided to inform this good news to their family and soon jotted down a letter as fast as they could. After finishing writing they delivered the mail to the nearby post office and waited for the mail to reach its destination so that they could at least imagine the exultation that letter would bring in their families. They felt lively and at the top of the world.

That night they went to bed so rapturous and looking forward to their coming days.

Next morning they quickly got up, took a bath and shaved. They both looked blessed and one could see the radiation radiating out of their young euphoric face. Both of their faces were lifted, packed with enthusiasm like a winner of a marathon race. They quickly took their tea and waited for the owner to arrive. At something like fifteen minutes past eight the owner arrived and asked them,

"Are you ready, have you decided to work as I had explained you?"

Both of them replied ecstatically at once, "Yes."

The owner introduced these men to his merchant friend and the employment was agreed upon.

The first day of the work was fine; just at first they had to be instructed about the shelves' items and their respective prices to sell.

Usually the customers rushed in the mornings and evenings but usually in the afternoon Kumar was almost free. So during his free time he thought of his family and the lovely old friend, Sathi in the jungle. These thoughts only made him alive, money was just an excuse.

In the village the entire family members were extremely elated to receive his first letter since he had left the village. It was not just a paper with some writing scattered on it, it was the writing of the one whom they adored the most. Their little son could not just stop gamboling and chortling all over the house.

He ran all over the neighbourhood and shouted,

"My father, letter, my father letter..."

It was somewhat difficult for Phul Maya to make him be quiet. Then Phul Maya shared the news with her neighbours and her neighbours came to meet her. Everyone seemed happy to hear that Kumar and Ghale were employed and were earning around twenty five hundred per month. That was handsome money for the poor villagers. It was as if the village was one family and everyone seemed to be happy for Kumar and Ghale.

Phul Maya made no delay in replying to Kumar with whatever she had learnt. Champa helped her a lot to complete the letter. She kept dictating while Champa continued writing but she would never stop. Phul Maya went on and on with her dictation until the letter was long enough.

"Now that is enough for the first reply mother," Champa said with a relief and taking a deep breath.

"Was that too long, Champa?" she said with a sparkle in her eyes.

"No Mother, that was alright."

But Phul Maya was still so exalted that she needed someone to pour down her exaltation otherwise she would drown on it. She could not wait so she ran towards the forest and informed this to Sathi; Sathi seemed much delighted and moved its branches in pure joy and ecstasy. News about Kumar brought bliss to everyone in the family and the village as well. Phul Maya remembered how her husband used to play his murali sitting underneath Sathi's branches and sometimes high among the branches. She reminded herself of those days; the times she felt enchanted by the music and the first time she had met Kumar just to fall in love, deep profound love.

So thus the mail communication began. The village was still at a great distance from the day when they would have towers installed for the mobile communication to take place, so the villagers had still to rely on mail that took days and sometimes days and days to arrive. But the genteel villagers were satisfied unlike the city dwellers who asked for more and more.

Kumar took his job very seriously. He would leave no stones unturned to accomplish the job at hand. Every time he received a letter he would create distance and read the letter with full emotion again and again. He lived for those mail moments and would always wait for the postman to surprise him with a letter from his village. Phul Maya though was not good at letter writing but she managed to compose letters easily understood by Kumar. He would take some time to write to her. It seemed as if an ordinary mail to him from his wife was the most precious thing in the world. The shop owner also inquired once upon seeing the excitement in Kumar's face upon receiving the letter.

"Kumar, you look very happy, is the letter from your wife?"

"No, sir, it is from my family," Kumar answered reverently.

"I see you are exceedingly fond of your family. Well, how many kids you have?" the owner asked him.

Then Kumar replied, "I have a wife and two children, er... one daughter and the younger one, my son..."

Then in no time Kumar would be busy with his customers.

Sometime he would not even have time to complete reading the letter as the store would get busy and full of customers; after all he was there to cater for the needs of his customers.

Chapter Nine

The Enchanting Vacation

Every day after his work was over, Kumar would find himself rushing back to the room which now he rented along with Ghale, needless to say to write letters mentioning all the events that had occurred during that day. They were very happy on the day that they had found this room.

He could not provide a good structure, a good start and a better ending to the letter but he could write a letter that was direct from his heart to the ones whom he adored with his sincerest passion. His eyes would just shine while his hands moved to jot down the words he had in his mind although he returned home with heavy steps overburdened with day's work. The shop owner had helped them find this room. It was just two rooms that they could afford that moment. A sleeping room with two wooden beds and room they called 'the kitchen' to cook. It was in this sleeping room that Kumar would come, sit, play his murali and write to his family. He always wished he could buy his wife a mobile phone but his village was at the farthest end of the world where no one perhaps cared to erect a mast for mobile communication As soon as he arrived in the room, he would fetch himself some paper and write down all his memory served him of the day's happenings. His heart would pound as he added words after words down on his paper. The writing gave him such an immense pleasure that it was beyond any material comforts and achievements for Kumar. He just wished he was better educated so he could express his heartfelt words in a better and educated way, It was then he would remember all the moments he had gone through his life, the day he had met her in the jungle nearby Sathi's place.

He would definitely even write at least a few lines to his daughter and son. He knew that made them happy.

He received letters from the village as well but sometimes they would be late by a week or so. Those letters were his more relished treasure as he would examine each and every line of the letter. He could see his small hut between the lines and the dwellers in it as well. His imaginative power was so strong that he would be quickly taken by it. Writing and receiving letters to and from his family was a noble experience for him. It was so strange that now that he had to rely on the mail carrier to receive the news about his family and village. Writing to Phul Maya was a different experience. He had never communicated to her through words. Every time he wrote her, he felt he was getting much closer to her He had never realized that he was so much closer to her. Phul Maya's writings, after crossing hundreds of miles, and valleys and rivers would fall into his hands. He could sense the fragrance through her words which was as melancholic and melodious as ever. He was even happier when he read the lines written by his children. They would be full of mischievous acts of his little son.

Sometimes his daughter would jot words of wisdom to him. The words would take him back to his family. Kumar would close his eyes and feel everything as being real and for several moments he would experience the same feelings and ecstasy as if he was really back with family in his little village. He would then hear his son calling him in his childish tone. But just then, Kumar would realise that he was not in the room and it would be time for Ghale to knock on the door.

That day Kumar received another mail from his home and as always Kumar could never wait to inform him about the letter. Ghale would feel glad. He had expected his wife to send him letters too. And she would do in no time. Ghale too would be happy. Both the men felt that their bad days were over. Both of them were satisfied with their work and the money they received in return.

Days passed.

So did the months. Indeed half a year passed in the same manner.

One day as they were sitting in their room Ghale started, "Kumar we have been here for quite a time now."

He did not say anything further, waiting for Kumar to start next. He wanted to see if Kumar also had the same idea lurking in his mind. Kumar waited for him to complete his phrase but Ghale did not say anything further.

"So what, I know it has been some time now," Kumar said suddenly giving Ghale a questioning look.

"So why don't we take some day's holiday and…?"

Ghale did not complete the sentence himself, he knew Kumar understood it. As he said that Kumar become so very excited with excitement that he looked right into Ghale's eyes with complete devotion and questioned with a deep and serious note on his voice, "Are you serious, Ghale?"

"Yes, I…"

With a broad smile and grinning cheerfully he said exuberantly, "I cannot imagine that we are planning to see our families."

He looked rather nervous and seemed to drift apart from his calm manly demeanour. He was lost and looked like a skittish mare. He was not in him and his very soul was already in the village waiting for his body to reach.

"Okay, let's talk with Sahuji tomorrow and make arrangements," whispered Kumar in half-conscious state. The way he said that was rather theatrical. Ghale never understood why he was whispering. It was tough for both the men to sleep later that night for their mind was already too occupied by the newly imagined vacation. A vacation that would lead them to their home where they really belonged.

Next day Kumar and Ghale collectively asked for a short trip with Sahuji.

"But how can I run the stores alone without you two?" exclaimed Sahuji with a frown on his face. Again he appealed, "Please don't do that…"

After much persuasion the owner granted them leave but only for three weeks' time. Later he laughed at himself for granting his men holidays. His agitation was reflected by his short laughs that recurred throughout the other half of the day.

The days rolled along quickly and the two friends made some minor purchases for their family and some neighbours.

Kumar and Ghale went back to the village for a short vacation. The bus dropped them at the station and they could sense the smell of land, they felt passionate pangs running through their blood vessels as they touched their homeland. The winds welcomed them and the villagers came running to greet them and expressed their happiness upon seeing them. It was the moment of sheer joy and bliss for all. The two men were cared about and counted not only as a living creature but as a man, as a friend, as a brother and most importantly as a guardian and a husband.

Kumar reached his home and found his wife at the store waiting for him with her passionate eyes. As soon as she saw him she leapt to her feet and threw herself out to welcome her hubby after long time of longing and meditation. They embraced like new lovers with solicitous looks in their eyes but found no words to convey their feelings for each other. Much later after they met they still had an empathetic look for each other.

"Where are the children?" Kumar broke the silence trying to hear some words from Champa.

Rubbing her eyes with her palm and looking straight into his eyes she said, "At this time they are at school. Now don't say you have forgotten their schedule after your visit to the city," she teasingly commented helping him carry his luggage inside.

The house was kept in better condition than before. Kumar could at once see the maintenance work done to keep the house in good condition and some new radical changes. Now the hut looked more spacious and luxurious.

Soon Phul Maya threw herself into his arms and gripped him violently as if to never let go. Her weeping started as she was so glad to have him home again after ages.

Kumar lifted her face and looked into her eyes and said in loving voice, "Now I am here and that is all that matters, let's not let the tears intervene between us. Soon the children will come and I don't want them to see your eyes red and swollen for whatever reason. Please cheer up."

And he began kissing her all over her mouth, cheeks, forehead and temple. Soon they made love violently and felt most of their distress go away. Love has such power.

Kumar felt asleep and by the time he woke up it was three in the afternoon and he became delighted feeling that his children would soon arrive home. He looked around for his wife and not finding her he went to the store. She was there, busy with a couple of local customers.

"Ah, so you are here," exclaimed one of the customer. "How do you feel being home after so long?"

"I can't say in words how I feel but I feel like I am in a never ending happiness," answered Kumar staring at his wife intently who looked even more spirited and elegant than ever before. There was a strange gleam in her eyes.

Later Champa and Manoj arrived home and looked quite shocked to find their father home again. He threw himself towards the entrance and embraced both his kids, one on the left and the other on the right and, with watery eyes kissed them on their forehead. It took some time for Kumar to get out of the turmoil of this emotional state, but finally he did with a glare in his eyes.

In his modulated voice he said, "So how are both doing at school? Champa, is your little brother conducting himself well at home and school?" he pretended to ask with authority.

"Oh Yes Papa! Now he is the most industrious student in his class," replied Champa giggling.

"Hurray, hurray Papa is here," shouted his son in a high pitch and as loud as he could. He was in high spirits.

"Yes, my son, I am back again, your Papa is back."

Kumar kissed and embraced his daughter and said, "Oh my love, I am back for three weeks to hear all your words of wisdom."

Manoj then started talking, asking his father incessant questions about city life, and again randomly mentioning all the facts about his friends at school. It was such a fun to see the entire family back again laughing and merry making. Soon the close neighbours came to meet Kumar and congratulate him on his homecoming, but deep down Kumar was also aware of the time clock that was ticking away and every tick brought them near to the day of departure to which he did not even wanted to give a tiniest fraction of his thought.

Later that day Kumar unfolded his luggage and handed them the little presents he had brought. The happiest one was the little brother Manoj whose feet were jumping at getting his presents. Champa thanked her father and snuggled close to him. Soon Phul brought fried rice with onions and garlic and the family had a grand feast. The store was closed for the evening that day.

Phul Maya watched everything and felt proud of her husband. The children were very, very happy to receive such wonderful gifts from their father. In fact this was the first time the children ever had gifts from someone.

Then, immediately that very evening, Kumar rushed to see Sathi in the jungle. He could not hold himself back any longer.-His immense desire to see Sathi was getting stronger and stronger as he marched his way towards the forest.

He envisioned all the past friendship of himself with his tree all his way and he looked triumphed. He felt victorious.

Finally he reached the spot and gave a triumphant cry. "I am here my friend."

He was already sentimental as he had the first glimpse of his tree. Sathi was already surrounded by other thick trees all around. Kumar ran and cuddled Sathi and murmured as if in sleep, "My friend, I am back with you."

He looked at Sathi and climbed up the branches, and jumped from one to the other, just to recollect all his previous experiences. He reminisced about the summers they had spent together and all the other long, long past days. All he had were memories. Kumar climbed as high as he could and looked around the forest like a conqueror. He encountered the same old Kumar he had left some time ago and now he was happy to reunite with all he had left. He felt very pleased.

Sathi also felt happy to see his friend after such a long interval. They talked a lot. Sathi said how much he had missed him in his absence. Now it was time for Kumar to entertain himself and his friend. He took out his murali and played it passionately. As his heart was filled with joy and happiness, nothing could restrain this young and gifted musician from composing everlasting and evergreen pieces of all times- The depth of his

167

conviction, dedication and consistency towards his music was insurmountable, so even while he was not playing, his soul was always weaving some melody even when Kumar was sad and distressed.

That evening he stayed late with Sathi in the jungle. He sat on one of the thick branches and was comfortable. He played innumerous melodies, every one of which was more than excellent, perhaps magnificent, like a king's palace. He closed his eyes and felt exuberant and highly exhilarated when he realized that he was with his beloved ones. But again soon the very thought of departure would depress him – it was like a demon that was always showing its unwanted and ugly face with the same saddening reminder. He did not even want to think about that day – that very day of departure that was sure to come no matter what he did to prevent it. It was surely inevitable. He was in fact very reluctant to face that day and doubted if he could make it. Soon it was getting dark and day was closing. He jumped down and saying goodbye to his friend went back to the village with a promise to come back the following day.

He reached his village and almost everyone gave him a warm welcome and many of the villagers inquired about the city life. It was the stuff of dreams and achievement to lead a city life so Kumar explained them everything he had witnessed and so far experienced in the city. Soon Ghale accompanied him and the two of them commented on the city life one by one. That would go on and on; the villagers never stopped asking them another question to receive an amusing reply to amuse themselves. That amused them a lot. Kumar and Ghale even talked about the hotel owner and the shop owner and many other vivid things that were only imaginable to those meek villagers.

And finally realizing that it was already too late, Kumar argued that he should return to his home otherwise Phul Maya would get worried.

Back at home, his little son was probably the happiest person on the earth and had put on the goggles given to him by his father. He felt like a superstar. Kumar took him in his arms and kissed him again and again.

Phul Maya asked, "Did you visit several places this evening?"

She wanted to know if he had visited Sathi. But when she realized that it was the time for the children, she kept quiet.

Kumar too was so engrossed with his children he even did not feel the need to talk to his wife. Deep down he was sure that he would be talking a lot with Phul Maya in bed till late night. Everyone had their own priorities.

Soon Phul Maya announced the dinner was ready.

"I have made chicken and rice along with some rice pudding," she energetically declared like a great dictator.

"Chicken, chicken, rice pudding, rice pudding..." cried Manoj again and again in his ringing voice. Having chicken to those poor villagers was like meeting a king; once in a lifetime. They had to wait for a very special occasion to eat chicken and rice pudding. It surely does sound strange but not everyone gets the same opportunity even while it comes down to chicken eating. For some it is a nutrient but some it is a privilege.

All the family went together and sat down for the dinner.

Little Manoj repeatedly burst into a repeated series of unrestrained short and long laughs. Something had gripped him so vigorously that he imagined nothing but sheer joy and had every reason to smile and laugh. He was after all the little prince of the household where all his guilt was absolved and he never had to ask for forgiveness. The little prince talked and talked all through the dinner. After dinner was over they enjoyed the supreme rice pudding as a dessert and enjoyed the family moment for a long time. Kumar's son started to narrate about his teacher.

"My teacher hit my friend with a stick and he went home crying."

"Ha hah... hah... haha."

"He never does his homework and..."

"He can't even spell apple..."

"I can spell everything from A to Z."

"And from one to twenty."

He would go on and on.

Perhaps if not stopped then he would continue going on and on.

It seemed as if he had waited for all this time to talk about how everyone in the classroom admired him when he stood first in his classroom, and how he was cheered by everyone. Everyone knew that his talk was not going to end. And all of a sudden he would burst into uncontrollable spasms of laughter.

Kumar's daughter talked a little as usual, she always had less to say and much to listen. Champa already had a sophisticated understanding of the world she lived in; perhaps she had inherited the same distinction and grace from her mother. She was quite so very wisely intelligent for her age and her beauty was no less than beauty itself. Everyone was floored by her beauty. Kumar considered himself charmed having such brilliant children and a wise mentor as his wife. He knew his happy home originated from his wife. Ultimately, after an hour or so both the children fell asleep and were taken to their room.

Finally Kumar and Phul Maya were left by themselves. The moment of solidarity had come again. Phul Maya came close to her husband.

Kumar said, "Now, thank God, our good days have already started; the money I make in the city is enough for us. My boss has promised to raise my salary."

He asked with a proud note, "Phul Maya, do you have any problems now? Is everything okay in the house?"

"Phul Maya answered in her shimmering tone, "Everything is fine with me and our children but we miss you a lot."

She remained quiet for a few seconds and again she asked, "How long will you still stay in the city, please come back soon? It is really difficult for every one of us to live without you."

She spontaneously said, "Whenever I see any other women with their husbands, I feel so…"

She stopped abruptly and threw herself into Kumar's arms. Kumar really had been waiting for this. His eyes watered, he held her tight as he could. He understood her sorrow – the grief she had to go through all the times he was away. He was not a woman but was fully capable of understanding a woman's feeling towards her husband.

He murmured, "Dear, do you think I went to the city just because I wanted to? It is all for you and our children. You deserve to live in a good home and our children deserve to have a good education and poverty can't reward us much luxuries and sophistication in life. All we have is poverty with just a very small glimpse of

171

wealth; we are just starting to grow economically. I know you understand me and do not think my leaving the village is for my own pleasure and satisfaction."

After a brief pause he added, "But do not worry, I am thinking of something else, and if I succeed in that then it will not take too long for us to prosper."

Phul Maya replied timidly, "Kumar, just do anything, but return as soon as possible and for good. I can't withstand the pain of leading a loveless life."

"Yes, I know."

Then Kumar pulled her again towards him and kissed her in a way that aroused her desire to make love and the only thing they thought afterwards was about making love. Kumar with his fullest passion kissed her lips and her tongue just to arouse her sexually. Phul Maya responded quickly as she held Kumar more tightly in her arms. Kumar slowly loosened her blouse and kissed her breasts all over. He gently revolved his tongue around her nipples which ultimately made Phul Maya moan in sheer ecstasy. In a few minutes Kumar was inside Phul Maya and finally both of them were exhausted and went into a deep slumber.

Next morning, Phul Maya woke up and got busy in her regular household activities. Afterward Kumar woke up and after having a cup of tea, he went all around his small hut – He cleaned the small garden his wife and children had maintained so beautifully where already ripe fruit and season's flowers were dancing along the breeze. He watered all the plants and removed unwanted dust and cleared the area. He even cleaned the spider's web in every corner of the house. Finally he then opened his shop and was amazed to find that the shop has grown even bigger than before. Since his arrival he had not noticed the growth that had taken place in the store.

There were so many new varieties on the rack. Kumar could not believe his eyes. He knew it was all his fortunate wife had done. Her execution was flawless.

Phul Maya later said that the money she had accumulated by selling the fruits from Sathi helped her a lot. Now the shop was in a much better condition than before. Many customers visited the shop and Kumar was much pleased to see his family slowly rising up economically because that was all that mattered.

Local villagers started to visit his home. Kumar welcomed them heartily while Phul Maya offered them tea and the biscuits he had brought from the city. The villagers enjoyed the biscuits more and asked him many more facts about the city dwellings. Kumar found it quite thrilling to engage himself with the other villagers and he would grab every opportunity to be with them. Later after tea the guest went away and the children also made their way to school. Soon after the children had departed, they were pleasantly surprised to see Phul Maya's parents.

Kumar cunningly inquired, "When, why...who... who...who...told you I had come?"

Both of the elder people smiled cunningly and replied, "What do you think; we do not care about you? We knew that you were coming. We just came here to surprise you and we very much thought that you would be more than happy to see us, but I see that you have expressed the opposite. If that is so then let us leave," added the old man ironically.

"No, no..." exclaimed Kumar in his high tone. "I did not mean that at all. I was just overwhelmed to see you all of a sudden like this, unannounced." Then they eased themselves in. Kumar had a wonderful conversation with Phul Maya's mother and she always gave an indication that she was longing to see the city life in her lifetime. She asked different over imaginative and unrealistic questions about the city life. They had envisioned that city was a place where one's all unfulfilled dreams were granted and all the inhabitants were blessed and lead a blissful life.

Kumar did not want them to change their perception about the city life; the innocent villagers were still not acquainted with the dark side of reality that was much more loathsome than the poverty that surrounded them. For them getting out of that prevailing poverty was the end to all the sufferings in life but they never knew the fact that the premises outside the poverty was more intense, brutal and untrustworthy.

Phul Maya showed the gifts Kumar had brought from the city. Kumar was little abashed for not having brought them anything.

He promised, "Next time when I come I promise to bring you something."

Kumar's mother-in-law replied, "Oh Kumar can't you see we are too old for these things. Now we only hope for the betterment of your life, that's all we want. May God always be with you."

Later in the evening when the children returned from school, they were extremely happy to find their grandfather and grandmother. They climbed on their shoulders and played. It seemed the elderly people were having the best time of their life. In the evening Kumar left the kids under their grandparents' custody and he went the jungle along with Phul Maya.

This walk flooded all the memories back from the past. All the way the couple kept silent being quite receptive to the memory and images that had started to present themselves so fluently and they were happy to have such moments back. For them it was like watching their gone moments on a projection wall.

On the way Phul Maya said finally, "Had our Sathi not been with us how could we... survive?"

Kumar did not say a word. There were no words that could justify all the help and support Sathi had provided.

So to consent his strong agreement to what Phul Maya said he kept just quiet, quiet and just quiet; quiet. He knew there was no existence of such words that could satisfyingly explain that.

She walked hand in hand as they marched along the way. On the way Kumar met different people. He had a brief conversation with every one of them and finally they reached the spot and found their dear old friend there with a smiling face ever waiting and expecting them. Sathi felt good to see both Kumar and Phul Maya together after such a long time interval. Phul Maya sat on the ground. Kumar chose a spot very close to her.

Soon Kumar took out his magical instrument and played different melodies to his wife's demand. Many of the melodies brought Phul Maya to their past, past days that made her recall everything. She was filled with nostalgia.

She requested Kumar, "Kumar, could you please play the melody that brought me to you the very first time?"

Instantly Kumar responded, "Oh yes, why not dear, luckily this happens to be my favorite melody too." He played from the beginning to the ending; it was so real, so pure and maintained in its originality that it was hard to believe. Kumar made sure not to miss a single interval. He knew he was playing for his love. Sathi gently swayed back his branches just to show that it enjoyed the melody. The melodies seemed never ending and Phul Maya was really influenced by the gentleness, sweetness and the softness of the music. For her the time had become timeless and she could live in that time forever. All these time away had not killed his music capabilities and now the same music had romanticized them altogether. Different far distance memories came flooding into her mind all at once and she felt over flooded with memories. She carefully managed to pick everyone up but still failed to collect every memory.

Then for the first time she told to Kumar, "You know Kumar I felt so amazed when you first introduced me to this friend. I was bewildered and confused at the same time."

Instantly Kumar replied, "Oh yes, Phul Maya, it happens with everyone. My friends still do not believe me in the city when I speak to them about this tree as my intimate friend. Some of them completely ignore me."

Thus the couple recalled everything.

Phul Maya said, "I was so afraid when you first proposed to me, I did not know how to respond to it. On the one hand, I was afraid of my father but in my heart I had some growing feeling for you."

Kumar then asked lovingly, "What was there in me that attracted you, those days I was so badly poor."

Then Phul Maya replied, "Diamonds maintain their originality no matter where they reside; the sweetness in your voice, the charm in your eyes was irresistible." They even talked how they spent the entire day resting under Sathi just talking and joking with one another.

Sathi witnessed this all and felt very much proud to find both of them together and happy after a long time. As it was getting darker, they decided to return back to their home. Kumar like always promised Sathi to come back the other day. Hearing this, the Sathi felt happy and patiently waited for the next day.

Soon they departed and both of them were in their old house where they found everything ready. Her mother had already prepared the dinner. The children as usual were busy playing. But both of them ran and kissed their parents as they entered the hut and very soon they all sat for the dinner like a happy family which they wore.

"Your mother's hand is really delicious, Phul Maya," said Kumar.

"What do you mean Kumar?" joked Phul Maya.

"No, no I mean you are excellent, but not like your mother," said Kumar blinking his eyes towards his mother-in-law.

Phul Maya's father retorted, "Stop this comparison, it is decided, both the mother and the daughter are equally experts, and any kind of comparison is foolishness." Then everyone laughed.

The little son popped up. "No, I know Granny is better than my mother."

Everyone laughed at his wit and keen intelligence.

Thus days passed.

The vacation was about to be over but Kumar just did not want to think about it. He seemed to ignore it as if ignoring the inevitable would make it less severe, perhaps less intense. It made him sad and had a sullen face. But after all he did not forget to visit his friend each and every day. Finally Ghale came to his home and announced the sad day they were to move. Everyone and everything got silent in the house.

Ghale quickly understood the situation and found inappropriate to stay there any longer.

He said before leaving, "Okay then Kumar, I will see you later,"

Kumar stopped him and took him outside the house. Kumar knew he had to face the truth, the very ultimate truth.

"Ghale, can't we postpone this date?" asked Kumar with full curiosity.

Ghale answered, "What do you think, I want to leave sooner than you? Even my heart is aching to leave my family and go to those crowded cities. But we have to leave and if we make any delay then our owner might have a negative impression and for the next time he might not grant any such vacation. We should not take advantage of someone's decency and modesty."

"You are right," said Kumar staring at Ghale with hard, hard eyes. His face was set and stern.

"Okay, then Ghale, we will leave together on the decided date, after all we must keep our words." Kumar did not know how he did manage to utter those words.

Ghale moved off. Kumar came in, he found sadness hovering in everyone's face. Phul Maya was nearly about to cry. Kumar finally strengthened his heart and said normally as if his going would be accompanied by happiness and celebration in his family,

"Phul Maya, we are leaving after three days so please pack up my clothes and something to eat."

She moved inside. His little son asked in a kid's tone, "When you go to the city, Papa, take me with you."

Kumar tried to make him happy.

"Well, that place is a not place for you; I will take you when you grow a little taller and bigger."

His son soon cried, "But Papa, when will I get taller and bigger?"

"Next month," answered Kumar.

"Then will you take me to city, next month, Papa?"

He was impossible.

Kumar replied, "Oh yes, why not, I will."

Finally, the day of departure approached. Phul Maya's parents too had woken up early in the morning. They assisted Phul Maya. Everything was packed and everything was ready. Kumar held both of his children on his sides and held them close. Champa was silent for a long time finally she questioned,

"Papa, when is the next time you will be back?"

But before Kumar could answer, his father-in-law said, "Yes, Kumar, it's better for everyone if you come back once in every six month. Phul Maya will really have many hard times in your absence, Kumar."

Kumar in his serious tone replied, "I can understand that but it is inconvenient, er... er... Sometimes it might not be possible, but I will use my best efforts to convince my owner to allow a quick short vacation." The room was silent for a longer time till Kumar said, "I will be back in a few minutes," and went out of the room," Both of his children followed him. He suggested them to stay in but they did not listen to Kumar. The three of them went together. In a few minutes' walk, they reached Sathi's place.

The children rushed towards it. Sathi took the children in its arms. Seeing Kumar, Sathi could understand the situation.

Kumar said, "My friend today I am moving back to the city and I cannot say when I will be back. But I will try to be back as soon as time and situation permits me; I request you to take care of my family, you know when I will be gone then they will be alone."

Sathi replied, "Do not say alone, they are not alone, they are never alone. Do not you people regard me as one of your family members – They can come to me whenever they want."

Kumar then took out has murali and played his last tune. The melody filled the environment. The sad notes made the entire environment gloomy and even the children were stunned with wonder. Sadness was in the air.

At last Kumar said farewell and went away. He did not even turn back to see his friend. His heart was in pain, he could hardly tolerate it. When they reached home, Ghale was already there.

"Come on Kumar now we have to move, we can't miss the bus," said Ghale hurriedly with an urgency to complete himself.

Ghale's family too looked very sad.

"Yes, I will be back in second," he said and went to his room followed by his wife. They embraced each other and kissed passionately.

"Please, do not forget, write me as much as you can," cried Phul Maya with a great insurmountable agony in her voice.

Kumar carried his bags and went to the other room and said to Ghale, "I'm ready, then let's…"

His words terminated abruptly.

His son and Champa cried but their grandfather took them under his control. For the last time, he said farewell to everyone and moved out. He did not want anyone of his family to follow him so beforehand he had given instructions no to do so. They went out of the gate and only once Kumar turned back to look at them. He could hear his children still weeping. He did not want to see their crying faces. After all he fathered them, he could hear the silent scream that prevailed in the air that day.

He moved on, Ghale was also silent, both of the men's' heart was filled with extreme pain and agony, but they did not reveal this to any one, not even to each other. The bus came and they rode off. The bus stopped at many stops as part of its routine. Almost all the other passengers disembarked to buy something to eat except Kumar and Ghale.

In the evening the bus reached the city.

They encountered the same rush of the people and the air covered with smoke. It was a part of life in the city. They reached their room and as they were so tired, they simply changed and went to bed. They remembered the time they were just so delighted with their family and friends. They were completely fatigued by the bus journey; they did not even know when they did go to deep slumber.

All through the night, Kumar dreamt of his family. The dream was over and the real formidable world was in front of them. They knew from the next dawn they would have no time for frivolity and playfulness as they had back home.

Chapter Ten

Back at Work Again

Kumar's owner was very happy to see him back at work again. He inquired about Kumar's family. He was also a family man, that's why could feel the charm of going home and pain of returning to work. He asked quite fervently, "How was your trip Kumar, hope you had a very wonderful vacation, and anyway how is your family?" Kumar was more than happy to answer him.

"Oh yes, yes, *Sahuji*, all of them are fine, extremely fine and even my friend is fine. How is business going on? I am so sorry for any inconvenience you had to face when we were away."

He admitted with confidence, "Well Kumar, the first few days were really awesome, I had to run everywhere; I checked the counter and even supplied goods to the customer; however, afterwards I got used to it."

Kumar was quick to reply, "Do not worry Sahuji, now you can concentrate just on the counter. I am back." "Hmm sounds great, and this is the wonderful part," said the owner with a shine on his face and evidently looked over complacent.

He instructed Kumar to arrange things. Kumar's absence had made the store a mess; in fact quite a mess. Items not placed in the proper rack, things out of stock; the store kept unclean. In fact the shop was not very well organized; God knows how many things were dislocated and misplaced. Kumar noticed it in no time and quickly organized the entire shop within two hours. The owner was really impressed to see Kumar performing his job like a maestro. He admired Kumar's skill at doing things so properly, neatly and efficiently.

He was moved by Kumar's love for his shop and admitted, "You know Kumar I have never been so good at arranging things, sometimes I think and doubt whether my life itself is organized or perilously disorganized?"

Kumar remained silent and felt it inappropriate to comment upon someone's life. This was at this moment a customer popped in,

"Sahuji, can I have one and half kilos of potatoes please?"

Kumar was back to his job.

The owner did not even bother to look at the customer since he had Kumar back to the job. He was self-assured now there would be no more problems in the store.

All kinds of customers visited the shop and kept Kumar very engaged. Each of them approached the store with their own list of shopping list and Kumar helped them purchase what they wanted to but Kumar was still amid his family in his deep imagination. He was standing there as a helper but he was not really there; rather at his village where he was sharing a very private life. Sometimes he felt irritated when too many customers came in and he would have no time to brood over his family. He felt disturbed, distracted and

183

interrupted. Sitting inside the store he could see the kids walking along their parents, hand in hand, affectionate, feeling protected. He could feel the domestic felicity all around him.

Kumar pondered to himself, "How happy these wonderful people must be as they can stay together all through their life with no pain of separation from the ones they were made to adore."

But deep down Kumar knew that life everywhere was very much the same; it was characterized as being onerous: inexplicably difficult, demanding, exhausting and very often punishing. He had learned about the Universal truth. The entire human race, no matter where they chose to survive, what circumstances prevailed, affluent or impoverished, they are never happy for long enough regardless of their long amassed accumulations. In fact, however, they are never meant to be happy as sorrow eventually will find its way and smile like a long lost friend upon reunion. His realization was intense. We must all lead an unhappy life; sounding quite pessimistic. But inwardly though, sometimes he would envy people living in the cities because they lived with their family. He did not consider the other fact that they too lived, or perhaps dragged, a pathetic life full with pain and misery embedded like all others did. However, other times, he would criticize them for being selfish, self-centered and egocentric. How could one be so self-centred? He would feel shocked. He realized that many people in the city pretended to be happy but inside they were so unhappy and depressed. In no time, he realized that most of the people cared for nothing in the world except money. They expected money and as long as they acquired it by whatever means, everything was all right, perfect and set as an example or even publicized.

People expect something in return for everything and lead a fallacious life. Even love is bargained and people are very meticulous when money matters, all the rest can all be compromised. He seemed to realize this indisputable fact.

Thus Kumar came to a conclusion that humanity was to come to an end in the city one day and they all deserved it. He sitting in his store philosophized that citizens in the city, instead of learning the art of living, giving, caring and sharing spent every bit of their energy in acquiring the skills of computing and electricity. Many a time, he cursed the evil thing called money as the greatest source of misery – he held money responsible for his having to leave this family. It was money he was out to acquire.

The first day at work after the vacation ended like every other day. Once he knew that it was time to shut down the shop, he did it so fast that he surprised himself.

Back in the room, he saw Ghale already taking his rest and asked, "What is the matter? Is everything ok? Why did you come back so early?"

Ghale replied sadly, "Kumar, I could not help thinking about my family and my mother. I just could not concentrate on my work, so I made up an excuse and returned. My manager seemed a little irritated," he added with remorse in his voice.

Kumar noticed that Ghale's eyes were full and almost overflowing. But Ghale was trying his best to hide his feelings although he could be seen failing again and again. It seems nothing could control his emotions.

It was Kumar's turn to prepare the dinner but he was not in the mood. So both of them decided to go out and have their dinner in the nearby hotel. In no time, they returned and retired to bed.

Kumar could not sleep. He got up and took out his murali and played it closing his eyes. It felt so strange, so bizarre to find himself again at the same place where he simply hated to be in. But suddenly the sound of the murali changed something in him, it was a revolution. He felt victorious and all at once waves of utter blissfulness overcame his despondency. He felt so radically different; the joy was so pure, untouched and virgin. As he was playing the melody he envisioned his son beside him, listening with acute attentiveness with his round eyes wide open. Now Kumar was reluctantly opening his eyes, he knew that he would find no one beside him except Ghale and the blunt stark walls, bluntly listening to him without any passion and rapture. At that hour of night he played different tunes just to entertain himself. He felt glad and relaxed and finally dozed off to sleep.

The very next morning early he wrote a long letter for his family. He expressed all his love and passion and he addressed at least a paragraph to each one in his home because he knew they all anticipated with eagerness at least a few words from him. He went to the nearby Post Office and sent them early in the morning. He was so happy to imagine that his wife and children were soon to read the texts aloud. He was overcome with happiness to realize that its readers would be happier than its sender. So by the time he returned back it was already time to be at work. But he was fresh and felt light that morning while Ghale could still be seen sitting gloomily and staring at one corner of the wall with his unblinking and penetrating eyes.

Kumar broke his meditation asking, "What are you up to, Ghale? Get up and get ready. Wake up and leave all your memories and catch up with them later tonight,"

Still Ghale maintained his position with no movements in his limbs. Kumar left him undisturbed.

"Yes, I am ready," remarked Ghale after some time. "Where you have been so early?"

"I went to the Post Office," replied Kumar, changing his dress for work.

"Wow, you are smart and faster than I assumed," retorted Ghale with his shining face.

Kumar just gave him friendly blank stare suggesting nothing useful.

Then as usual they went to their work and got busy. The entire day both worked in the shop and came back home. Both the men were happy. Now they felt a sense of unbounded pride and gratification sending money back home. It was not much, but it was at least something and they could buy something out of it if not everything .Frequently they received mail from their family.

So as usual they starting earning and saving and sending it back home just to give more and more happiness with the money that has so much purchasing power. Every three months they sent their families money they had earned. Both the men spent as little as possible just to send more and that was all they could do that moment to make their family happy. Kumar was really a generous man. The happiness that prevailed in the Kumar's family was insurmountable every time they received mail which was highly prized more than that money. The family was poor though not money oriented, but rather love oriented. Rejoicing filled their small hut and the entire hut seemed illuminated with sufficient light emerging from every corner of the hut. The boy would hold the letter in his tiny hands and just jostle here and there until someone came and seized from him.

During the season, Phul Maya would visit Sathi to get ripe fruit for her family and to sell in the market. She received good money from the market. Phul Maya thanked Sathi with her knee bent with gratitude. "You are really a true friend of ours; we just do not know how to thank you for all you have done for us, especially when Kumar is not present,"

Sathi stayed as ever, smiled gently and answered, "I should be more grateful to Kumar, you know he is the one who saved me when I was so delicate and could not protect myself from anything. Kumar taught me to live. In fact, he taught me what a real friendship is and how a friend should be related to another friend."

Then it further added, "Had not Kumar met me then I could never have been a member of such a wonderful family who adores and cares for me so much. So please, Phul Maya, I request don't ever thank me, whenever you thank me I feel as if I am communicating with a stranger who is just interested in my fruit; and under such circumstances I fail to recognize you. I find somebody else who is thanking me pitifully for all I have done and that help means nothing to him. So, Phul Maya, I expect you will not thank me again."

Sathi noticed that Phul Maya looked gloomy. Then and there it quickly changed the subject and asked, "Anyway how is my friend? Is he all right? Is he earning?"

Phul Maya quickly recovered and said, "Yes, yes," wiping tears from her eyes. "Yesterday we received his mail, he is just absolutely well and asks lots and lots about you."

Sathi answered gravely, "My love and best wishes are always with him."

Phul Maya then returned home later that evening. She was again busy with her family and her little shop. Her neighbours helped her a lot, they gave her some valuable suggestions regarding how to deal with the customers and organize things and not to be at loss. She was really thankful towards them. Not always, but sometimes she invited them for a tea party and she was always aware that she could need their help anytime and anywhere. She was intelligent but not astute. She realized she was not alone, although Kumar was far away she had very warm, affectionate and loving neighbours. She never tried to reveal her pain about the absence of Kumar. She never separated herself from the rest of the society and energetically she took advantage of each and every opportunity that brought her near to the society. She never backed out; she went and helped the village women in their *pujas* and ritual ceremonies. And that was the requirement of self-respect.

Even though Kumar was far away from his family, they had regular contacts through mails. Kumar mailed them every so often with each piece of new, old or stale information that had gathered up in his soul. The very act of writing and receiving mail made the two men very receptive and served them with an abundance reason to survive and not just live. He shared everything with Ghale and Ghale shared with Kumar. The two men talked and laughed recalling the days back in their village.

Champa once wrote a little piece of poem, addressing her father, that the mailman brought while Kumar was not so very absorbed with his customers. He was a bit unoccupied that very moment when the postman appeared in the store with a broad grin on his elongated brown face. He knew how much Kumar

189

cherished the moments when he would bring him this mail.

The mailman shouted openly from a little further away, "Mail for you, Kumar."

With that news distracted Kumar said in a very high repetitive tone, "T... thank you. Thanks s...o... o very much now." He opened up the mail with an unrestrained haste and read the below lines:

On her Demise

Never did I feel so alone,
Since the day you were gone.
You strode all the ways to my heart,
And made me feel a thousand times alive.

Oh! What can I say to you?
The one with the bright views.
Always showing me the ways;
Incessantly, like a rain in a rainy day.

You told me why the daffodils bloom,
And sang a song that pushed me in gloom.
In a voice so mellifluent never I heard,
Even during the spring time from the Cuckoo bird.

Your loving daughter,
Champa.

Kumar was really happy to see his daughter write so well. Although he could not understand everything behind most of the words, and the meaning, Sahuji helped him a lot to clarify the actual meaning of the poem. Even Sahuji liked the poem and appreciated his daughter poetical abilities. He at once said in his high-spirited mood, "Kumar, why do not you bring your children here in the city for better education; it seems your children deserve better school and good teachers."

Kumar remained quiet; he clearly knew what the problem was. After a few weeks Champa wrote next poem to her father, but this time it was even a challenge for Sahuji to decipher the meaning of the poem. He read the poem several times and could not make out the entire poem's theme. It went as follows:

Revenge

Oh! What a horrifying movie it was,
Alas! Fear and fear that it was made of.
All the others faked to enjoy,
But do you know, somebody was about to die?
As I was watching the movie intensely;
I felt something shuddering beside me
I gave it a damn thinking it a mere thing.
Assuming someone might be moving something.
Again moments later I felt the same.
And this time I could not constrain anyway,
Irritated, I turned my head around to see
Can you imagine it was unbelievable to me?
An old women on the wrong side of seventy

Had turned up alone even without a relative.
One of the scenes had such an impact on her,
She was trembling and tears rolling with fear.
Taking pity on her I spoke to her real softly.
Attempting to console her that it was only a movie.
But nothing I said made her sorry.
She was terribly quivering and on tears with even more velocity.
Ultimately I got annoyed and swore inside;
To direct a movie with such terrible horror for the world to see.
And let this old woman hear about the movie,
As a romantic one and full of tragedy.
ANYHOW, I would manage her seat as near as possible to the screen.

Without even a human soul near,
And let her die with fear.

Your loving daughter, Champa.

Almost everybody who read this poem would admire the poem and comment.

"How could such a girl of that age think so deep and write in such a way? A talented girl," remarked Sahuji with a strange appreciative expression lingering on his face for quite some time. It did really strike delight to Kumar's heart.

After that during the following days Sahuji constantly argued him to bring his children to the town for a proper education. Kumar knew he was helpless, all

192

those new arrivals would mean more money and he could never afford it.

Gradually the days flew by and Kumar had made many new acquaintances and some had even converted to good close friends in the city. He would often talk to them on his cell phone which he had bought recently. For him he could talk to everyone he knew except his beloved ones. What a pity!

Many of them were helpful and supportive. Kumar was really liked and admired by all the new friends for his integrity, honesty, thoroughness and, of course indeed, for his hospitability. Kumar was a nice and amicable man, his hospitality and resilience was admired by all surrounding him. He cooperated with his friends in all the ways he could cooperate and often in the evenings it had become his usual routine to play his murali for his new audience that was composed of his admirers and most of all, his loyal friends. Ghale knew that it gave Kumar peace and relief inside so he pretended to remain quiet even though sometimes he wished to go to bed early. But most of the times he liked the accompaniments. It was not that he disliked Kumar or the friends coming to their room; it was just that he needed his own privacy sometimes which was not unusual.

One of those days their new friend, named Bishnu Thapa, dropped in their room at about eight o'clock in the morning when Kumar and Ghale were getting ready to go to work.

Kumar was surprised to see him at this hour of yet another busy day,

"Bishnu, you at this time, what, what... and how are you? What made you come so early?" questioned Kumar all in one breath.

Bishnu replied in an ironic manner and made a face. "Ghale, I guess Kumar is not very happy to see me here, I suppose I better move off." Ghale caught his arms and said, "Oh! Bishnu try to understand this Kumar is a little psychic, he is just joking; come on, today I will serve you a cup of tea with my own hands."

"Yes, that's the spirit of true friendship," jumped up Bishnu.

Kumar was a little shamed though he did not mean to convey disrespect from his side or be rude. Sometimes things just happen without one being alarmed of it as if someone else wanted that to happen.

"Bishnu, I was just … leave it, okay tell me how are you, *Bhauju*, and of course your daughter. Is not her name Preeti?"

"Yes, Preeti, she is just fine and also your *Bhauju* is pretty good. We are all happy together as we can be."

Kumar said, "Convey my Namaskar to her."

At once Ghale shouted, "Mine too, Bishnu, please do not forget otherwise from the next time onwards I will not be allowed to enter your house or served tea ha, ha…" He kept on laughing.

"Ghale, do not you worry, if she kicks you out, I will always be there to take you in, that's what friends are for," said Bishnu, joking with widening smile.

Bishnu looked at Kumar and asked, "So how is your work getting on; is there much pressure?"

"No, there is not much pressure, but sometimes if there are too many customers then I hardly get chance to sit down and rest," replied Kumar calmly.

Bishnu said he was working as a gate keeper and the job was pretty simple.

"You see guys, I am extremely satisfied with my job, no work, no tension, my duty is simply to sit down and see the people passing by, but yes sometimes I have to stand and salute my boss whenever he comes in and goes out."

Ghale asked, "And your salary, are you well paid?"

"Yes, definitely, my boss is a very good man of decent character, he likes me and admires my diligence at work. He has never complained anything about me and I am content with the salary I get every month."

The three men shared each other's life story with great humour, civility and sincerity. The men enjoyed it.

Finally, Bishnu announced quite enthusiastically, "Oh, I forgot to inform you that today is my daughter's sixth birthday, so you are all invited at seven in my house tonight, and I mean seven p.m."

"Oh, thanks for the invitation. We will surely come to your daughter's birthday," said Ghale with a huge grin upon his face.

Kumar added, "After all she is now even our daughter."

"Then, okay now I must leave, I have to do some customary purchases for the evening, the main thing is that my Boss is also coming, so everything needs to be planned and well organized," said Bishnu as he was about to leave the room.

From the door he said,

From the door he said, "Oh! One thing, I nearly forgot. Kumar, this evening you have to perform and please do not embarrass me by saying 'No', I have already talked about this to my boss."

"Bishnu, but, but, you…" remarked Kumar.

But before Kumar could finish Bishnu broke in and said,

"No buts... No maybe... No excuse please, I know that you are a very good murali player and you have the ability to perform anytime and anywhere," cried Bishnu.

Kumar could not say anything observing the sincerity and discretion in his words.

"You just told that my daughter is also your daughter, right?" boldly said Bishnu.

"Do not worry Bishnu, Kumar will perform this evening. It is my word to you, I know him very well," Ghale jumped in to resolve the matter.

"So then, see you this evening exactly on time," said Bishnu and left the room.

Soon both went to work and agreed to return a little earlier than usual. Kumar was nervous whenever he thought of his performance. The whole day he was a little worried. He had never performed under such circumstances and for the unknown public. Anyway he believed that everything would be all right. Kumar requested his owner for the early leave and his owner readily agreed to leave him a little earlier that day. He did not even ask the reason why. So had it been with Ghale. Around seven o'clock both the men were in the room. Quickly both of them took a bath and put on their new clothes set aside for such occasions.

"Don't forget to carry your murali, otherwise, you know Bishnu will not allow you in," Ghale said.

"Yes. Yes I know, no need to remind me. I knew it very well, but what present should we give to Thapa's daughter?" asked Kumar.

They liked to call Bishnu by his surname.

Both the men shared their ideas but ultimately it was decided to buy a small car toy. On the way to Bishnu's house, men bought a toy car. They both contributed a little amount from their side. The gift was wrapped and packed beautifully and it looked pretty.

They reached the place and found there were approximately twenty people invited to the party. They went inside, Bishnu and his good wife greeted them in good terms, "Namaskar welcome, come in. I am so glad that you both came."

"How could we miss such a wonderful party and especially when Bishnu has invited us personally," replied Ghale at once.

Kumar simply smiled. Bishnu's daughter was amid her friends and looked very pretty and overwhelmed to receive new presents from everyone. Kumar and Ghale went forward, hugged the little girl and gave her the present.

She was now even happier and said in her childish accent, "Thank you, Uncle."

Bishnu announced, "Actually, we are waiting for my Boss to arrive; please a little longer more,"

"Yes, why not, never mind, we are prepared for the whole night," said Kumar politely and rather in a jocular manner.

Everyone burst into laughter.

"Prepared, prepared for what? Oh yes, you mean to play the murali? Anyway, best of luck! All of my guests and my daughter's friends are waiting to hear your murali come to life," said Bishnu.

Then his wife supported him, "Yes, Kumar *Dai* there is no way today, you cannot create any lame excuse, you have to play something for us. In fact I have not heard anything from you as of yet, your friend Bishnu always tells me about you that you are superb murali player."

Kumar heaved a sigh and cast his eyes scrutinizing about the well decorated room with some restlessness. Ghale was quick to study the flush that had appeared on his friend's cheeks.

He approached Kumar meekly and whispered, "You can do it; you have done it so many times." Those words made Kumar get off his mounting stress and nervousness.

Suddenly it was announced that the boss had arrived. He was a little late, but Bishnu thanked God that at least he came. He was with his wife. She was a plump woman in her late thirties while his boss was a huge and tall man of dark complexion with a huge hanging belly. He wore fitted clothes and his shoes were also neat and classy. He was a man with scholarly appearance and a tenacious personality. Kumar did not know that shoes could be so shiny. Both of them approached and congratulated Bishnu's daughter. His wife kissed her and whispered something; hardly audible. Then she cracked a smile. Then afterwards they presented her with a huge present; it was packed neatly with a thin piece of colourful paper. In fact it was too huge for Thapa's daughter. All the rest of the people looked at the present all the time wondering what it could be and guessing the possibilities among each other with their random probability. It was the first time those people had had such a grand opportunity to come in to close contact with such a rich personality. As the couple moved around, the fragrance of their perfume prevailed in the room. The way they talked and even moved their hands impressed everyone. Ghale just could not stop staring at them. He thought they had simply an irresistible charming personality.

Finally it was announced and the ceremony began. Thapa's daughter cut the cake and everyone clapped their hands and sang a birthday song. Everybody in the party kissed Thapa's daughter congratulating her. She looked pretty with her new clothes and a big proud smile lingering on her face all the while. After that a small party was organized. Thapa and his wife served the guest. Thapa really admired his boss and was always in constant eagerness to serve him. First he invited his boss and his wife. They had prepared a couple of varieties of chicken meat with parboiled rice over it and side dish of spicy mango pickles. For sure the guests enjoyed the party. From time to time the guests even cut jokes which reverberated the room and made the party wonderful. All these birthday parties and cake was anew to Kumar and Ghale. In their village, they could not afford to throw such a party. Actually, they had only heard that birthday parties were organized where a number of guests were called in. But that day they got a chance to witness it.

Observing the happiness of Thapa along with his wife and daughter made Kumar a little gloomy. He looked at them with a distinct lack of enthusiasm. No, he was not jealous of Bishnu at all. He was depressed. He realized he could not deliver such luxuriance to his family, which they deserved; they deserved the glee that was profound in that birthday party at that very moment. For Kumar and his family there was no going out, no cinema and theatre, no birthday parties, no vacation or other such festivities. The only place he took them was to his friend's place in the jungle.

He had just recovered from his thought when Thapa announced, "Well I am so glad that you all came here and made this small party a huge success. My family can never ever forget this day and thank you all; this day has become a memorable day for us,"

199

With a quick smile he added,

"I guess you might have got a little bored due to all this noise and lack of good music. I know this kind of situation should be entertaining and definitely calls for wonderfully soothing music. So I am proud to announce here among the guests we have a wonderful murali player and he is my friend Kumar." Thapa pointed towards Kumar.

With this everyone in the room started to stare at him with huge expectant eyes. Kumar looked a little nervous and confused. They clapped their hands and a huge applaud was audible even out on the streets.

Kumar slowly got up from his sitting posture. At first he found a hard time to take out his murali and take it to his lips. He expected someone to ask for it. Perhaps he needed a catalyst.

Thapa's boss started up, "Kumar, come on, play some wonderful tunes for every one of us. You can call it a celebratory music," he said showing his white array of teeth.

Kumar's eye glimpsed with a kind of energy and he at once gathered all his confidence to face the crowd. This was his first time he was ever playing for audience completely strange, unknown and unprepared.

In a nervous accent Kumar said hesitatingly,

"I am thankful, my friend Bishnu, thank you for providing me this chance and thinking me as a good player, and to be exactly frank, I am doing this for a first time in my life, so I am sorry if I make some mistakes,"

Thapa approached Kumar and whispered, "My friend, I know you can make it, just concentrate."

Kumar moved his eyes swiftly across the room and then began to blow his instrument. The first few notes were not clear and probably missed the intervals. Also the tempo was irregular but soon he managed to stand up to his real form. The music filled the room with a certain kind of magic; with a kind of enchanting aura. It seemed as if the music was floating in that room and vicinity. The sweetness of the music embalmed the entire atmosphere of the room. Everyone was enchanted to hear such a mellifluous pure music, it was beyond the imagination of the city people that someone from a remote place can play so beautifully, so majestically and many of the guests even gasped for breath from time to time. Kumar was a musician of the first order. All the people in the room sat in complete silent adoration and for sure they were enchanted by the overwhelming strength of the melody.

Kumar stood in the middle of the room with his eyes closed tightly and his fingers hitting the notes, totally immersed. He knew he had to entertain his audience and nothing could stop him now. He was already weaving his music. Thapa's boss just could not believe his ears; he even had forgotten to smoke his cigarette that he was holding on his right hand.

At last, the music was over and the guests clapped their hands with excitement and contentment. The applause was even louder and longer than before. Kumar knew it was from their heart. All of the gathered audience marvelled at the power of his untiring spirit by which he could impact and give such joy to others. Some of them did not even know that music had that strength, that aptitude to make some cry or smile. For some music was no more than a couple of songs from a movie played on cinema and sometimes on the streets.

201

Then the guests requested for more and more songs. He tried all his best to satisfy them with his quenchless desire to play and perform music. It seemed it would never stop; it seemed Kumar would never get tired of playing music. Finally, the last request was put forward by Bishnu's boss.

"Well, you did perform wonderfully and to be honest, the way you played it was far beyond my imagination.

"I am interested in music, but I do not play any instruments. In fact I tried but I found these hands were not gifted, maybe God does not want me to be a musician," he said modestly.

"So, Kumar can you play something serious, something utterly sad, something magnificently gloomy yet provocative and still maintain the spirit and vigour of this birthday party," said the boss with newly found excitement in his same old accent.

Kumar answered slowly, "Yes, sir, I will try my best."

And then he was on and began. All his trepidation and dreadfulness melted away just leaving him alone to do what he was best at, unparalleled at; incomparable at.

And then it was a grand one. All the music Kumar had performed moments before seemed weaker and less enchanting compared to the one he played now. He played like professionals would. His fingers were so swift and sensitive. This time, the music touched the heart of everyone. Kumar played that melody which his friend has taught him in the jungle, the melody which his painful and tortured childhood had taught him, and the melody which his first love had taught him and of all the melody that was in his soul until now captivated and longing to be freed. And now it was free and everyone present in the room could feel it. It spread an aura of enchantment like that of the havoc spread in the village by the news of a prowling mad tiger. He played with all his energy and passion. It seemed a combo of all the expert musicians. He completely stole the show and succeeded to win the heart of his audience, every one of them. The audience reacted as if they were invited there to listen to Kumar's performance and not to celebrate any birthday party.

The one who was the most impressed was the boss. After the party was over he summoned Kumar and patted him on his shoulder and said, "Kumar you know I still find it incredible to believe what you have performed, I know that I cannot play music, but at least I can understand someone else playing it, at least I can appreciate it." Do not just think I am making fake words to cheer you up; in fact you are an excellent murali player.

"Do you play any other instrument?"

"No sir, it's just the murali I have my hands on," answered Kumar humbly.

Soon few other visitors hovered around to listen to the conversation. They seemed just so eager to know what the conversation was about.

"Anyway, who taught you music and such wonderful techniques?"

Kumar said a little cunningly,

"Sir, actually nobody taught me. My mother gave me this murali when I was a small boy; since then I have been playing whatever I can."

The Boss said with an air of dignity, "Then you are a self-trained man. Excellent!"

The Boss's wife even admired him for his capability and said, "One day you will be a great musician."

Despite all this appreciation and admiration Kumar seemed modest.

Gradually, the guests began to leave. Thapa and his wife thanked everyone for coming to the party. Then the boss asked Thapa to bring Kumar to his office some days later and went off with his wife.

"Congratulations, Kumar, my boss has asked me to bring you to his office in a few days. Maybe he wants to give you some job or help you; he is a kind hearted man. Maybe he does not understand art, but he really seems to admire the artist," added Thapa.

The show was over and all returned back.

Chapter Eleven

An Offer; Just Can't Refuse

By the time Kumar and Ghale reached their room, it was already nine o'clock.

Ghale in his excited spirit said, "No matter what, the party items were delicious; the *pulaw* and spices were so tasty but I thought it to be a little salty, didn't you think so, Kumar?"

"Oh, Ghale, I think of nothing but the time I spent with my murali. You know I never believed that I could perform in front of so many people," replied Kumar.

With little excitement, Ghale added, "Yes Kumar, undoubtedly, you were wonderful tonight, your music made everyone spellbound. Really it was your magic that kept the party alive."

Kumar looked towards the heavens and sighed, took a long breath and murmured, "Thanks God, thanks for everything."

He talked to himself, "My family would have been really happy had they seen me performing tonight."

He just could not stop thinking of his family. He kept on talking to himself, whispering something, some vivid words to himself almost in a mute whisper. Ghale was already in a deep trance by then. He thought of his family and in no time began writing another piece of a letter. He used all the words he knew to explain the evening to his family.

He wrote several lines to his family, addressing every individual. He wanted to write everything about the evening, he wished to explain each and every moment in precise description; he was dead sure not to miss even the minutest detail but again he was limited by the extremities of his language and writing capabilities, he knew this too; his impediment. All along he wanted to emphasise his performance. He wanted to write how everyone in the party admired and appreciated his talent. He also wanted to write that he had never heard such a loud applause before. Finally, he mentioned Thapa's boss, how he was influenced by his murali performance and how he had even called him to his office for some unknown reason. He finally managed to write:

Phul Maya,

How I longed for all of you to be here tonight when I was playing my murali. My eyes were looking for someone who was really happy from within and really cheered but unfortunately I could find none, except Ghale and memories of you back in my head.

[And so he continued....]

Back in the village, Phul Maya received the mail and was tremendously happy. She just wished for more and more letters to come from Kumar. As she went through the lines she could hear Kumar's voice as if he was dictating the words for her. The advent of the mails brought real bliss to the family; she ran and told all her neighbours about this. She looked so happy. Her

206

intensity of happiness was immeasurable and insurmountable as well. She even went to her parent's home in the next nearby village during her children's vacation. She just could not stop talking about Kumar and his musical talent. She was overwhelmed by all the success Kumar was achieving.

A few days later, Kumar was in his shop busy serving his customers; it was midday when Thapa came in.

"Hello, Sahuji. How are you? And how is the business going on?" Thapa looked very happy and excited.

"Just well, no problems so far as God has provided me with food at least twice a day. You have come after a long time, come on, have a seat."

Turning to Kumar, the owner said, "Kumar, go and order two cups of tea and if you want to have some you can add one more."

When Kumar came back, the two men were busy in their gossip. They talked about different people whom Kumar hardly knew, so he preferred to keep silent and kept himself busy with the customers that visited the store.

Soon the tea arrived. A small boy with ragged clothes brought three cups of tea, shouting right from outside, "Tea, tea, hot, hot tea. Where shall I keep it, tell me?"

Kumar's owner was a man of humour, he said jokingly, "Look, if you find nowhere to keep them then you can rely on my head, it is really a good place for three cups of tea, what do you think Thapa?" This is how he would create some ambience of humour almost every day.

207

Thapa too was a man of similar sense. He replied, "Oh! Yes, perfectly, why not, there is positively no doubt in that."

Kumar threw a silent laugh, he got up and handed the tea to the other men and at last for himself. Kumar wanted to maintain his politeness in every action and word.

Thapa finally asked for a favour with the Owner.

"A small request: can you allow Kumar to go with me today just for an hour or two, my boss wants to see him today?"

Kumar's owner replied with a little hesitation on his face, "You could take but…"

Before he could finish his words, Thapa interrupted him, "Do not worry. It will not take more than two hours."

Finally, they agreed and the matter was settled but the owner's face still radiated very sharp questioning remarks.

Kumar turned to Thapa and asked, "Bishnu, are my clothes okay, or should I change?"

Thapa assured Kumar. "Oh, no, it is perfectly okay and by the way my boss seems not to give a damn about these types of things, he looks inside of you rather than your clothes, he looks and can instantly penetrate a man's soul and comprehend what he is composed of."

After a few minutes' walk the men reached the office.

It was not a huge office at all. But it was clean, tidy and well managed. Outside the boss's office, the peon was standing and Thapa said something to him.

The peon went inside the boss's office and came back promptly.

He said,

"Wait for a while, there are a few people in the office."

While they were waiting Thapa introduced Kumar to his friend to whom Kumar had already been introduced at the party. One of his colleagues came forward, shook his hand and said,

"I can still hear the music, it has been recorded right inside my head."

Further, he added with an air of appreciation,

"You were splendid, I just have no words to tell how I still feel, I am stuck for words, you see."

Just then the visitors left the boss's room and the peon announced,

"Thapa sir, now you can get in, the boss is alone."

Kumar entered the room with a gentle smile and brightness in his eyes. When Kumar and Bishnu entered the office the boss was busy talking on the telephone. Kumar could smell the same fragrance he had experienced in the party. His room was neatly washed, the tablecloth was neatly fitted, and not a single stain was visible. On the walls small paintings were hung. Among all the other paintings, there was a painting of a bigger size and Thapa whispered in his ears, "It is the Boss's favourite painting of all you see in this room."

Although Kumar could not make out a lot from the painting, he liked them. Quickly he summarized: The Boss is a lover of foreign art and a disciplined man as well.

Soon his telephone conversation was over and he turned his attention towards these men.

Kumar at once said, with a little nervousness in his shaking voice, "Namaste, sir, you are well?"

The boss replied, "Oh yes have a seat please, after all, why should you stand?"

The boss called the peon and ordered three cups of tea, which were soon ready on the table. But still the tea was superior to the one they had an hour ago.

"So, Kumar, where is your murali?" the boss asked in a child-like manner.

Kumar smiled and said nothing. He knew he was just making jokes.

The boss confessed,

"You were amazing that evening, I was really mesmerized by your music and the colours it produced in my mind. Tell me, who taught you to play so beautifully and artistically because the last time I asked you this question you replied nobody taught you music, but I find this a little hard to believe."

Kumar replied respectfully. "Sir, you see I belong to a very poor family, my mother gave me this murali while I was still a small kid. Our family circumstances were too miserable and it was impossible for us to hire a tutor; I was not even sent to school."

The boss was surprised to hear this and said, "You mean, you did not attend any primary school. That means you cannot read and write?"

"Just a little bit, just to get by," assured Kumar.

"And what about your father, what did he used to do?" asked the boss again.

The speaking of the word 'father' at once brought a type of coldness and hatred in Kumar. He heard it as if it was an announcement for a jail sentence for the remaining years of his life. He at once recalled his father's face and all the torture he had while his father was still alive – many things flashed in his memories –

He remembered how he used to scold and torment his dear mother while his mother remained in one corner of the room just saying nothing, simply allowing him to treat her the way he wanted to. His entire childhood revisited his mind like a devastating flood and this flood disturbed him and made him feeble. He lowered his head down and said nothing. The boss was highly sensitive to his pain. He at once discerned that there was something about Kumar's father that he did not want to mention.

To overcome his sorrow, the boss immediately changed the subject and asked, "Yes Kumar, have your tea, the tea loses its taste after it gets cold, and by the way, what do you do here, you work somewhere?"

Kumar found it difficult to find his voice, so he hid his nervousness and his sorrow in the cup, pretending to be taking a sip. Gradually he came out of his depression and he answered, "Sir, I work in a small grocery store in the market."

"And in the village, you live with your family, your mother and..." The boss gradually diminished his voice; he did not want to hurt Kumar any more.

Kumar sadly answered, "Sir, my mother and my father died when I was a kid. I was brought up by some of my neighbours and in my village, I have a wife and two children."

"And here, you are living alone, or...?"

"No, sir, I am living with my friend, Ghale. We are sharing a room."

"For how long have you been in this place and... er... er?" the Boss wanted to ask something more, but he was hesitating to do so.

Eventually, he got strong and asked, "Well, it is not right, but let me ask, what is your salary now?"

Surprisingly, Kumar felt free to answer this question. He told him his actual salary. The boss again asked, "Kumar don't you have difficulty, I mean you have to eat and live here and send some money to your family as well."

"No sir, we can adjust with that little amount and my wife even works in the village. She looks after a small shop." Kumar added, "Besides these, our needs are not much, we know we cannot afford any luxury so we never desire."

For a moment there prevailed a momentous silence.

Breaking the silence, Thapa spoke up,

"Sir, Kumar is very anxious because of your calling. He kept asking me the reason, but I am also ignorant about it. Actually, why have you called him, Sir?"

The boss gently smiled and replied in a grave and influential voice, "Now, can you simply guess why I have called Kumar here?"

Both the men shook their heads.

"Kumar, just try and guess the reason for it, you might find an answer."

Kumar was nervous. "I'm afraid, I cannot figure it out."

Then the boss said, "See Kumar, I could not be an artist, maybe God does not want me to be an artist, but I am sure he cannot stop me from admiring, appreciating and encouraging another fellow artist. As you can guess my life is always reflecting around arts. In fact, I love arts and fine arts of every type. There is not one which I can select and say that this is my favourite – perhaps that would be totally discriminatory. So to sum up this entire matter, I just want to say that I'm willing to help the artist in you to prosper."

Kumar was confused.

"I appreciate that sir, thank you. But to be precise I wonder, how can you help me? As you can see I am just an illiterate man from an undeveloped village."

With another very brief pause, Kumar asked ironically,

"And what do you expect out of me in return?"

It was then the boss made another long speech.

"Now there's the point Kumar. This is only the greatest drawback of human civilization. Today you switch on to any television channel or pick up any newspaper and you find people lust for money, sex, blood and many other things. The desires of people have mounted to unlimited heights. Nowadays people just talk to each other because they expect something out of each other. If you possess affluent money, you will always have people all around you to help you, but once you are broke the same people will disappear into thin air.

Kumar, just imagine for a moment, well this is virtually impossible, about a system in which the one who gives anticipates nothing in return. I mean the giver just gives without expecting absolutely anything in return. I guess this system is called Humanism, which seems to be at the point of extinction from this earth. And I am sure once this is extinct; the scope of human growth and civilization reduces to null. So sad to say but this is a fact."

There was a sudden rise in his voice and he said a little harshly, "Kumar, can I not help you without expecting anything in return?"

Kumar and Thapa were both silent. They were both so confused; they were not making sense of what the boss was trying to say.

Just then the telephone rang. The Boss answered and said the caller was to call back later. They could see his mood was not in the right place; perhaps something disturbed him. He seemed restless and in a duel with himself.

"Kumar, I know how great a musician you are, now I know that you haven't had any formal training of music at all, but still you play with such a beauty and wonder, so do you not think that is a miracle?

Kumar, try to understand that Nature is your tutor, you are your very own tutor, your sorrow and pain are your tutor and you are a self-trained man. Today there are so many music universities, music institutions, but the products from those institutions are not even qualified to match your talent in any respect. They lack many artistic abilities a pure musician should possess. They learn music as a hobby; they learn music because their fathers have presented them with a guitar or a piano for their birthday. They take music for granted. But they fail to realize that music is a boon, a pure gift from heaven which none but lucky people like you acquire.

Under all these circumstances I want you to work as an artist, I suggest to you why not use your music to earn your living. If you search, then you will find many people work as a professional musician. Now, just see the condition. People like you work in a small shop for a few hundreds, the place where art and an artist are both condemned and not admired. Just realize, Kumar, you have worked so long there, but can you recall a single day when a man comes to you just to appreciate you and your ability. Can you recall a day, when you Sahuji talks about your talent and suggests to you to find a better job?"

Without even waiting for response he continued.

"No, Kumar. You don't seem to understand but someone like you can bring revolution into the world. Remember, there is only a single man behind every great work ever accomplished and there may be many people to assist him, but the ideas are the mere product of a solo supreme brain. I find many people just live for money and luxury, and this very desire has killed humanism, creativity and morality from inside of us.

"Let's try an experiment. If you agree to help a man, say, lend him some money without expecting anything in return, not even the money he has borrowed, then surprisingly he will simply reject the offer because he suspects something uncanny. He is not ready to believe that there could ever be a man so generous who gives money for free without any expectation. Sometimes I feel that there exists only one kind of art in this world, and that art is money and we all are experts in that art and always ready to claim superiority over others."

Kumar and Ghale were both very afraid to utter a word. Rather they decided to keep their mouth shut.

Then the boss added again with a little relief in this voice.

"I have a friend, not in this city, but the city is six hundred and thirty kilometres south from here, he runs a restaurant. And every evening he hires musicians for singing and for playing instruments. I suggest you go and join the restaurant. I think the money you get there every month is better than the money you earn here."

"Also, the job is of your type and it suits you. In that job, I see many prospects. The first one is you earn more than what you earn here, next is you will have more practice on your instrument and the last one is that the city I am talking about is a big city. So if you're lucky then you can move to other places if they offer a better salary. But here, I see and I have already seen, that you have a dark future, Kumar."

After a momentary pause, releasing the air heavily through his nostrils he said,

"Maybe you can see some future here but I don't see any..."

"If you are interested, then I can call my friend and fix your job as a murali player. Well, I will not compel you to do so; maybe you have other, better plans than I can see. Maybe you believe in something else or maybe something else interests you more than this."

It was very difficult for Kumar to give a prompt decision there and then. He hesitated to say anything. His reluctance to jump to a conclusion was natural.

Understanding Kumar's hesitation, the boss said, "Well Kumar there is no haste and you are not under compulsion, it's entirely your choice and your will, if you like my proposal it is excellent, if you dislike, it is okay. Please do not feel yourself under any obligation," he said with finality in his voice as he looked out through the window.

"Let me know when you make up your mind; maybe you have to talk to your family."

Then they left the office. All the way back Kumar's mind was completely blown away by the proposal put forward by Thapa's boss. He could not decide but the more he thought the more he felt distracted from the situation.

Kumar asked Thapa, "What do you say, Bishnu, your boss does not mean any harm, I suspect."

"Oh no, Kumar, he is a man of his principles, he does not take any interest in other's matters unnecessarily. But still I cannot show you the best way under these circumstances. What I feel is that you should rely on your own instincts, family and closest friends," Thapa concluded.

After a brief conversation, the friends departed.

Kumar reached his store. He saw his owner busy dealing with the customers. Seeing Kumar, the owner felt excited.

"Oh Kumar, you have come in time. Come on, help me to take out all the items in this list. The customer will be here any moment, so you'd better hurry up."

Kumar soon got engrossed in this his usual work.

All the rest of the day Kumar could not focus on his work. The meeting with the boss had disturbed him and put him completely at sixes and sevens. Many different ideas popped in and out his head. Sometimes he would get optimistic about the proposal and the very next time he would feel pessimistic about it. He argued and reargued with himself but consequently he found himself in the same state as he was before: lost and confused. After the duty was over, he went straight to his room.

Ghale finally came. He found Kumar holding his murali but was surprised as he was not playing it. As usual Ghale seemed happy and gay. He entered the room and changed his clothes but failed to notice some changes in Kumar's deportment. At last he felt suspicious about Kumar and, going near to him touched his shoulders gently and asked,

"Kumar, is everything all right?"

With a grave voice Kumar replied,

"Well, what should I say to you my friend, everything seems fine one moment and the very next moment I see things falling apart."

After a second's pause he continued,

217

"I am so muddled up, I just can't say what to do and how to act."

Ghale quickly calculated the intensity of the problem, he rarely found Kumar in these moods and that day talked in a different tone.

He inquired, "Then tell me, Kumar, I may be able to help you, after all I'm your friend."

Kumar did not want to hurt him.

"No, Ghale, there is nothing you can help me with. It is a struggle within me that is making me so uneasy. It is so intense."

He was mute for some seconds.

"This struggle has grown with me and is equally capable as I am. Only death can end this struggle, I know."

Soon Kumar related everything to Ghale. He elaborately explained everything said by Thapa's boss that day. He barely missed out a word or two. He dictated every detail of the day and the subject matter. After listening to all the details, Ghale too was quite nervous. Even he did not say anything.

At last, Ghale spoke up.

"Now see, Kumar, I think whatever the boss has said today is correct and practical. In fact, it is a very personal matter. To be honest, I too think that you are wasting your life with the work you are engaged presently. Great men are born to be great but for that they need and have to pay something and that's what you are paying now, perhaps your sweat and toil."

"Kumar, just speak your heart and tell me, are you satisfied with your job?" Ghale asked targeting Kumar directly.

"I am sure you are not."

"Are you satisfied with the money you are earning?"

"I am dead damn sure you are not."

"Are you utilizing your talent?"

"No, not at all."

"I have to confess that it is such an insult to see you in this position."

"So, then under these circumstances I think Thapa's Boss is correct and has talked sensibly."

Ghale had struck him with very pertinent questions.

Then Kumar spoke up.

"Then what do you suggest, Ghale. Should I leave this permanent job and go to another city where the job is not secure and I hardly know anything about it?"

"There is no hurry Kumar, think, take your time, talk to your family, and think over every aspect of it," Ghale answered in a low tone.

He added further, "You know Kumar, we go and take suggestions from others expecting to get a proper answer but we never ask ourselves. It seems that you and I have failed to understand that there lies the answer to every question that is so pure and chaste within our hearts. We ourselves are the supreme masters, we just need to meditate upon and manifest it."

"Try to understand Kumar, self-manifestation is the key," he said softly as a preacher.

Kumar thought of writing to his wife and getting her views on this matter. But he thought that it would make her confused and she would worry even more so he decided not to write her that moment.

After that the men spoke no more and retired to bed. Kumar had a hell of a time on his bed. He tried to sleep but he soon found he was disturbed with that interview.

Next day, as usual both the men prepared their breakfast and left for work at their usual time. That morning the two friends talked less. The whole day was disturbing and distracting for both Kumar and Ghale. Ghale was even distracted and it made him think deep and hard.

Later that evening Ghale said something to Kumar that Kumar had never expected.

"Kumar, I have given it a fair amount of thought, pondered the subject from every possible view and have concluded that it is safe for you to follow Thapa's boss's advice."

Kumar could not say anything.

Ghale added, "Life is nothing but a game of chance, so try your luck."

With a very serious note in his voice Kumar said, "And if I fail in this game then I and my family will fall into ruination and I would never be able to tolerate this. I can't be responsible for the sorrow of my family."

Perhaps his soul was bleeding at that point and struggling to reach a stage of mental equilibrium.

After this the conversation stopped abruptly.

Next early morning Kumar woke up quickly and went to see Thapa. When he reached his home he found Thapa was still in his bed. His wife was working in the kitchen. He entered the room and asked,

"Namaste Bhauja, How are you? What are you doing?"

"Oh! Namaste *babu*, yes, I am fine and doing the usual homework. That's what my life is confined to. And see your friend is still in bed."

She pointed Kumar to a nearby chair. "Please have a seat, I'll soon wake up your friend."

Soon, after a few minutes, Thapa woke up. Over tea, Kumar asked him many different questions about his doubts to which Thapa responded positively.

Thapa gently said,

"Kumar, you can trust my boss. He is a very sensitive man and he never means harm or hurt to others. The greatest joy he gets in the world is by helping others."

Thapa provided him with valuable friendly advice and encouraged him. In about half an hour or so Kumar returned to his room as he was also getting late for his work. Back in the room Kumar described everything to Ghale and meditated on his newly acquired decision.

Ghale finally realized that it was already time to congratulate Kumar.

Chapter Twelve

There Must be More Money

The same night after spending a busy day at the store Kumar decided to inform his wife about his newly made decision. He knew he had to be very selective in choosing the words that would otherwise bewilder her and the kids. He pondered hard before he started to write down the words he had to write. He gently introduced her to his new plan.

He wrote:

Dear Phul,

How are you and how are my kids?

I know they must be doing good and behaving.

I am also fine here. I just had to inform you of a plan, a new venture I am about to undertake.

Let me put everything in short. I am planning to quit this job for another one as a murali player in a restaurant. I have a very good friend here named Bishnu Thapa, and his boss heard me playing the murali. He is so impressed that he wants me to work as a murali player in his friend's restaurant in another city. He believes in that way I can use my murali playing skills and make more than what I make here at the grocery store. See, Phul Maya, I know what you are going through at this point, I know it is hard for you to understand and it is even more difficult for me to make you understand as well but trust me it seems good to me. It is for the betterment of the family. I have now realized that I don't have much future in this grocery store.

I will send you my new address once I reach there. Everything else is all fine here and I know that you will understand.

Just yours

Kumar.

In the city, Kumar ran to meet Thapa and reported everything the very next morning.

Thapa said, "You have made the right decision. Today I will go and talk to my boss."

Soon everything was planned and the date of the departure was fixed. Kumar felt nervous to inform his owner about his quitting the job. Kumar knew that such a good man as a boss and as a human being was hard to find. After several attempts, he briefly summarized the whole story.

The owner said finally,

"Well, it's your decision, good luck, if you think you have a better future there, then what can I say? Well, very well. Anyway, in the future if ever you want my help and this job then you can always rely on me. You have really impressed me by your faithful service and diligent work."

A quick frown seemed to appear and then quickly disappear all over his face.

He further said with some reluctance in his voice,

"I know it is not easy to find someone as intelligent and diligent as you. No one can replace you."

Kumar bowed his head and said, "Thank you Sahib."

"Okay, then Kumar, you can collect your money anytime you want; after all you deserve it, it's all your money. By the way when are you moving and before that are you visiting your family?" the owner asked in a very humble manner.

Kumar replied, "I want to visit them once before I leave but I have to move in four days from now so I guess I will not be able to go to the village and return back in time."

His owner finally congratulated him. Next day Kumar collected his money. Both the men felt uneasy during the moment of departure. A special relationship had already grown between them.

Back in the room Ghale also felt the same way. He was not happy to miss his true friend.

"I will always remember you and I will come to see you sometimes," said Ghale crying.

"And let me know if there are other vacancies in your place," Ghale added with a quiver in his voice.

Kumar found his speech was lost; he tried but could not speak. He bit his lower lips just to hide that he was about to explode.

Kumar said, "Ghale, the day after tomorrow I'm leaving to this new place and have no idea what my new boss, new friends, and new work will be like. It may also be that I might not be able to go back to my family for a long time, so please take care of them whenever you get a chance to visit our village. I have already informed Phul about my new job."

Hearing this Ghale burst into crying like a small baby. Both the friends embraced each other with tears in their eyes.

Ghale replied, "I promise Kumar, I will protect your family as I do mine."

Time passed, who could ever stop it.

Finally, the day of departure came and Kumar was not very happy even though sometime he secretly believed that the city life would bring more money, success, prosperity and better opportunities.

He all of a sudden thought of composing another letter to his family before he departed.

He began:

Hello Phul, how are you?

So I am leaving today for my new job, I guess everything will be all right. Let's hope together for the prosperity of our future.

Please do not panic. I am right with you all the time and I will write you again when I reach to my new destination.

Just yours

Kumar

He soon posted the letter in the nearby post office. Kumar knew that his wife would never ever be dismayed at whatever decisions he would reach. He knew she wanted him to be happy for all and everything that he ever did. He knew he was true in his heart and there was nothing to be afraid of. God was on his side.

Walking clumsily Kumar reached his room where he found every object staring at him. He looked at his packed luggage and felt sad. Just then Ghale arrived and they both went to the bus station.

On the way they did not say much to each other as both their hearts were filled with pangs of pain.

"Okay, now the time is here and I must be going," announced Kumar breaking the silence.

Ghale stared into his eyes and had nothing to say except give some best wishes.

Then the bus left the station.

Phul Maya received the letter from her husband. She read the letter, reread it and starting sobbing. Soon Phul Maya rushed to the jungle and cried a lot to Sathi. She said and expressed her every drop of pain to Sathi. She let him know how sad she was about Kumar's leaving to a new place.

She asked him, "Why does he need more money? The money he earns is enough for us; at least we do not starve."

It then said, "So did you not tell him and say not to go anywhere?"

"I could not do it though I wanted to, but..." She resumed crying.

Sathi laid its arms on her shoulder and consoled her,

"Phul Maya, do not cry, our Kumar will be all right, God is with us; he sees everything and knows everything."

That day she felt like spending the entire night under the embrace of Sathi. This was the only means of true consolation she could find. She felt free of pain and all the uneasiness that had enchained her. Finally, it alarmed her to go back to her home for the sake of her children, in case they would get afraid. That night was a restless one for Phul Maya. She kept thinking about Kumar. She prayed to God for her family's eternal peace and happiness.

What else could she ask with God at that point?

That whole night Kumar did not even sleep a wink on the bus. The face of his entire family, his village and his friend kept rushing in his head even though he mustered all this energy to avoid it. He looked up into the sky; the sky was full of stars, it was a starry night. The moon was full. He at once remembered how they spent their time in the jungle with their friend whenever there was a full moon. He recollected everything as far as his memory allowed him. But finally he made himself strong.

He talked to himself,

"A real man is not supposed to be weak along his way."

Before he left, Thapa's boss had already informed the owner of the restaurant where Kumar was to work. Everything was fixed. A man was even to come to receive Kumar at the bus stop. Kumar was a complete stranger to the place. Before he left his village, Ghale was with him but this time no one was beside him. He wondered if he could ever find someone like Ghale in the city.

The next morning the bus reached its destination on time. This city was bigger, more crowded and more advanced than the previous one; it happened to be one of those metropolitan cities. There were tall buildings all around him and people wore neat clothes and spoke politely. He saw many different vehicles running everywhere. Kumar noticed that the people were extremely busy. It seemed as if every one of them was running after something. Even the little boys and girls who were going to school had a very huge satchel in their backs and walked sluggishly to school. The uniform they were on was perfect and clean and this reminded him of his own children. They looked similar when they were on their school uniform. Kumar at first could not even guess where and what the people were after. He stood at one corner and waited for someone to receive him. After waiting for fifteen minutes a young man with a long hair and a soft moustache confronted Kumar and asked softly,

"Are you Kumar?"

Kumar at once said nervously, "Oh! Yes, I'm Kumar, the murali player."

"I am Bishal," said the young man, putting forward his hand. He had a lean and equine face with white, even teeth; and he was dandy in his short jacket and frilled shirt. It seemed he had a great national love of fine clothes.

"And I have come to pick you up."

"Let's go…"

They got into a crowded bus.

Kumar saw people of all types in the bus. Some were talking and were extremely loud while some were silent. Kumar noticed girls and boys, their dress and attitude, the way they talked, walked and even the way they moved their head which he thought was attractively different. After a few minutes' bus ride, Kumar and Bishal got off the bus.

On their way Kumar asked Bishal, "Are these people really busy or are they moving just to pass their time?"

Bishal laughed gently and said, "Within a month, soon you will discover everything."

After that Bishal spoke of nothing and Kumar also hesitated to ask him anything despite his willingness to talk further. He was just curious to know about the things that he was seeing all around him.

On the way Kumar noticed varieties of goods put on sale. The mall was really a wonderful place to visit; people were all lined up like ants scattered and roaming in all the possible directions. He even noticed how the small kids talked. They were really smart.

At last with some determination he said to himself, "Yes this is the place my family should live, these are the posh schools my children should attend and these are the streets and societies my wife should be acquainted with. One day I will earn lots of money and settle down in this wonderful city. Indeed my family deserves a better place than that poor village where people live under such miserable conditions – the only thing the people think there is the way to procure some food to fill up their stomach and nothing more. Those people never live, they only exist."

At last they reached a beautiful three storey magnificent building, which was finely decorated. The gatekeeper was a fat man who had a protruded belly bulging out on all sides; he was a really huge man with a thick stick in his hand. He had high boots on and had a thick moustache. To be honest the gatekeeper was a perfect match with the moustache. The big belly added charms to his so called personality. He saluted to them.

On one side of the restaurant Kumar could see many motorbikes and a few cars as well. Gentle soothing music was oozing out from the restaurant. Many people were constantly coming in and going out of the restaurant. Many of them were young but few were elderly. Two young boys came and shook hands with Bishal. They murmured something to Bishal, so did

Bishal back to them. Both the boys at once looked at Kumar and smiled. Kumar got embarrassed and he could not make the reason why. He preferred to be quiet and followed Bishal up the stairs. Kumar felt so strange and afraid.

They climbed through the elevated stairs and reached the top floor. The rooms on the top floor were much bigger. They were highly illuminated and dazzling with lights everywhere. The tables were much bigger inside; this was the first time he had ever seen such huge and nicely furnished room in his life. The cloth spread on every table was notably neat, not even a single spot or stain was to be seen, even upon close and distinct observation. Rich and well-dressed men and women were seating and eating from their plates that were occupied with such eatables Kumar had ever seen. All of them seemed so happy and filled with life. They merrily laughed and enjoyed; sorrow, pain and misery seemed miles and miles away from them. Kumar repented, he could never afford his family such luxury and provide them that level of entertainment, lifestyle and luxury.

As he crossed the rooms, Bishal stopped at a door and turned around to Kumar and whispered,

"Now we are going to enter the boss's office, his name is Deepak Manandhar. He owns this place, so be polite as much as possible and answer only when you are asked. Let's go."

Kumar nodded his head. Everyone there seemed to be in such haste that Kumar found no time to respond.

When they got in Mr Manandhar was working on his computer. Kumar had never ever seen such a thing in his entire life. He misunderstood it to be a television but he could not understand why Mr. Manandhar was constantly hitting a small piece of rectangular board and why there were not any songs being played on the screen. He was bewildered. After a minute or so he looked around.

Bishal said, "Sir, this is the man your friend has recommended, he is that murali player."

Deepak then looked at him, "Oh yes, I remember now … What is your name?"

Kumar was pretty nervous while answering, "Kumar."

"Is this your first time in this city?"

"Yes, Sir this is my first time in the city."

"My friend has really admired your musical skills and has highly recommended you. He believes no one in the world can play and perform like you do, is that right, Kumar?"

Kumar did not reply. Then Mr Manandhar said something to Bishal, in some foreign tone Kumar could hardly understand.

"Kumar, let's see how you perform. Do not feel nervous, just play anything you like; you are absolutely free to decide," said Mr Manandhar.

Bishal then took him to a small room. The room was full of musical instruments. Kumar had never seen such a great collection of instruments at all. Kumar could only differentiate a few of them.

Bishal then picked up a classical guitar and tuned the strings properly and said, "So what can you play, Kumar?"

Kumar replied, "I cannot understand your question."

Then Bishal mentioned him many new popular songs that were really on top of the charts on all the radio and television channels. Unfortunately Kumar had never heard even a single one of them. Bishal got depressed and said nothing at all.

Kumar asked, "You play this instrument?"

"Yes," replied Bishal.

"Can you play something, I have not heard this instrument so closely."

Soon Bishal gave a very short description about the guitar and played a beautiful melody. It was really ear pleasing. He played a piece for near about six minutes and while he was playing, a new boy came in and said nothing but sat on the drums and began playing the drum beats to accompany Bishal. The percussion beautified the guitar's music. Finally they stopped. Then Bishal introduced Kumar to the drummer. He was a professional drummer.

"Oh then what are you waiting for? Just perform something in that murali, I really love it," shouted the drummer with much excitement.

But depression was all over Bishal's face.

The very next minute something happened that left Bishal with his eyes wide open. Kumar played the entire melody he had just heard on the guitar. He did not even miss a note or phrase. The drummer was too embarrassed that he didn't accompany him with his drums. The same melody sounded even better on the murali than on the guitar. Others flocked up hearing such mellifluous music. Everyone there just got bedazzled seeing his skills in playing the murali and as a musician.

Someone said, "He can play by ear – the greatest asset for all musicians."

"Where did you learn to play so beautifully?" asked the drummer.

"Nowhere, just a little practice," replied Kumar.

"You call that a little practice!" exclaimed Bishal with his eyes wide open.

This time he was off his feet,

"Oh! My God, you are terrific. Kumar tell me frankly had you heard this melody before somewhere?"

Kumar replied,

"No, this is my first time, you just played it on your guitar. Did I make any mistake?" Kumar asked with a slight shiver in his voice.

All at once Bishal rushed out of the room and came back along with Mr Manandhar. They again conversed privately. Soon they made him play a couple of songs he had heard. Mr Manandhar could not readily believe it. He left the room without even saying a word.

Then, both Kumar and Bishal went to Mr Manandhar's room.

Mr Manandhar said, "Yes, you are appointed here as a new murali player, congratulations. Take a little rest and from the next week you can join the band, you have to play every evening from five p.m. onwards to ten p.m. And yes, tomorrow go to the market with Bishal and buy a new Murali for yourself, yours seems a little old."

Kumar did not like the idea, but he kept quiet and did as he was told. He could never abandon his gift from his beloved mother. Next day, he bought a new murali that sounded better than his older one but still he was content with his older one. It was not the sound but the love and fond memories that connected him with the murali.

With the new Murali he practised with his new band. The band members admired his efficiency and his talent as a music virtuoso. Mr Manandhar provided him with a nice room. Although it was a small one it was clean, except for some cobwebs in the corner of the room. He slept comfortably.

Soon after he was left alone in his room he started writing to his wife. He was overwhelmed to write or start to write anything. He did not know where to start and how to start.

Finally he did:

Dear Phul,
Yes I have reached the city and the city looks so beautiful and elegant. All I can see is tall buildings around me and cars running here and there, I wish you were all with me here.
Don't worry about me, I will be fine here and you take care of your health and keep writing. You know everyone have admired me for my musical talent and my boss hired me. So now onwards I will send you more money than before. I have made new friends here and they are friendly.
You know I got the job, here at the new place the people are so excited seeing my murali playing. The boss also bought me a new murali and it sounds better than the one I have now.
The boss has also provided me with a small and clean room. It seems as if our unhappy days are soon to be over. I promise I will work day and night to make my boss happy and try to bring all of you here.
I have not asked him about my salary and I feel so uncomfortable to discuss that. Don't worry, I will ask with him tomorrow.
And how are my kids. All my love to them.
Okay, I am very tired today. I will write to you later with more and more beautiful news.
Just your
Kumar

Kumar was very happy that night as he wrote the letter addressing his family. He felt safe.

Phul Maya revealed this great news to her kids.

Champa was extremely happy to hear this. Although they knew Kumar was far away they felt good thinking that Kumar would be back soon with lots of money, perhaps lots and lots.

Sadly, that season Sathi did not give them enough fruit. The fruit Phul Maya sold in the market returned them less money than in the previous years. Sathi felt sorry. But it was helpless. It is not that everything can be accessed and possessed with hard efforts. It is also the luck and fortune that counts. But Phul Maya didn't mention any of these happenings to Kumar as it was of no use. There was nothing Kumar could do about it, but adversely it could have a negative effect and Kumar could get depressed. So Phul Maya decided not to tell anything about this to Kumar. After that they had regular mail exchange but she never let Kumar know her secret financial condition; so sensitive was she.

Sathi was gradually getting older and weaker. Its fruit bearing capacity was decreasing every year. The Sathi did not possess that energy it had years before. It felt ashamed for its helplessness but still it was helpless and could do nothing to improve the situation. But Sathi felt proud to be associated with such a family. They never abandoned Sathi, not even now when his fruit production power was on the verge of failure. Capacity had decreased and was almost of no use.

In the city, Kumar was content in his happy days. Every evening he had to play his murali. Doing something he was truly passionate about and had passion for. He really enjoyed and thanked God for this. The guests would request songs and Kumar would play for them. Their applause filled him with enchantment that nurtured and refined him. Now his taste for music had completely changed. Now he listened to the all kinds of music ranging from rap to the new generation. His task was to play music and he had to feed his memory with all the different kinds of musical styles. His boss Mr Manandhar was really impressed by his talent. His gentleness intertwined with kindness soon made him the favourite of all; he never mocked others but always sympathised with others and always established peace.

Like the saying goes, 'Every rose has its thorn'. There was a thorn in that surrounding group who was slowly beginning to despise Kumar for his growing popularity and prestige he had earned as a fine musician. The band member, Rakesh, disliked Kumar's performance. He was jealous of Kumar for what he had accomplished since his arrival. He was ill-natured and for sure contemptible.

"How this new one could win everyone's heart," he said to himself with wrath in this voice.

The very look of Kumar brought extreme pain and wrath in him; his eyes would redden and he clutched his heart as though the agony would make it stop beating. Kumar's music vexed him, irritated him and the most predominantly was killing him from inside. Rakesh played the bass guitar for the band. Whenever anyone appreciated Kumar he did nothing but leave the place. He had not spoken about this to anyone because he knew everyone else admired Kumar for his talent, faithfulness and simplicity. He secretly despised and envied Kumar for this talent.

Days passed in the city. Kumar was now completely engrossed in his musical world. He made more money than before. The entire day he kept himself busy. He practised with the band for the evenings. Among the music lovers the rehearsals would never come to an end. There was always another last song to play.

But back in the village, Phul Maya realized that her time was going to be more difficult. The children had now grown and their demands had also grown, so more money was needed. But still she did not say anything to Kumar. It was not that Kumar was not sending money. Kumar would get so busy that sometimes he sent only once in three months. Kumar was assured that Phul was the candle of his house and she would never let the house go dark.

Whenever she had any sort of trouble she went straight to the Sathi and spilled out all her sorrow. Sathi cried as well but never let Phul Maya know about it. It knew that would make Phul Maya unhappier and emotionally weaker. She wrote to Kumar but never let him know the challenges she was involved in and was dealing with, alone without him being by her side. To some extent Kumar did not know about the financial status of this family. Even though he sent money every month we all know money is never enough. Finally, she decided to write a long letter. Deep down, she knew that letters are letters, they are much dearer and can carry greater load of love, influence and have greater capability to impact others. She wrote a letter and mailed it to Kumar.

In the restaurant, many different people came every day. The restaurant was clean and less expensive than the other restaurants in the town. On one such occasion, a man came with his family in the restaurant. As he was taking his dinner his attention was constantly attracted by Kumar's music. He was surprised. Again after a few days, the same man visited the place but this time he was alone. That day he stayed there for the entire evening

237

until it was time for the restaurant to be closed for the night listening to Kumar.

The letter Phul Maya had sent Kumar reached the restaurant but it was placed in the wrong hands. The man at the reception handed Kumar's letter to Rakesh to deliver it to him thinking they both belonged to the same band. But out of envy and jealousness, Rakesh did not give the letter to Kumar but instead tore it into pieces.

Back at home, Phul Maya, could not understand why Kumar did not reply to her letter. But she consoled herself thinking that Kumar might be busy due to some work. Phul Maya could not ask for help from anyone. Everyone in the village was too poor to help her, but still she managed to run the house with the little money she had. She worked harder than before. She tried every attempt not to let her children down if they ever requested for anything. Champa understood everything. So she made no demands at all. But her brother did not understand anything all. All the money Phul Maya had saved was not enough to run the house and buy new books for the children.

The shop was also not running properly as before.

Now there were already many such shops in the village.

One particular evening, the man approached Kumar when his performance was over,

"Hello, I am Prabin Gurung and I produce songs and music. I have been watching you for many days and I have come to believe that I have never heard anything like this before," he said.

At first Kumar did not know just what to say. He felt himself at lost for words but before he could say anything Prabin asked,

"Well, if you have time then can you help me with some of my recordings. Currently I am working on a project and is soon about to get accomplished in a month or two."

He did not know what to answer. He was surprised to realise that he had already uttered the words, "Sure, yes, why not, *dai*?"

Prabin dai smiled in return and left the place.

Kumar talked about it with Bishal, who was very happy to know about it.

He said, "See Kumar, these types of opportunities never come twice, you are lucky that Prabin dai picked you up, so I suggest you should not let this opportunity go."

Kumar was at a total confusion for not knowing how to react under such circumstances. Soon his band members knew about this and all of them repeated the same thing told by Bishal.

Finally Mr Manandhar heard about this and called Kumar,

"If you are interested then you can work during the daytime, as you are almost free every day. And please don't rely on me for your next decision, just do not hamper my show time, that is simply all I want and expect from you."

With a little encouragement from his friends he gathered a little confident. He thought of writing to his family but soon dropped the idea thinking of it as a nonsense act.

"I can't confuse them anymore."

He said to himself, "I love my family but it is not necessary to inform them about everything as they might get unnecessarily worried about me."

Worst happened, Rakesh blocked several other letters. The letters written by Phul Maya never reached Kumar. The situation back home was getting tense with each passing day which Kumar was so awfully unaware of.

Kumar was now completely engrossed in his job. The best part was that Mr Manandhar had already given him permission to work with Prabin. Then for the next few days nothing happened. Kumar performed every evening in the restaurant. He was just overwhelmed by the idea of the new job and how much he would enjoy it. Most of all it was the double pay that lured him.

Then finally Prabin dai approached Kumar that week. That evening Kumar had just completed his first interval in the restaurant. Kumar had not noticed Prabin dai among the guests. The men greeted each other and shook hands. Kumar took him to one corner of the hall and made him sit on one table. They talked about different issues.

The most interesting part for Kumar was when Prabin dai said,

"You will get four hundred rupees for every piece you play, and may be that someday you may have seven or eight recordings and someday no recordings at all."

"That is all right," timidly replied Kumar.

He was already busy making the calculations in his head.

Soon Prabin dai let him know some of the business rules and left the restaurant. Kumar resumed his second part of the show at the restaurant.

The day arrived and Kumar was for the first time playing in a music studio. He was not recording with the professionals.

At first Kumar was nervous, as he did not know how to face the people and play so well at the same time. It was a recording so now error was desired.

The first time he went into the studio was memorable for him. He had never seen such big speakers and such an excellent sound system. The studio room was well furnished and well decorated. The entire room exuded a sweet type of fragrance. Soon, after a few minutes Prabin dai introduced Kumar to everyone in the room. Basically all the others in the room were musicians and performers. Prabin dai introduced him as a master murali player for which Kumar felt a little uncomfortable. Kumar read the others' faces. They all anticipated a lot from him, especially Prabin dai, who was in his mid-forties, seemed to be the happiest of all.

Then the recordist turned to Kumar and said, "You'll have to fill up some bars for this track, listen to it very much carefully, just do the best you can."

Prabin dai patted on Kumar's shoulder and gave him an encouraging look. It was rather more a warning look than an encouraging look.

He silently whispered in Kumar's ear with an air of finality and certitude, "Just go on and let these people see who you are and what you can do."

Now Kumar was even more afraid but he successfully managed to hide his nervousness. The track Kumar had just heard was a complete noble one; Kumar had never heard such music before. It was a sort of fusion music, but Kumar could hardly differentiate this. In the restaurant all he had to do was to copy the music of others and simply play it. But here the case was on the other side. He could not copy anyone but compose whatever his instinct allowed him to. This was a real place for Kumar to show his musical talent. These were many different types of music like classical, semi-classical, funky and the notorious of all, the rap music. It was like things coming out of Pandora's Box. Kumar had never been exposed to music composition for all those different types of musical styles. Kumar was not classically trained like others nor did he have any formal music training. No one but his instincts and nature had taught him to play the song; the song of the earth; the earth song.

His heart began to sound like accelerating train on its track, he just did not know from where to start, what to play and how to play.

He heard the track repeated six times and then the recordist asked,

"Now if you are ready then can you move in to the recording room and do some trails?"

Suddenly Prabin dai interrupted,

"Kumar, but only if you are ready. If you'd like to hear it more please do not hesitate to ask, otherwise..."

Out of sheer nervousness Kumar did not know what to say, he suddenly said,

"Okay I'm ready, let's try and see what happens."

But Kumar was not aware when he said this. Everything came out voluntarily, as if someone else was doing the speaking for him. The recordist took him to the recording room and helped him adjust the microphone on his head. Then the recordist went outside asking Kumar to seal the door properly. As the door was closed, Kumar felt hot inside. There was not even a single hole for the air to pass. On the other side he could see

242

everyone through the transparent thick glass. He could see Prabin dai smiling at him and cheering him up.

Over the microphone, Kumar heard the voice of the recordist,

"Kumar here we go, adjust your phone and your murali and give it a try, just a try."

Again, Prabin dai was heard over the microphone. "Kumar do not worry, it is just a try. You can try as many times as you want until you are confident."

Then the musical track was played and Kumar had to fill up some bars with the murali. He remembered where to play but was not clear what and how to play. He closed his eyes and took the murali on his lips and thought of his family. Everybody's face came smiling up to him. He felt as if his son was saying,

"Papa, you can do it."

His wife said, "Keep the faith."

At once he recalled the days on the branches of Sathi where he played so beautifully without any fear, frustrations and hesitations. He recalled how Sathi supported him but here there was no one to support him here except its vivid visions and imaginations.

On the first go, he missed the timing. He started a little late.

Soon the recordist reminded him, "You missed the timing, so try again."

With his heart pounding Kumar put the murali to his lips, but this time a miracle happened. Kumar performed incredibly well and excellently. Kumar himself could not believe he played it. He felt someone else played for him. He knew it was his instincts after all that had again helped him. All those on the other side of the room were amazed to hear such a magnificent melody; it was certainly a noble experience for them.

Prabin dai shouted over the microphone, "Yes, Kumar you did it, I knew you could do it."

The final take was done and that was not less in comparison to the previous one. It was even better later on; the other musicians congratulated Kumar and patted him on the shoulder.

"You were terrific."

Then the recording was over.

Later, back in the restaurant Bishal and others heard about the recording and they all praised Kumar. Now Kumar's confident had even accelerated to a greater height. He knew he could do it. He believed he could rule the world and he was the King.

Many proposals started coming to Kumar.

Soon his fame as a veteran murali performer spread and nearly all music people knew about it. Now he was not the same old Kumar as he was before. His personality had changed and everyone respected him as a musical genius. He just knew how to handle different musical situations. He quickly began to make more and more money as time passed. He practised a lot at his room. He practised regularly. After two months he was recording seven to ten tracks a day. He had to visit different studios for that. Kumar was invited for musical performances.

He got busier and he had hardly time to eat and sleep. Sometimes, he had to spend many days in a studio arranging and performing music.

Once he found himself asking forgiveness with Mr Deepak for not being able to play the following evening. Many different people and restaurant owners came and made proposals to Kumar and promised better money if he agreed to play for them. But Kumar realized that he just could not leave Mr Deepak. Kumar knew what he had done for him; how he had encouraged him in at every step and most of all treated him as his own brother. He knew that he could never leave Mr Deepak Manandhar no matter what happened.

He was now already a start famed as a veteran murali player. He was the entertainer but deep inside he felt alone like a solitary candle sitting in one corner of the room just to eliminate the darkness.

He felt deeply apologetic that his family could not share the light.

Chapter Thirteen

The Architect of his own Demise

Kumar deeply felt that Mr Deepak provided him the real opportunity. He could feel that Mr. Deepak had really cared and loved for him and above all had a profound affection for him. He made sure to return every evening to the restaurant. But still sometimes he missed the evenings. He would feel very bad. He did not want to hurt Mr Deepak come what may.

Time passed.

Kumar made so much money he could hardly believe it. His life style started to change. Often he wanted to go back to his village to meet his family but he was so busy he could only think of it. Kumar kept a diary to fix his appointments with his clients. Everyone liked Kumar as he was the man of his words and faith. He did not care much for the money but he cared for the quality of music he played. He tried and put his heart and soul whenever a new project came over. He was living a prosperous life. In no time, Kumar became very busy. He wanted to spend more time with the murali. He wanted to practise more; he loved meeting artists and he extremely liked the group rehearsals. He had a genuine feeling for invention every time he walked on stage or stepped into the recording studio. That's why he would always think of arranging some private time for him.

In one meeting Mr Parbin Gurung announced that he had organised a solo concert for Kumar.

Kumar could not believe it.

He thought that he was going to take another birth again; rebirth.

"Yes. I need to try my best. The moment has come," he said to himself.

Kumar got more and more busy with his life and work that eventually he drifted a little apart from everything he had acquired and unfortunately even from his own family. Temptation had possessed him completely and all he could see was his popularity and the money that was flowing in.

Finally he decided,

"Ok let me finish this solo concert and then I will go back to my village for good now that I have made enough money."

He waited for the concert to end and go back to the village unannounced as a complete surprise to his family. Even that thought ran shivers up and down his spine. He was excited, nervous and agitated at the same time; he saw the success for the first time in his miserable little life.

But destiny had some other plans.

Back in the village something unexpected had cropped up. A serious unnamed disease attacked Champa. In no time, many people in the village became bedridden. Children were the main victims. Champa's situation got worse; Phul Maya did all she could. Her neighbours were too helpless since they too did not know what to do in such a situation. The disease was new, they did not know any medicine, they approached the local small hospital but the doctors said that they were doing their best. On top of that the villagers were poor.

Phul Maya tried very hard to contact Kumar. She wrote letter after letter to his new address but Kumar would never reply any of them. His band mate Rakesh never let Kumar read all those letters. He was determined not to see Kumar happy and prosper and now how could he hand over those letters from his family that would inevitably cheer him up. He simply disposed all these letters in the gutter. Champa could not go to school. Since many schoolgoing children were sick, the school too announced closed until the fever was terminated.

Next day, Phul Maya saw that her son too was becoming sick perhaps chances were he had contracted the disease. He too felt weak and feeble and both the children wanted their father. Champa asked for Kumar again and again even when she was unconscious and completely to herself.

Phul Maya looked at Champa. She was calling her father even whilst in her deepest slumbers.

The girl was whimpering.

The situation was really worst for Phul Maya and getting worse day after day.

She wrote to him again. She wanted to take her to the hospital in the city. She did not know how. Perhaps she was too ignorant to figure her ways to the hospital.

Destiny was playing a cruel game with her. It was such an act of disgrace she was witnessing.

Kumar was totally unaware of this and was busy in his musical world. The day of his solo concert was approaching nearer and nearer and he was getting busier and busier. And he was counting the days for the concert to be over and he would return back home for good.

Kumar was to going to hit it. He was going to add some more melodies in the world of the music that was sure to hit the charts. This was to be his debut stage performance as a professional musician.

The concert date was already fixed and tickets were on sale. Many people were expected to visit the concert and tickets sold like hot cakes.

So due to all this Kumar was not free even to hear his inner voice. Now he had to find extra time for his upcoming music concert. He put all his heart and soul in it. He knew he was getting a lot of money from this concert if it did succeed. He thought that after the concert he was going to go to his village to his family directly. He would not compromise and he began to envisage the good days he would be spending with his family.

He always thought that his family might be fine and enjoying their dandy days, it did never occurred to him that his daughter could be at risk back home, it just never hit him; his mind was busily preoccupied temporarily and there was no place for any other thought to linger for long.

Phul Maya could not hold any more. She went to Ghale's home and wrote another letter addressing Ghale asking for immediate help describing the turmoil and the ruthless God exhibiting himself in a very eerie way. She wrote in detail, every detail to him. She wrote him enough to realize how serious Champa was and how much Kumar was needed at the moment. She requested Ghale to send Kumar home as soon as possible.

After a couple of days Ghale read the letter and was so shocked. He reread the letter. He simply could not fathom how a man such as Kumar could be so negligent and remiss with the issue that had prevailed over his family.

Ghale too was helpless and his face turned red with anger and confusion.

"I have to take some days leave and go in search of Kumar," he declared to his store manager.

The manager was more than overwhelmed to hear this from Ghale.

"Ok… but what is the matter?"

"I have no time to explain all that now," he replied bluntly concentrating his eyes on something though not observing anything.

He tried calling Kumar but his mobile was off.

He at once rushed to Thapa's work to find out the address of the place where Kumar was employed at the restaurant. Thapa soon contacted his boss and acquired the phone number of the restaurant Kumar was supposed to be working.

Ghale called, "Hello can talk with Kumar. It is urgent please."

"Well he is tremendously busy for his upcoming concert."

"What!" shrieked Ghale with bitterness in his bassy voice.

"And when is this concert?"

"Two days from now at the City Hall."

"Can you connect me there?" breathed Ghale in his rising voice.

'Sorry, he can't be disturbed and I can't do it even if I wanted to."

Ghale hung up the phone with fire radiating all over his face.

He cried.

He knew that Kumar loved his family more than anything else in this world. So he wondered how he could ever be so different all at once. How could anyone change so quickly within months? Ghale was so confused and he felt really bad. He too got anxious about his own family. He came back to his room.

He could not sleep.

"Is everything okay at my home?"

"Are my family members all right?"

He decided to go to the city to bring Kumar home the next morning.

His store owner hesitated to grant him leave but Ghale did not listen to him and made his way to the city stating that something very serious had happened.

Ghale reached the city. He knew Kumar's address. He went to the restaurant, but he was informed that the next day Kumar was having a grand debut performance and was really busy with the rehearsals and hardly had time to meet any one. He requested the watchman to let him in but in vain. The watchman could not help him. That day Ghale tried but he could not find Kumar, then the night he spent in the lodge.

Early next morning he went to the restaurant. He said everything to the watchman and even showed him all the letters he had received from Phul Maya. Perhaps the watchman's heart softened.

The watchman took him to Bishal who was talking on the phone. Later, briefly, Ghale was able to narrate him the entire collapse in Kumar's family.

Bishal said to Ghale, "Today is a grand day for Kumar, many people are coming to listen to him play his magical murali. There was no question that he should be disturbed."

Ghale begged and explained him everything in full detail.

Bishal finally got convinced that this needed to be reported to Kumar as soon as possible.

He said,

"Come with me. In half an hour his concert is due to begin. Maybe you can talk to him after the concert."

They went together to the city hall. It was a great and huge hall built to accommodate thousands of people. Bishal helped Ghale to enter the hall.

He said, "See, you can sit here now and listen to Kumar and after the show is over you can talk to him."

"All right," replied Ghale.

"If Kumar learns about his family, then he might not be on his feet to perform tonight."

Then Bishal left towards the stage. In the hall there were thousands of people and they were so enthusiastic to hear and see Kumar at play. Back in the seat Ghale felt utterly miserable like a fish out of pond. He remembered the painful words of Phul Maya.

He thought,

"Should I inform Kumar before or after the show?" Then again his heart asked a question.

"But what if it is too late after the show, who will be responsible for it?"

Innumerous questions checked in Ghale's mind. He could not curb his sentimentality anymore, and not thinking of the consequences he took quick and rapid steps towards the stage. He made his way behind the curtain. He asked the people there about Kumar. They were so busy they did not even have time to listen attentively.

Finally one man answered, "… in that room."

Ghale made quick steps towards the room. As he was about to enter, he was stopped by a man. Ghale made his way forcibly into the room.

In the room, Kumar was practising with all other musicians. Kumar was really surprised to see Ghale there and then, when he was expected the least.

Kumar read in Ghale's face, the fear and confusion. Ghale took Kumar's hand and took him aside to one corner of the room. He explained everything without missing a word and in great detail. He also showed him the letter sent by Phul Maya.

Kumar now realized the mistake he had done by not writing to his home. The result was irreparable. He felt culpable.

"Oh, poor me and my Phul Maya. But no serious things should happen to my children."

Ghale then said, "This is not the time to talk all about this, make your decision."

Kumar felt very guilty. He heart flooded with pain; he experienced the same feeling as he had felt when his father used to torment him. He felt so frightened and afraid like a motherless child. He began to cry and hugged Ghale. He remembered his family's face and mostly Champa. Now he felt that he was living in a phony world all for the money; the fraudulent world that had so truly captured him. He realized that money had taken him in. He looked at the stage and found it all false. He found himself engulfed by the city's life. He found himself lost. He realized how he had abandoned his family for the fake applause and praise from the people who just wish to be entertained. He regretted so much, indeed he did.

Soon he decided to quit everything.

"Ghale, we are moving, right now," Kumar said unexpectedly.

Ghale asked, "What about these people... This concert, Kumar?"

"Nothing in the world is more important to me than my family," replied Kumar in one go. He left the room with eyes full of tears while Ghale followed him. On his way Kumar came across Mr Prabin who asked in his overwhelmed tone,

"Are you ready Kumar, the audience are dying for you?"

Kumar said nothing and made his way out from the back door where no one could see him. Ghale and Kumar reached Kumar's room. Kumar collected all the money he had earned so far. He had saved all the money in the pot that he had hidden from his father; the same pot that belonged to his mother.

Soon they reached the bus stand and were on the bus for their village. All through the journey, Kumar did not even say a word; he felt utterly speechless and in fact could not face Ghale for the negligence he had exhibited towards his family. His eyes remained watery all the time and his face was gravely serious. Ghale thought it better not to disturb him as he was amidst the sea of trouble and seemed captivated in that panic of turbulence. On the way, Kumar counted all the miscalculations and fallacies he had carried out under the misapprehension of a better future. His soul was filled with remorse and tragedy and often suicidal thoughts visited his chaotic mind. However, he maintained his spirits and struggled to remain calm all through the way with little or no interaction with anyone on the bus. He just kept starting at the floating clouds high in the sky and felt at complete loss and agony.

"Why did I stop writing home?"

"What a fool and complete idiot I had been under the influence of temporary applause and wealth."

"I have been tempted."

"How will I ever face Phul and my children?"

Such recollections hit his mind repeatedly making him fragile every time it did. However, he never wondered why Phul Maya had not written to him while she was going through such hard times. He was too ignorant to recognize the devil, and the vicious act he had carried out with exact precision and perfection. He was too gentle and perhaps too genteel to suspect the culprit.

He tried hard but he could not suspect anything or anyone. Kumar just wanted to get to his family and be part of the pain they were going through. He sadly regretted the negligence and for the lack of his responsibility.

All at once the face the Mr Prabin would show up and that would torment him the most. He had cheated everyone that had proved his or her loyalty and had been the most reliable while he was going through the thick and thin of his life and had never deserted him and left him in his isolation. His emotion and pain was incalculable. It was way beyond expression but he was going through it quite alone; bleeding all the way.

The bus finally reached the village. He glanced all around the bus station still seated on his seat with his reddened bulging eyes. He was the last to disembark the bus and that only happened when Ghale prompted him.

"We have arrived!"

He cast his mournful and deprived face towards Ghale with poignancy.

Kumar struggled towards his home as fast as his feet could take him. He never felt such feeling of dejection, forlornness and tribulation while he was on his way home. For him his home was always a sanctuary, perhaps more, perhaps a paradise. When he reached his home, he found the gate wide open as if no one ever inhabited there. It was silent, terribly silent and still, like a breeze on a hot and humid summer day. The store was closed and looked as if it had been unopened for ages and ages. The front garden surely looked neglected and deserted and he could hear the dolefully weary welcome notes from the drooping flowers.

The house was so quiet and so very silent; like never before, more silent than the silence of the Universe. The ear piercing silence was so deafening and intolerable and that certainly aroused suspicion that something was terribly wrong. He made his way silently through the door, afraid as he made another step.

He saw Champa asleep and Phul Maya nursing her son.

Seeing Kumar at once she ran and embraced him bursting into huge sobs of crying and complaints.

She asked with suggested violence in her voice, "Why did you not reply to my mails. I wrote you thousands of letters and none replied to."

Kumar remained in his position pondering how he missed the letters.

Kumar knew that it was not time to think about the past. He asked, "How is our son?"

"Now, he is okay, but I am afraid...?" Phul Maya began to cry violently than before.

Kumar was so sorry that he thought he did not have the right to console her. He approached his daughter, she was very cold and still. She did not even feel her father standing there. Kumar cried.

He said, "Let us take her to the city, where there are better doctors... now."

Phul Maya cried, "Let's wait, we cannot take her in this condition, she cannot even open her mouth to eat?"

"What do the doctors say?" cried Kumar. The local hospital had a few medical compounders, whom people called 'the doctor' in the villages.

"They did the best they could and always said she will be fine," cried Phul Maya with a little hope in her trembling voice.

That day ended and Kumar tried to sleep with his son. Later that evening his son woke up and kissed his father with no energy and enthusiasm as he had previously whenever he met his father.

He trembled and said, "Pa, at last you've come, I knew you would come, sister is sick but she will be fine and we will all go to the jungle."

Kumar held him close.

The same night around two o'clock Kumar suddenly woke up hearing the violent cries of Phul Maya. She was standing beside Champa's bed and moving and shaking her. Bubbles of froth appeared at mouth's corner.

Kumar ran to her and shouted, "Champa, wake up, your pa... is back." Kumar cried bitterly.

257

But Champa did not move even a single muscle. At once, Kumar ran to get a local hospital. After few minutes, he came back with a compounder. After performing some examination here and there on her body, the compounder sadly announced that Champa had passed away.

Phul Maya fainted and collapsed on the ground.

Neighbours soon poured in on hearing the news. They nursed her and provided moral support to Kumar – that was all those poor neighbours could do.

Kumar was grief-stricken and tremendously depressed. He had lost his beloved daughter. His son came beside him and hugged him with tears.

Later it was heard that many schoolgoing children in the village and nearby villages died due to the same mysterious disease, which was never to be identified and diagnosed in that poor village and the surrounding areas.

The days began to pass as usual, quite ignoring the pain Kumar was going through .One day Kumar noticed that his wife was getting feeble and she had developed peculiarly heavy black areas underneath her eyes. Now she resembled nothing more than a living skeleton, crying all the time.

She was getting lonelier but she was still so aggressive to fulfill her spousal activities though she was less active than ever before. She would stare all of a sudden at any corner or wherever her eyes landed and then just keep looking and looking. Kumar could feel that something terrible was eating her soul and mind and consuming her physically, mentally and spiritually.

It is so rightly said, 'Poverty is the root of all evil'. With the pervading illness and starvation in the village the local rascals even took to stealing and robbing. After all they all needed money to buy things and, most of all, the medicine. Mostly were reduced to beggary.

One particular night, Kumar forgot to close the main door of his house and went to sleep. Next morning he was terrified to find all his money was stolen. Now he was the same old Kumar of times long ago who had no money and had gone to the city with a strong desire to earn money. Many had known Kumar had returned with money from the city. The village was full impecunious people, and every one needed money very badly. Therefore, somebody did it.

Kumar did not know what to do. He did not suspect anyone. But he knew his destiny was the robber of his blissful life.

All seemed to be his friends.

He gathered courage to inform his wife about the money that was stolen right from the home. But Phul Maya did not respond. She said nothing about it. She looked at Kumar blankly while he was addressing her. The loss of her daughter could not be compared to this loss. She had already lost the most desirous thing in her life – her daughter, Champa.

Phul Maya got weaker than ever before. She stopped working. She thought that her life was nearing to an end. She did not say anything about it to Kumar. She did not want to make him unhappy even though her life was at stake. She did not want to burden him and as always she tried her best to conceal her pain. Kumar would often ask her about her health,

"Dear, I'm all right… just a little tired, that's all. I'm so sorry you'll have to look after the kitchen for a few days," Phul Maya would reply feebly.

"That's nothing," Kumar was ready to sacrifice his whole life for her.

Phul Maya could not stop crying, thinking about Champa.

The next evening Kumar went to Sathi's place.

Sathi was happy to see his friend back. The two friends embraced each other.

Sathi asked, "Kumar, why did you return so late? Did you not know your child was sick? How is she now?"

Kumar did not know how to say that Champa had already passed away. With a crying voice,

"My friend, our daughter has gone. It has been two days."

"What?" Sathi could not believe. It stopped moving and cried.

Kumar consoled him,

"Please, my friend it is all done, do not cry."

But Sathi could not stop.

Kumar then repeated himself.

"You know, I'm responsible for all this... my greed for money and fame. I was so happy here in the village with you and my family, we were not so rich but happy with whatever we had."

He further added, "But from the day I left my family I have never been happy. I had accumulated some riches but my heart was never at ease and in fact I longed for you and my family, and now I'm back and it's already too late."

Sathi did not answer for a long time. It did not respond to Kumar.

At last it said, "The greed for money and power is accountable for every misery in this world. Just imagine a world where people do not fight for money and power, where people do not have hungry eyes for another's wealth,"

At last, his depraved soul confessed. Kumar knew he had completely whored his life and ideals perhaps in every possible way though he never intended to. He had already sold his soul to the devil himself.

He felt belittled, rather shrunk and belittled.

Kumar sadly replied, "We have already lost that flavour and essence of life."

The friends stayed together for a long time until Sathi demanded his leave as it was getting late.

He came back home and found Phul Maya asleep. Even during her sleep, she maintained her beauty. The dazzling light of her face had never left and the charm was always there no matter what happened.

She woke and seeing Kumar, she asked,

"You are back...?"

"Oh! You're awake I thought you were fast asleep," replied Kumar with surprise.

He sat very close to Phul Maya. Phul Maya again wept over their lost daughter next day. Their son did not to go to school. The regular pattern of the house was somewhat lost. Finally, one day Kumar opened his shop. It was all dirty and covered with dust and surely had been unattended by months. As he sat waiting for the customers, he thought of Mr Deepak and Mr Prabin. He again felt guilty for the betrayal. He had left the stage without even informing anyone. What would Mr Prabin have thought of me, after all he had done so much for me. He truly regretted it but it was already too late.

"May God forgive me for my negligence and cowardice."

Many days passed.

A few customers visited the shop. Kumar could not welcome his customers like the way he used to do.

Ghale and other neighbours sometime attended his place. Even Ghale decided not to return back after the terrible incident.

But Kumar loved to be left alone. Whenever he was surrounded by people, he stood up and used to say,

"Please leave me alone,"

Many days passed. But Phul Maya never recovered. She seemed perhaps in the high stage of some kind of syndrome and had turned lean and thin – a clear and precise indication that her health was declining. Her figure was emaciated. Many people would visit her and nurse her. Phul Maya's parents came. They tried their best to take care of her but all of them failed to see that she was dying from the inside until one day when Phul Maya passed away silently without anyone noticing it.

Kumar was now beyond any grief and so was his son.

But apart from grieving and lamenting there was nothing else he could possibly do. He swore that he would never ever run after money. Had he not been so attached to money and fame, his daughter would not have died, his wife would not have died and he would not have seen this terrible day. Cursed are the poor persons like him.

Her parents did not know what to do. They had seen so many deaths in their lives that they were ready to die rather than to cry on someone's death. They looked very sad. For them, to go away from the village, their daughter's home was the only remedy. Kumar could feel their mind. He requested them to leave the place for he felt the need to be alone and his heart desired complete isolation. Kumar did not want them around in mourning mood.

His son did not believe, even now, that his mother was gone. He continuously kept staring at one corner of the room, relentlessly. However, deep inside, he understood everything perfectly. He had already seen two deaths in a row of someone most precious and too important for him. He was young but life's harsh truths had already made him an experienced youth. He was familiar with severe pain and longing and he seemed to realize that weeping was not the solution at all.

Days passed and flowed liked a river in one direction never to consult the father and son about the grief they were going through. Father and son were bound to live at home. They looked very sad, pathetic and vulnerable. Sometimes their neighbours would come to assist them otherwise father and son took care of each other and looked after their home and the store.

Late at night, Kumar would take out his murali and play, radiating a heavy wave of sad life he was leading. They would mostly be sad tunes which made not only the audiences, but also fairies of the night, cry.

Years passed; it never stopped.

Kumar had now turned into an old man in his late sixties with grey hair, dark brown complexion and eyes deep in their sockets. His son had already turned into a young man with thick dark hair, black eyes and hairy chest. He had stopped going to school from the very day his elder sister had passed away. He did not miss the school nor his friends. After his mother died, he thought that it was better to become deaf to the world, and he tried his best to avoid contact with the rest of the world and locked himself up in his room.

Kumar wanted his son to go out and enjoy life. His son still had a good part of his life waiting ahead. With the help of some neighbours, including Ghale and his wife, Kumar tried his best to convince his son to get married.

After Kumar's experience, Ghale never returned to the city. He seemed to realize that family togetherness and unity was the greatest asset a man could ever amass in his life and rest was just a show.

Kumar talked to his son,

"Son, now you've to look at your age. If not today then tomorrow you must definitely marry, so why not today? I can simply request but I cannot insist that you do."

During the conversation, the son said nothing at all and remained silent. His heart was so full of agony and bitter sensations that he never believed that he could ever be happy simply by uniting with another female. The whole idea of marriage did not entice him.

Finally after much persuasion things were finalized and Kumar's son agreed to come to a marriage deal.

Ghale's wife arranged a deal with a beautiful girl from the nearby village. The marriage ceremony took place and only a few people were invited. Kumar was so exhausted he could hardly do anything by himself. The entire ceremony was accomplished by the help of the neighbours. Ghale's wife played a vital role in this marriage. After the marriage Kumar's son started concentrating more on his business. He started looking after the store and sold vegetables. Since the family was small, the earnings from the shop and vegetable were enough for them and he seemed uninterested in gathering more and more wealth. Wealth counts as zero if destiny holds nothing.

Kumar got older and older and older. He looked older than his age. He did not bother with anything. He rarely changed his clothes and rarely shaved. His trousers were tattered and covered with dust. Kumar looked as if he did not belong to this world. He began to spend all his time with Sathi in the jungle in a deep trance like state. Every day, they would share all the memories. Kumar would rant on about the unfairness of it and all that had happened to him. Perhaps he felt he had suffered injustice.

One day Kumar gasped, "Friend, I have lost everything in my life, now I feel so naked and poor. I left the village to earn the money for my family, but ultimately what did I earn? I lost everything and earned nothing at all. It was all due to my carelessness, my greed for more and more money and fame."

Kumar kept talking about different incidents that had happened in his life, using long-winded phrases. Waves of despair and sorrow had ascended upon him and would never ever leave him alone. Emptiness had found him again and there was no escape even if he tried.

It was utterly impossible for Kumar to remain calm and composed and yet justify himself after all he been through. He lay in front of his friend with his head drooped as a victim submissively bowing down before an executioner, without any struggle, waiting and longing for it all to end soon, very soon. He felt incarcerated for a broken promise. Sathi stopped Kumar abruptly and said,

"Don't blame yourself my friend, that's what life is all about. We endeavor our best in life to achieve something but it all depends on your luck and belief in God."

Sathi further objected.

"Kumar, do you think every man who has laboured hard enough in his life has turned out to be a very successful man, ended happily"?

"Does happiness always follow sorrow?

"Are failures always the pillars of prosperity and triumph?

"Is every sorrow balanced by happiness?

"No.

"Just remember we are a very miniature part of this entire creation and Universe. We came here on a given time with no idea of what happened before us while we were there all the time from the time immemorial. Our soul has never ceased to exist while we simply change this body quite so very often. God has just given us the ability to comprehend what is before us and a very weak judgmental ability to foresee what lies ahead of us in the times yet to come. We are not that educated to understand such matters. Very few people try to understand life, but their explanation is so baffling and arouses confusion that everything seemed muddled up."

As Sathi was saying all these things, Kumar managed to climb the branches; he realized that his strength had all gone.

He whimpered to himself – "I was deaf but now I am languid too."

Sathi also had turned out to be an old ordinary tree with its delicate branches. Its leaves had already turned pale. There were very little fruit on the tree.

Sathi had witnessed everything in Kumar's life. It had never separated himself from the family. It too had already lost Champa and Phul Maya. It too was exhausted and broken from inside. The condition of his friend made it even more frustrated and weak. It was clearly visible that it was the last it could offer anyone. Kumar sat on one of the thickest branches and began to play his murali, but now all the charm was all lost. He was no more a maestro murali player. His fingers betrayed him and he could not blow the required amount of air into the murali. He still tried his best but it all turned out to be a useless attempt – it was just a series of useless notes.

At last, Kumar gave up playing the murali.

Sathi had realized this but said nothing.

That night Kumar spent the night under the branches of Sathi. Kumar did not know when he went to sleep.

Back at home, his son and his daughter-in-law were very anxious and worried about Kumar.

His son went to inquire at Ghale's home but he did not find his father there. Seeing the anxiety, Ghale decided to help him find his father. They searched everywhere but they could not find him.

Kumar's son got uncontrollably worried. Then suddenly, something came rushing by in Ghale's mind and he said,

"Wait son, I think I'll be back with your father," and went away without even looking back. Marching straight, forward with confidence.

Ghale made his way towards the jungle. Kumar's son followed him. At last they found Kumar who was sound asleep under Sathi's huge old trunk. He looked safe and secure like an infant cuddled up in his mother's arm. The tree was no doubt his heavenly sanctuary.

Ghale felt that it was very inappropriate to disturb him, so they left the place silently and returned to the village.

Later that morning Kumar returned home sluggishly.

His daughter-in-law cried, "At least you should have informed us, we were so worried about you."

Kumar gave a pitiful smile and asked for a cup of tea. Soon his son came; he had been working on his land. He looked at his father but did not say anything at all. He could find all his answers in his serene eyes. Manoj had seen all he had gone through.

Kumar beady black eyes kept targeting back towards the muddy floor. He remained in a complete motionless state except sometimes his black eyes flashed a bacchanalian smile, involuntarily, perhaps for no reason, other than perhaps to show that he was at the least still alive.

He exhibited a gesture of complete solidarity.

And the solitude looked overwhelming that seemed pregnant with nothing except remorse and pain.

Days passed and Kumar turned more and more depressed. How could he ever forgive himself?

"Am I responsible for all the losses?"

Many times, he cursed himself. He was utterly remorseful; He was in constant pain and torture all the time. The pain was not a proper thing for a solitary person but he could not muster any strength to overcome it. He was deprived of all the happiness around him, he could not even smell the sweet fragrance the air bought in, perhaps it was on God's order.

His son Manoj got finer and full of life and just went on working for the family.

Kumar rarely spoke to anyone. More often he would look at things that belonged to his daughter and cry violently. It seemed nothing in the world could stop him from doing so.

A fine day. Around three o'clock. Kumar left his home.

Kumar's son did not find his father in the evening. He asked his wife about him. His wife too did not know anything at all. He was too tired to go out in search for his father.

His wife said,

"Father is not back yet, why do you not go and bring him back? You know it is not safe to stay out at nights."

In his trance like state he replied,

"Oh! Do not worry. He is surely safe with his friend."

Needless to say that Kumar was with Sathi in the jungle.

That night, Kumar sat beneath Sathi, almost embracing it. He tried to play the murali but he could hardly produce any sweet melody. He looked deep into the sky at the stars. He recalled his past life. He recalled his youth days, the day he had first met Phul Maya, the first night and his children. He recalled how he and his family spent their time with Sathi. The more he recalled, the more his heart ached. He tried to scream but he could not.

Sathi hinted, "It seems you are more sad today, Kumar."

The tree could not even give him false hope, perhaps as it was not human who could play smoothly with words and manipulate them. It was unable to speak like humans and the beauty of its inability to speak was the inability to lie and feed false hope.

Kumar did not respond. He seemed to have lost his path to God and his glance expressed nothing significant except longing and pain and the surrender. Importantly he seemed to be forgetting that every breath was a gift from God and should be valued.

He did not feel the need to move his limbs.

"How can you help me?" said Kumar, frowning with vexation.

Sathi replied, "That I have always done, given you peace and shelter."

That engendered some peace in Kumar but not for long. He wished he could drown in his grief and wished it very dearly that to happen.

Kumar said, "My friend, now you are old like me, your branches looks so tender and all your life you have helped and protected me and my family. Now I cannot take your last fruit. You might not be able to bear any fruits so keep something for yourself my friend, I've lost so many things and I'm tired. I need some rest." And he closed his eyes.

Kumar did not return to his home the following morning too. His son took it lightly; he thought he would be with Sathi. He felt sure that his father would be unharmed wherever he might be.

The day was almost at its end when Manoj inquired of his wife,

"Did he come?"

"No," was the sudden answer from his wife.

That evening about seven, Manoj went in search of his father. He went to Ghale's home.

Ghale did not take the matter seriously and said,

"Oh that old insane might be with his beloved Sathi in the jungle, you go back and sleep soundly. He is just fine there."

At Ghale's word, he returned back and prayed to God for his father. But deep inside his heart he suspected something was wrong. His father had only once before done such a thing.

Next morning, Manoj woke up and got busy with his duties. His wife was worried about Kumar. She complained to her husband. Finally, he decided to go and search for his father. This time he did not go to anyone else's house, he headed directly towards the jungle.

His heart pounded. Different things popped into his mind. His father had never done such a thing. He had not left his son and daughter-in-law for two days. As he was approaching near the tree, his heart began to pound heavily making heavy thuds.

At last he saw his father from a distance. He was lying underneath the tree. He laid there motionless. The two friends were seen to be embracing each other. The branches of the tree were completely lowered down and he could clearly see the scene, but he did not go near the tree to wake his father. He could so clearly see the long friendship had come to an end. He also noticed the murali that still lay in his father's hand.

With tears in his eyes, he looked at his father from a distance without even trying to move any further. Puffs of cool air, really heavy with enfeebling odor gently floated by him.

His father held the murali in his hand and Manoj looked at his father and his tree. Silently though he genuflected the legacy of his father and his tree – the legacy that would be told again and again as long as the friendship existed in human emotions – so as long as enmity and hostility never condemned friendship.

He knew that his father would never play his murali again.

*****

Applaud my friends, the comedy is over.

Ludwig Van Beethoven